Reviews

'This novel, a convoluted thriller New World and Orwell's 1984, gives a Nostradamus-like prediction of the rise of the Right in the Britain of the not-too-distant future. After a coup, life in Britain has changed beyond recognition. Fear and intimidation reign. The only law is meted out by the New Dawn security force. The only citizens that prosper are the lickspittle followers of the fascist regime. Corruption is widespread, especially amongst the new political elite. Gripping from the outset, To Retribution, is a fast paced narrative which leads its youthful protagonists into the very heart of a truly evil conspiracy. A definite page turner.' *Bookmuse UK*

'Having spent most of my adult life living in places where freedom was limited for many years, I found it remarkably easy to become immersed in the scenario. This time, however, the action takes place in the future and the novel is set in Britain, which led to a certain uneasiness as the story unfolded. I quickly warmed to the characters and became absorbed by the story. How would I have behaved in each scenario? I could not wait to keep reading to find out what would happen. Fast-paced and very relevant to our world of corruption and political intrigue, this story is a fantastic debut covering social and ethical issues in such a way that compels you to keep reading.' *Hannah Shipman*

'A brilliant book that really got me thinking about what could potentially happen at some point in the future, and that is a disturbing thought indeed and given all the uncertainty at the moment it is all the more worrying and real. All of the characters are believable and well thought out and their various purposes within the plot are not predictable or dull. I read this at every available opportunity and truly enjoyed it, as it has the right mixture of what is needed for a good read and is written it such a way that I was immersed in the world created by the author. Highly recommended.' *Baattyaboutbooks*

'Fast paced. Intriguing and unexpected. Enjoyed the read from start to finish. I fully recommend to anyone with a functioning moral compass, an interest in corruption and conspiracy, or reading thrillers.' *Haribo Mack*

'I had to stay up until it was finished! A frightening warning of what can happen if people accept the politics of fear. The story twists and turns and you never know who to trust. Thoroughly recommended.' *PJ Lai-Fang*

'I couldn't put this book down!! A tense thriller, fast paced, but the characters had a depth to them. I was constantly trying to second guess where the plot would go next, and was constantly proved wrong!! A great read, that I'm still thinking and talking about a week later (always a sign of a good book!!).' *Joy Vee*

'This is a fast paced political thriller set in a potentially not too future Britain. I found it compulsive reading & was engrossed to find out what happens to the principal characters who are portrayed with insight & empathy. The story covers a number of contemporary social & political issues set in an all too possible near future scenario. A riveting read from an exciting new author.' *Keith Simpson*

TO RETRIBUTION
by
F. J. CURLEW

PART I

1

Jake sat on the barstool, as usual, hunched over his laptop: faded jeans, a Hardcore Help Foundation hoodie, spiky Mohican. The remnants of the pub could barely be seen through the glow of the three screens throwing shadows across the walls. Everything of value had been stripped months ago. Piping, panelling, brass fittings, pictures, even the old pool table, had all been taken, most of them during the riots, after which the owners had given up and left. The windows and doors had been boarded up and Jake and his colleagues had covered them in blackout blinds, just to be sure. What had once been a friendly local had become their latest safe house.

'I don't like the look of this at all,' Jake said, with a note of panic in his voice, his leg beating a nervous rhythm. 'We're down,' he added, his fingers clicking the staccato of his anxiety as they flitted across the keyboard. Checking, checking, checking.

'Could it be just a glitch, a technical thing?' Suze asked, as she hurried across to him, the stench of stale alcohol and mould creeping out behind each footstep. She leant one arm on the wooden bar, the other on Jake's shoulder.

'Uh-uh,' he shook his head. 'The computer's fine,

Internet's up, but the site's vanished. It's gone. I mean completely. Just gone.' His face drained of colour as he frantically racked his brain for any possible, innocuous reasons. None sprang to mind.

'We're still secure, right? I mean, even if they've managed to close us down they can't track us?' she asked as she watched him, concerned by the disappearance of his usual cool façade.

Brian sat at a table with his laptop open, lost in his own investigations; hacking was what he did, what made him tick. His work was invaluable to the team, but sometimes he went a little bit too far. Took a risk too many.

'Bri?'

Brian's attention flicked back to where he was, what he was meant to be doing. Checking their security. Removing infiltrators' comments – hackers from the other side. Disinformation was a continual threat. Lies spread to undermine their exposés. He had to be at the top of his game; one step ahead, as he tracked dodgy posts, infiltrated back, annoyed them. He switched computers and checked their site, watching the black screen flicker.

'What do you reckon, Bri?' Jake asked. 'You're the expert here.'

'We're on a shifting proxy chain to hide the IP, black firewalls all over the place, so safe as possible but– dunno, it's dangerous–if they've managed to hack us, trace us back somehow. Shit, shit, shit.' He nervously played with the collection of silver earrings which curled around his ear.

'Okay, so do we need to make another move then?' Suze asked. 'I mean, is it that time again?'

'For sure,' Brian replied with increased urgency, as

he caught an almost invisible pin-prick of light blink on the screen. A tiny flicker of red that you wouldn't notice if you didn't know what to look for. Brian did. There was no doubt that it was a spy. He shook his head. 'Definitely been taken down. Not only that. They've got us.'

'How? What do you mean?' Suze asked.

'They're through. Right there.' He showed her the light. 'Christ knows how much they've got,' he whispered. 'I'm for getting out of here right now. And they,' he pointed skywards, 'are sounding far too close tonight.'

Outside the air rang with the menacing clatter of helicopters; their searchlights sweeping the deserted streets. The curfew sirens shrieked above the clamour, warning all good citizens to remain indoors. Curtains were drawn; doors were locked and bolted; residents withdrew inside the flickering lives of approved media.

Jake scanned the old bar which had been the nerve centre of their operation for the past few months. 'Shit,' he mumbled.

This day was going to come. They knew that. And they had prepared for it. They gathered everything of importance, making sure nothing was left behind which might leave a trail back to them. The place returned to its state of abandonment.

The sound of heavily booted feet attempting to be quiet drew closer. The click of weapons.

'You hearing that?' Jake whispered.

Suze nodded, throwing on her biker's jacket and shoulder bag. 'Out of here,' she mouthed.

One of the reasons they had used the old pub was its delivery hatch, which left a secluded rear exit – a top priority these days. Jake hurried behind what was left of

3

the wooden bar, broken glass crunching under his feet. He lifted the hatch in the floor and climbed down the small flight of wooden steps to the old beer cellar. Something scurried across the floor in front of him. It felt too big for a mouse. He guessed it was one of the many rats who had become prevalent and somehow more brazen these days. He made his way carefully in the dark, across the cold stone floor, fumbling for the delivery hatch. Feeling the coolness of the metal he pulled the latch across, raising the hatch just far enough to give him a letterbox view of the disused car park at the back of the pub. He paused, scanned, raised the hatch as quickly as he dared, until he could see the entire car park. Their escape.

'Okay. It's all clear,' Jake whispered over his shoulder.

They slunk silently out through the hatch and sidled, their backs to the wall, along the edge of the tarmac, where weeds and grass now defiantly forced themselves between the cracks; the charred skeleton of a burned out car its only occupant; a stark reminder of what had happened here not so long ago. Their behaviour was almost military as they crept towards the exit. The metal gate squeaked as they tugged it open. No time to check. They ran along the alleyway at the back of the car park.

Flowing beyond the track was the canal; once a place where Jake and Brian would sneak off to, disobeying the warnings of well meaning grown-ups, in pursuit of mischievous play. Here they'd thrown stones at bottles and cans which casually bobbed their way along the water. Sometimes they'd raced things from one bridge to the next, twigs, leaves, lollipop sticks, anything which would float. The most difficult part was getting past the weir, where now the eyeless head of a doll spun

4

grotesquely, caught in the eddy at its foot. Rancid brown water churned and spat.

They kept to the shadows, focussing only on the way ahead. This was now about speed, not caution. Their footsteps echoed through the old canal bridge, slimy and dripping, foetid and claustrophobic. They carried on in silence past the crumbling walls of a disused warehouse, a half-sunk canal boat, the overhang of unruly trees. Half an hour later they had reached the back of the railway embankment, with its brick arches and assortment of workshops. They scrambled up the incline, which was littered with broken bottles, rusted cans and discarded needles. Suze caught a cry in the back of her throat as a sharp pain seared across her shin. *Shit!* She felt a trickle of warm blood begin to creep down her leg.

Jake fumbled nervously with his keys, checking left and right up the dimly lit cobbled lane. Only one street-light remained unbroken; its power almost ineffective, casting more shadows than light. There appeared to be nothing else about; no-one that he could sense. Sometimes that was more effective than sight. Just feeling – tuning in. His lock-up appeared to be a desolate place; nothing but a decrepit old metal door, taken over by rust, set amongst crumbling red brick ravaged by weeds, fronting an unused space. That was the intention. This was a place of no interest. He clicked open the padlock, paused, checking left and right again, listening, before opening the door and ducking in. Suze followed.

He'd been given this place by his dad, ostensibly as somewhere to work on his bikes, but they both knew the real reason. It was a place of escape, a sanctuary away from the madness. He had converted it into something habitable. It served its purpose.

'We should be okay here for a while,' Jake said, as he flicked the light switch on.

'Brian? Where the hell is Brian, Jake?' Suze asked, her voice uncharacteristically fraught. 'Christ. He was there at the bridge. I could hear him right behind me.'

'Shit. I'd better go check. Hold tight and don't move. All right?'

'All right. Be safe.'

'Yeah. You know me,' he replied, smiling with a reassurance he didn't feel. The last thing he wanted to do right now was to go back out there. But you look after your friends. You keep them close. Keep them safe.

He padlocked the door behind him to keep Suze safe, before slipping back down the hill, towards the canal. This time he crept along slowly, staring through every break in the bushes, gap in the fence, hole in the wall. He had a torch, but wouldn't dare use it. His heart was thumping as he tried to control his breathing. Even that sounded too loud. If he came across anyone now, well past curfew, it could only mean trouble. Muggings had become prevalent with the loss of income, the loss of hope, for so many people, but he feared that less than New Dawn. Some of the muggers might just be people like him; ordinary people who had stood up and said "No!" People who wouldn't keep quiet. People who had fallen down because there was no-one to pick them up. When you have nothing left what else can you do but break the law?

It seemed to take such a long time to retrace his steps. After he had crept through the old bridge, he stopped and stared. A helicopter hovered around the area where the pub stood. This wasn't the standard curfew time sweep. This was definitely focused. Focused on them. Its searchlight glinted off the water of the canal, the wall, up and down, up and down. Through the shrubbery and rubble smaller lights flickered to the beat of footsteps. Dozens of them. They were drawing closer. He had no choice but to turn back.

Brian was the most fastidious of the three. He was the studious one, the techy geek, the one who paid attention to the tiniest of details. He might have noticed something, paused, left distance between them; realised he, and they, had a better chance of escape if they split up. He would be fine. He had to be fine. Right now all Jake could think of was getting back to Suze safely, discreetly.

2

Suze wandered around the lock-up, taking in its tall, vaulted ceiling, bare brick walls, and tiny windows set high in the wall. He had obviously made an attempt to personalise it with some posters of classic motorbikes, a picture of an old foreign looking town with tall spires caked in snow and, most interestingly to her, photographs, which she took to be of his family. Jake, aged about nine or ten – there was no mistaking that smile – with an older girl; a man and a woman sitting around a bonfire on a beach rimmed by pine trees with a pale, pale blue sky caught between night and day in the background. It made her smile. There were a few more of the girl, at different ages, laughing, flowers in long braided hair, playing with a pet rabbit, sledging.

She flicked through some magazines which were lying on a table made out of a couple of tyres covered with a piece of old plywood. They were about bikes and politics, no big surprise. Her attention was drawn by a letter poking out of an envelope, well fingered, tattered. She picked it up and turned it over in her hands. The handwriting was spidery and smudged. It was addressed to Jake. The temptation to read was strong, but guilt quickly replaced it. She carefully put it back on the space it had left clear of dust. Her hands were trembling and she suddenly felt dizzy. She steadied herself on the back of the rickety old armchair and gratefully slumped into its seat. Her leg was throbbing, her head pounding. The walls seemed to pulse, to sway. She passed out.

She came to with the scrape of the door closing. Turning to face the entrance she thought she could make out two figures. Her vision was blurred. She rubbed at her eyes. Two became one. Jake was alone. He locked the door behind him and scratched his head.

'I couldn't see him anywhere.' He thought for a bit, wondering about what to say. He didn't want to upset her, worry her, but he knew better than to lie. They were beyond that and she could see through him anyway; read him so easily. 'He knows this area so well though, I'm sure he'll be fine. Maybe he headed off to his folks' place?'

'I hope so. And New Dawn?'

'Yeah. Crawling all over the place.' His brow was furrowed showing off the little scar that ran through his eyebrow up to his hairline.

'Too much of a coincidence for it not to be us they're after then?'

'Yeah, 'fraid so.' He took a double take at his friend and colleague. 'Shit, Suze, look at you! You're shaking like you've got the DTs. You okay? Jeez.' He fetched a blanket from his rickety little camp bed and wrapped her up. She winced.

'Are you hurt?' he asked.

'It's just a scratch. I'll be fine,' she replied.

'Let me look, okay?'

He gently pulled her trouser leg up and raised his pierced eyebrow at her. 'That's more than a scratch, sweetheart. Nasty. I'm sure there's an old first aid kit here somewhere,' he said, as he rummaged around under the sink.

He cleaned the gash as best he could and covered it with a creatively applied assortment of sticking plasters. 'That'll have to do for now, but I reckon it needs stitching.'

'Yeah, yeah. That's the least of our worries right now. Do you think someone's grassed on us?' Suze asked, as she huddled in front of the two bar electric heater which sent out crackles and spits in protest, its warmth gradually beginning to seep through her. Though why she felt cold, she wasn't sure. It was a typically humid August night in London.

'Can't imagine who,' Jake replied. 'I mean, who else knew? It's always just been the three of us at that place, at least as far as I know.'

He looked across at Suze for confirmation, knowing full well what her response would be. They were always careful, always secretive, always together. That was the deal they'd made when they had started publishing openly online; taking it seriously. It had begun as an experiment, a project for their journalism course, but as the country changed, as fear and distrust became the norm, as traditional media became the government's puppet, it slipped into something altogether different. Concerned citizens began contacting them about what they had witnessed. Random arrests, disappearances, ransacked houses. And behind it all, New Dawn. Now it had taken over their lives. Everything else had been left behind.

Suze nodded that confirmation. Nothing had slipped. No-one had infiltrated. Their unit was as tight as it had ever been.

'Maybe they just hacked the system, like Bri thought, and somehow traced us,' Jake suggested. 'You know anything we can do they can do better, right?'

'Yeah, I guess so. What about here? Are we safe? I mean...'

'No worries there. This place is so far off the radar it doesn't even exist. Anyway, best try and get some shut eye.'

'Yeah, right. Night then.'

He feigned sleep until he was sure that Suze had drifted off. Yes, he was quite confident that this place was as safe as possible. It had no address, no registration, but New Dawn were New Dawn and you could never let your guard down. He pulled his chair next to the door and did his best to stay awake, listening for anything. Anything at all.

3

Suze woke up to the smell of coffee. 'You're a star, Jake. Cheers,' she said, gratefully wrapping her hands around his favourite old Banksy mug; "Keep your coins, I want change", it read. 'And in THE mug, I am honoured.' She smiled up at him.

She remembered buying it with him at a second hand stall in Camden, not long after they'd first met. He'd been really chuffed with it. They'd bumped into each other during registration for their journalism degrees at L.S.E., discovered they shared classes and causes, and begun hanging out. They talked media control, politics, conspiracies, and corruption, never imagining it would become their reality so quickly, so easily.

'And you are welcome,' he smiled in return, graciously, mock bowing. 'How are you feeling?'

'Not bad, thanks. No sign of Brian then?'

'Uh-uh, nothing. But whatever, we need to decide what we're gonna do. Do we hang on here and hope that we're just being overly paranoid and it'll quieten down, or do we hide out somewhere? Personally I'm for getting as far away from Lewisham as possible, laying low till we find out what's going on. What do you reckon?'

'I guess so,' she agreed, with resignation in her voice. It was what their lives had become. It was necessary, but it was tedious. Constantly on the move, on edge, suspicious. She sighed. 'Where to though?'

'Somewhere safe, out of the way, out of town maybe. Dunno.'

'How about my parents place? It's in the middle of nowhere and they're, well, my parents.' She smiled across at him.

'Are you sure? I mean, will they be okay with us just turning up? It's not as if we can risk calling them.'

'Yes. Of course. It's been far too long since I saw them anyway. They'll be fine with it. It's quite a trek though.'

'How much of a trek?'

'Cornwall.'

'Ah! A three hundred mile trek. Cool! We could pretend we're off on holiday,' he said laughing. 'One of the happy campers.'

'We could, if you happen to have a travel pass in your ID,' she replied, with an expression of feigned expectation.

'Sadly not.'

'No, me neither. Ah well. We'll just have to keep out of sight then.'

In an attempt to tighten things up, increase security, the government had made all travel beyond your designated area illegal without a pass authorised through your ID card. It made it easier for them to round up troublemakers, control possible dissidence, keep a tight grip on things. It was mandatory that ID cards be carried at all times. Being caught without one meant immediate arrest. Black marks were given to lawbreakers, dissidents, and anti government activists, meaning no possibility of changing jobs, if you were lucky enough to have one, no transfer of accommodation, and definitely no travel permits. And, of course, the levelling up of surveillance. IDs were used for everything: cash-cards, medical records, club memberships. Everything. Unbeknown to the general populace, they also contained trackers.

'Cornwall it is then!' he said, handing her a crash helmet.

'By bike.' she replied, enthusiastically. 'Cool. Just like old times.'

He smiled at her. 'Yeah! I reckon it'll be safest too, just so long as we don't get pulled over. We can go off road when we need to, to avoid check points and the likes. Should be okay. Once we get out of London, that is.'

They discussed the safest ways of getting out. There were some disused railway tracks, but not enough, and if they were seen, or heard, they would be drawing attention to themselves. The main roads were littered with closed circuit cameras; random spot checks were always a possibility. Vehicles that weren't listed as safe were fair game to New Dawn. They decided to ride slowly through the residential areas in the rougher parts of town, one borough to the next, making regular stops, acting as casually as they could. Just a normal couple.

In these estates the signs of the riots lay everywhere. Unlike in the nicer parts of the city nothing had been cleared. Evidence was left sitting. A statement. "Look at what you've done." Charred buildings, broken windows, burnt out cars. Graffiti had spread like a disease across the walls. Racist slurs battled with anarchist slogans and signs; anti-state, pro-democracy phrases fought for their space. There was even some poetry. Eloquence to base profanities. It was all there.

It wasn't possible to avoid all of the cameras. Of

course they would be seen, but their crash helmets offered decent cover. They just had to hope that they weren't flagged, pulled over, identified, taken in. Suze tapped Jake's shoulder, meaning pull over. He stopped the bike at the foot of a block of flats where the space between lock-ups offered a place to hide from the obvious CCTVs. He couldn't be sure that there wasn't something watching them somewhere. Drones could appear from nowhere; random sweeps in known trouble spots, security in more affluent areas. This was the best he could do.

'What's up?' he asked, keeping his helmet on, his visor down.

'I thought we had a tail. The same car. That grey one, right there,' she said, as a grey hatchback crawled by. 'It keeps appearing, then disappearing.'

'Okay. Could just be some cruisers looking for a score. We'll give it a couple of minutes, double back, and see what happens.'

They waited until the car was out of sight, turned around, and took one of the parallel roads. It seemed to be okay. No tail. At last they had reached the edge of the city. Countryside beckoned.

4

Now that the city was behind them they almost relaxed a bit. Almost let their guard down. The countryside appeared strangely untouched by the "disturbances" – as they were called by the powers that be – offering a false sense of safety. Of the old normality. Out here they were far more obvious. Easily spotted if they were being followed, looked for, hunted. They had taken side roads, stuck to quiet places where they hoped New Dawn hadn't bothered to install any checkpoints. So far, so good. They kept heading west, riding past fields of cattle casually grazing, rows of hops standing tall, awaiting transformation into the sweet nectar of a glass of beer – simple pleasures, now a rarity and more appreciated than ever. A stream gently gurgled its way to the consuming ocean. Calm, idyllic, deceptive. It would have been easy to drift into a state of that old normality, when life just carried on and, really, it was okay, but they knew that they couldn't. Senses had to be kept alert.

Evening began to close in bringing a chill to the air. Suze shivered and clung tightly on to Jake's back. He pulled over, exhausted, after so little sleep.

'You need to stop, babe?' he asked. 'We could maybe camp over there for the night. The cover looks good,' he said, as he studied the small copse in the distance.

'What is it with you these days? Babe! Sweetheart! For Christ's sake I hate it! Drop it will you?'

'Shit, sorry,' he said, taken aback. Hurt spoke through his dark brown eyes. 'It's just, well, yeah, sorry Suze.'

'Uh-huh. I could do with a break though,' she conceded

'I can see that. Best check that leg of yours.'

'No. It's fine really! For Christ's sake, I'm okay!' she snapped at him.

He held his hands up in a gesture of surrender. 'Okay, okay.' Her mood concerned him. It wasn't like her and he guessed stress, pain; perhaps most worryingly an infection, were leaving her on edge.

They lay under the cover of the trees for a few hours, neither managing anything resembling real sleep. Drifting off would be broken by the scurry of a mouse, the crawl of an insect, the call of an owl. Attention snapped back to the here and now. Their perilous situation. They both sat up, alarmed, at the sound of breaking twigs, footsteps. Staring through the darkness they could only imagine what it might be. There was no need for words. Intuitively they crept over to where the bike stood against a tree and wheeled it across the grass, slowly, stealthily, biting back the desire to run. A couple of steps, a pause, a look behind them, around them, over and over until they reached the road again. There was no curfew out here, but they still had to be careful. Unusual movement, lights, engine noise, were all liable to attract attention from anyone who happened to be awake at this hour. Concerned citizens who had been warned of the dangers of outsiders. People didn't take risks. They called in. Reported strangers, odd activity, anything outside the norm. Report it. Stay safe.

It would soon be daybreak, but until then they would walk, pushing the bike beside the road. It was painfully slow, made more so by the depth of their fatigue. Legs complained, heads buzzed, arms ached. Finally the darkness broke, the sun rose and lit up the way ahead in a warm soft orange that would normally cause comment, a pause to stare at the beauty of it all. All that concerned them now was that it allowed them to see. They could make out nothing untoward. Nobody following them. No army vehicles. No sign of New Dawn.

'We were just imagining things, I guess,' Suze whispered, although there was no need for silence any more.

'Yeah. Seems that way. Maybe just deer or something.'

They straddled the bike and rode off. It felt good to be on the move again, drawing more distance between them and the New Dawn squad that had been after them in London. They stayed away from the main roads again, skirting villages and towns, avoiding any signs of habitation, sticking to quiet back roads, cutting through woods, off-roading as often as they could.

Traffic was sparse. They focused in on any vehicles, looking for signs: a uniform, a badge, anything out of the ordinary. Those that passed seemed innocuous enough. Delivery drivers, farm workers, people whose lives seemed to have been barely affected. Life carried on.

They decided to cut across Dartmoor. It was more direct, but so open, so desolate. Bleak moors devoid of trees, rough grassland grazed by sheep. A place where you could feel truly alone. A place where you could see for miles. A place where you could be picked out just as easily.

'I'm not sure I like this,' Jake said, pulling to a stop, pointing ahead.

There was a helicopter far on the horizon. Another. They were drawing closer.

'We're fine,' Suze said. 'They're always playing army games up here, practising manoeuvres. It's normal.'

'You sure?'

'Yes. And if I'm wrong we're a bit late. Sitting ducks and all that!'

'Keep going?'

'Keep going!'

The sun was now high above them. A bank of clouds clustered far on the horizon of an otherwise pure blue sky. The desolate landscape began to change. Signs of cultivation. Hedges surrounding fields, copses of trees. Dry stone walls coated with thick green moss lined the road which had become wider, well surfaced, better looked after. An army Jeep suddenly rose from the brow of a hill in front of them. Jake started, causing the bike to wobble slightly as his attention jumped to the approaching vehicle. What would be normal? To ignore it. Normal people would just ignore it.

'Fuck!' Suze mumbled and held her breath as they drove on by, trying not to look, but she couldn't resist a glance back as they slipped behind the hill. 'We're all right. They're not interested.'

Small towns appeared as the moors fell away. Finally, the gentle hills gave way to a coast Suze recognised. Curlews shrieked in the distance, as if heralding her homecoming. She flipped up her visor, closed her eyes, and threw her head back, drawing in a deep breath of the salty sweet air. She found herself caught in a delicious reverie. She was a child again in the hidden, sandy coves where she danced to the rhythm of the waves crashing on the shore, twirling, laughing, through the magic of her imagination. The feel of her long wet curls gently flopped against her sunburnt skin. She was standing on the tall grey cliffs where she balanced precariously, leaning forward, arms outstretched, fingers wiggling, imagining that she was a bird in flight. One of the gulls that swirled above her. Reluctantly, she snapped herself out of it, just as her mother's warning calls had done all those years ago.

She directed them down a dirt-track, not wide enough for a car, which crept through the woods, so dense that it was completely enclosed. Branches twisted together over their heads like the grasping fingers of desperate lovers. Jealous threads of sunlight forced their way between them. She smiled, feeling that familiar relief of arriving at the sanctity of her parents' realm.

'Home,' she said, her voice sounding drained and croaky. 'It smells of home.'

They were soon met by the joyous yelping of the family's collies as they bounded towards the bike. Suze removed her helmet and gingerly climbed off, trying to suppress a wince as she did so.

'John, Yoko! Hi guys!' She bent down to stroke them. Their tails wagging furiously, tongues lolling. An instant release of everything that was wrong with the world. 'So good to see you!'

Jake laughed, 'John and Yoko – really?'

'Well, yes. It's a family tradition. We've also had Ché and Fidel, Nye and Jennie. The closest I ever came to getting a slap from my mum was when I suggested Maggie and Denis for two of the kittens!'

'Oh brilliant! I love it,' Jake said, laughing. He

swung the heavy metal latch off the wooden gate post and they walked in to the cobbled yard. A clamour of clucking chickens ran around in a panic. Feathers and straw speckled the ground.

On one side of the yard stood the main house. A traditional old Cornish farmhouse, painted a brilliant white, with grey slate tiles and tall chimneys. Swallows darted in and out from nooks and crannies under the eaves which supported the muddy balls of their nests. Around the courtyard stood a curious assortment of buildings and sheds. There was a working barnyard, where cats contentedly stretched and yawned; their bellies full of mice. Two quirky wooden hen-houses, lovingly crafted by Suze's father, Geoffrey, stood close to the barn. One of the long, low, stone sheds, once housing cattle, had been converted into a self-contained apartment for a select few who came to escape the mayhem of city life and enjoy the tranquillity of a retreat. It had also been a place of safety, a temporary shelter for those in need. Refugees, dissidents, dreamers. Stained glass stood in place of windows sending patterns of suns and moons, birds and flowers dancing over the whitewashed walls and stone floors.

'Mum. Hi. God are you a sight for sore eyes!' She was such a constant in her battered dungarees, rainbow Doc Marten boots and hand knitted cardigan. Her outrageously orange hair tied back with a rustic Celtic clip. Thankfully, Suze thought, some things never change.

'Suzanna!' Katherine's green eyes twinkled with a combination of relief and delight, followed quickly by concern. 'My dear child you look absolutely terrible,' she said, as she took in the full effect of her bedraggled daughter's sickly pallor, her eyes settling on the

21

bloodstained jeans. 'Whatever has happened to you?'

'It's been a rough couple of days, Mum, but I'm fine, really.'

'This is not what fine looks like to me!'

'Mum, this is Jake. Jake this is my mum, Katherine.'

'Hello, Jake. So lovely to meet you, at last!'

'Likewise Katherine.' Jake smiled and held out his hand, which she used to pull him close and give him a strong hug, kissing both of his cheeks. She smelled of a combination of roses and earth.

'Come in, come in. Let's get you cleaned up and fed then you can tell us all about it. We've been so worried, you've no idea. Ever since your site went down. Of course we knew that something was wrong. Oh my dears, I am so relieved. Wonderful! Your father's out "creating" she said, drawing quotation marks with her fingers and smiling a knowing smile. 'He'll be so pleased you're here.' She swept an imaginary piece of hair from her face.

'Great to see you, Mum!' Suze enthused, opening her arms for another hug. 'Great to see you.' She did her best to hold back tears but failed miserably.

'Right my girl. Upstairs. Bath and change, then I'll have a proper look at you.'

It felt good. It felt safe. It felt like home. She peeled her jeans off slowly and carefully, disconnecting the denim from the scab. The relief was palpable as she sank into the roll top bath and immersed herself in the warm, soothing water. Once the initial sting had subsided, body and soul were benefiting from the familiar concoction of herbs and oils as they worked their magic. *Thanks Mum.* She could hear the gentle murmur of voices from the kitchen below; the occasional clatter of copper pots sliding across the range. Bliss.

5

Katherine knocked gently on the bathroom door. 'Are you all right in there Suzanna? It's almost dinner time,' she called.

'Yes, I'm fine. Sorry, I drifted off. I'll be down in a few minutes. God, I look like a prune!'

She climbed tentatively out of the bath and wrapped herself in the sumptuous white towel she had pulled off the heated rail. It smelled gorgeous, fresh and somehow wholesome. She held it to her face and inhaled slowly.

'Will you let me have a look at that wound before you get dressed?' her mum called through the door. 'Best get it seen to!'

Suze opened the door and sat on the wicker chair that still bore the pink and green stains of her childhood crayoning. Little pieces of her early life had been left in odd places as mementos. Evidence of happiness and joy and the love that still lived on in this house.

Her mum cleaned the wound, chatting away as she did so about nothing in particular. Soft words that soothed, that swathed everything in goodness. That said it was all okay. She covered the gash with a turmeric paste before bandaging it.

'Let's hope that does the trick. You must say if you feel unwell. We might need to get something stronger.'

Suze dressed in the clean clothes laid out for her and

followed her mother down the well worn stairs, smiling to herself at the creak three from the top. It was sneaking down for a midnight snack, creeping in after a late night out, spying on grown up parties after bedtime.

'Oh, something smells great. What have you been cooking?' Suze asked, as she walked across the slate tiled kitchen floor and sat with the others around the wooden table crafted by her dad from a single slice of tree trunk. Jake was deep in conversation with Geoffrey on the art of its creation. His reputation had spread and his pieces now sold to a select few for a decent amount.

'Spinach and cheese pie followed by a clafouti,' replied Katherine.

'Oh, delicious. I'm starving! We haven't eaten since yesterday.'

'Come. Sit!' Katherine insisted, as she doled out the pie onto wooden plates. 'Sautéed potatoes, salad, tuck in,' she added, gesturing to the bowls all ready on the table.

Little was said as Suze and Jake greedily ploughed their way through the main course. Katherine and Geoffrey smiled at each other across the table. He winked at her, his bushy grey eyebrows like two hairy caterpillars crawling across his forehead.

'And you made it safely, I mean without drawing attention to yourselves?' Katherine asked, as she sat down with her desert.

'As far as we know, yeah,' Jake replied.

'We were so careful,' Suze added, reassuringly, emphasising the so. 'We came across both moors then in the back way, through the woods too. Just to make sure.'

'Good, good. You know there's a reward for

25

reporting strangers? Well, of course you do! Isn't that despicable? People actually call in as well. It's quite beyond me, really. How can anyone?...I mean—' Katherine shook her head despondently. She took a deep breath to calm herself. 'Ah well, it's the world in which we live now isn't it? So sad, so very sad.'

'It's a bloody disgrace, my love,' added Geoffrey, shaking his gloriously thick head of shoulder length grey hair, his mouth overfull of cherry clafouti, some of which dribbled onto his paisley neckerchief and ancient denim shirt. 'Apologies for my atrocious table manners,' he said, dabbing at his spillage, 'but this is quite simply delicious,' his eyes twinkling adoringly at his wife. 'She never feeds me as well as this you know? You really should visit more often.' He winked at Jake.

'Geoffrey!' Katherine chastised and laughed.

'So, the cell, thingamajig? Has that been disbanded then?'

'For now yeah. At least for a while,' Jake replied. 'Way too risky. We don't know what happened to the site yet and there was more than the usual amount of New Dawn in the area so...'

'Yes, of course. Damned shame. You were doing such a splendid job of keeping us all informed. Can't rely on the bloody press these days can you? Propagandist poppycock, the lot of it!'

'Yeah, tell me about it,' Jake confirmed.

After dinner they relaxed into glasses of Bordeaux, trying to keep the talk light, avoiding discussion of the deportations, the demonstrations, the riots, the coup, the complete upheaval of everything they knew, despite it being uppermost in all of their minds. Tonight was a celebration. A rejoicing of family, of love, of all things good. The antithesis of what their world had become.

26

Too easily. Too quickly. The loss of something so integral that it allowed people to be swayed, taken in by mass media and those who control it. Fear.

'Divide and conquer, my dears. Divide and bloody conquer,' Geoffrey would say emphatically, but not tonight. Tonight his eyes twinkled, his smile was almost constant, his joy at the safe return of his daughter was everything.

'Do you mind if we head on up? We're absolutely exhausted,' Suze asked, feeling somewhat remorseful, not wanting to break from this precious moment in time, but barely able to keep her eyes open.

'Of course, of course,' Katherine replied, apologetically. 'I should have thought. Sorry! It's just so lovely to see you. I've made up the beds. Jake's in the spare room. You in yours. Goodnight, dears.'

'Yes, yes. Goodnight. Sleep tight,' added Geoffrey, with a reassuring nod, blowing a kiss to his daughter.

Sleep came almost instantaneously.

*

Suze awoke with a start. 'What the...?' Her mother was urgently shaking her.

'Get dressed, quickly. Someone's coming. Your father thinks it's a patrol. Come on.'

'How...?' Suze shook her head in dejected disbelief and threw on her clothes. As they hurried down the stairs she could see her father and Jake waiting by the back door which stood open to the gentle hues of the breaking dawn.

'Dad, I...we...'

'Not to worry. It's probably nothing. You know what they're like. Best if you two hide yourselves in the barn for now,' said Geoffrey, attempting to disguise his concern. 'Just to be on the safe side. Off you go.'

27

They scurried across the yard and into the barn where bales of straw were piled almost up to the roof, six deep. It smelled of lazy summer days, school holidays, hide and seek, searching for eggs with her dad. Somehow she always won the game; found more than him. She knew that he cheated, but it didn't matter.

Clambering up to the top they made a makeshift hiding place, then pulled bales over themselves so that they were completely hidden. Hens clucked and scratched, pecking at ears of corn. A cat walked over them mewing softly, sniffing at the straw above them. Suze sat clenching her knees, crouched, eyes closed. The gentle sounds of the countryside were shattered by the insidious rumblings of approaching military vehicles. The screeching of brakes, slamming of doors and stomping of feet echoed around the courtyard. The barking of John and Yoko was silenced with a yelp. *Oh good God, what have we done?* She couldn't make out the voices, just the barrage of boots thundering through the house, furniture being overturned, glass and china crashing to the ground, splintering on the polished wooden floors.

Her father's voice. 'How dare you!'

Her mother's voice. 'You have no right!'

A scream.

No! Tears streamed down Suze's face as she stared at Jake, clutching his hands, drawing blood. Time became an unknown quantity. She had no idea if this was taking hours or minutes.

The barn door flew open. The hens squawked and scattered, their useless wings flapping, their dry eyes panicking.

'Torch it!'

The spit of the fire as the first bale caught light was

signal enough. They clambered out of their hiding place and tumbled down the back of the bales of straw, hidden from the intruders. Hitting the ground they ran from the flames that licked at the fodder. Ran to the back of the barn and out the rear entrance. Shadows drifted through the smoke behind them.

Suze turned to look back. She thought she could make out her father. Flames were flickering around him.

Her mother's screams rose above the cacophony. 'No! Oh my God. Please no!' Then indiscernible wailing, inhuman, agonizing. A gunshot. Another. Suze couldn't breathe. She couldn't draw her eyes away. She stumbled.

Jake pulled her up and dragged her after him, over the brow of the hill that stood behind the barn, then raced down the other side and into the woods. The trees were dense, confusing. The foliage thick, hampering their progress. Birds rose in alarm, screeching, betraying their whereabouts. Jake ran in the direction he thought would lead them away from the farm, but wasn't sure any more. He stopped and listened, trying to get his bearings; straining to make out if anyone was in pursuit. He couldn't hear anything now, even the dawn chorus had strangely quieted. The smell of the fire was strong in the air, but he couldn't see the smoke through the dense foliage. He couldn't see anything other than trees. He pulled Suze close and held her to him, felt her trembling, gasping for breath.

'Suze. Fuck! Come on girl. I need you to keep it together,' he whispered in desperation. 'Please. Suze,' stroking her hair. 'You know this place. You need to get us out of here. You can do this Suze. Come on.'

Her eyes stared blankly. It was as if he wasn't there. As if she wasn't there. As if there was nothing.

6

The pale morning sun was breaking through the dense canopy of the woods, sending slivers of light dancing amongst the fluttering leaves. Suze's shoulders heaved as she struggled for breath in between silent sobs. Jake sat her up against a tree and held her face firmly in his two hands. Her eyes seemed not to be registering anything, maintaining their blank stare. He was frightened.

'Suze. Suze babe. Which way?'

No response.

'Forgive me,' he said, as he slapped her. Shook her. His eyes red; his face tear stained. 'Which way? Which way, Suze?'

She started, stared at him, turned from him and began to run. Pushing herself through the undergrowth. He followed, hoping to hell she was aware of what she was doing. Tangles of brambles, sticky willies and nettles leapt at their ankles, clawing, sticking, stinging. Each snap of a twig a Judas shouting their presence to the uniforms of the New Dawn Militia, if that's who they were. Though they had little doubt. No-one else would behave like that.

As if from nowhere Yoko was suddenly beside them, limping but silent, as if she knew, sniffing, purposeful. She looked up at Suze. *Good girl Yoko. Quiet now. We need to get away. Far away.*

The dog took over leading the way, Suze and Jake trusting her instinct. She was leading them north, towards the coast. At the edge of the woods she hesitated, looking back. Her ears pricked. Jake and Suze both froze. Checking, scanning.

'You hear anything?' Jake whispered, relieved to see Suze's eyes focused. She was back with him.

She shook her head. 'It's okay girl, on you go,' she whispered to Yoko. The dog led them along the hedgerow which separated them from the road, silent, free of traffic. They crept through a break, running across the single track road, through another hedge then on towards the coast. *The caves, of course. You're a bloody genius, Yoko!* They slid down the steep, grassy slope soaked with dew which led to the cliff's edge. They took their time on the cliff. It was steep and dangerous, with perhaps a one hundred metre drop straight down to the sea below. They clambered down, zig-zagging along the haphazard track, barely visible to anyone who didn't know of its existence. The rock was damp with dew, slippery, treacherous. Care had to be taken, but it was difficult to fight the urge to run. The closer to the bottom they got, the more they picked up speed.

Reaching the ground they ran on round the edge of the sandy cove to the point. The waves of the incoming tide crashed against the rocks. Seaweed swirled brown and green in great swathes. Kittiwakes and gulls squealed and screeched overhead, swooping down to catch their slithering silvery breakfast.

They had to wade through the surging waters, Yoko swimming at their side, to reach the entrance of the cave which was only just large enough for Jake to clamber through. It opened up into a large cavern with several layers of grey rock, like giant steps, tunnelling back, far under the cliffs; its ending not in sight. Yoko shook herself, sending translucent silver droplets flying around them. The only sound they could hear was the tumultuous crashing of the waves. An old smuggler's cave. Centuries of refuge from the authorities. A temporary haven?

Suze pulled herself up on to the lowest ledge and sat breathing heavily, with her back against the wall of the cave, green and slimy. Her wet jeans stuck to her, uncomfortably, stinging against her cut. She pulled her legs close, her head bowed. She felt trickles of sweat dribbling their way indecently down her back. Jake sat down beside her.

'I am so sorry, Suze,' he said, feeling so inadequate. Sorry? So much more was needed, but he couldn't find the words. He put his arm around her shoulders and pulled her gently in to him. She rested her head on his chest and began to cry. 'Let it out Suze,' he added, holding her tight. 'Let it all out.' Yoko's gentle pink tongue licked at her tears.

The tide had now risen above the entrance. The sea lapped softly against the walls of the cave below them. There was no way for anyone to find them until the tide turned again and the water retreated. Neither was there a way out.

'We should go on up.' Suze gestured towards the higher ledges behind them. 'Keep away from the water.' She wiped her nose with the back of her hand and sniffed. 'It rises, fills the place up.'

It had been another of those forbidden places of her childhood which had made it all the more appealing. Of course she hadn't listened to her parents warnings. It was far too exciting flirting with the danger of the water. Playing at being a smuggler, a pirate, a heroine in a romantic novel. She would hear her parents calling and would stay hidden for as long as she dared, before diving down and swimming out into the breaking waves. Of course, if they had known where she had been, she would be in trouble, but it was worth it. Danger had always attracted her.

'Come on.' She stood up and patted her thigh. 'Come on, Yoko. Good girl.' Yoko padded after her. The smell of wet dog brought an unexpected smile to her face. Memories. Beautiful, comforting memories. Reaching home after a day's adventuring with her dogs. Getting drenched in a storm. Settling down in front of the fire. The tingle on her cheeks. Safe. Secure. Her family.

She and Jake sat down again on the highest ledge, Yoko panting beside them.

'How long do you think we should stay here for?' Jake asked.

'Oh God, I've no idea. Were they looking for us? Are they still? I have no god-damned clue.'

'I reckon they must have been. Again. Too much of a coincidence. Don't you think? I mean, your mum and dad?'

'Yes, I guess so. But how? Do you think someone saw us and called in?'

'Maybe. Or maybe they've got everything on us. Families, friends, the lot, and they've been watching.'

'Christ, this is such a nightmare.' She pulled at her hair with both hands, squeezing her head. Squeezing. Squeezing. 'They do have history you know, my mum and dad, demo's and such like. A while ago though.'

'Really?'

'Yes. That's how they officially met. They went to

the same uni, shared classes, but had barely spoken. Then, a few years later they both happened to be at the same demonstration. Mum was throwing eggs at the police.' She smiled. 'Dad rushed in to try and stop them from handcuffing her and they both ended up in jail.'

'Oh priceless! I can just picture it,' Jake laughed. 'They're so lovely and polite and...radical! You must have had an amazing childhood.'

She sighed, 'Anti-establishmentarianism was very much a part of my upbringing. They were great parents.' She closed her eyes as tears began to fall again. 'Fuck, fuck, fuck! Bastards!' She stamped her feet as her screams echoed around the cave 'Fu..cking ba..stards,' then broke into sobs and more tears.

Jake held her close again. She felt strangely small and vulnerable. He wasn't used to this. She had always seemed so strong. So independent. 'I don't know what to do Suze. I–I'm so sorry. We don't know for sure what happened though, do we? Maybe – I dunno – maybe things'll work out. You know? You have to keep that in your head.'

'They...are great parents. You hear that you sons of bitches? They ARE great parents!' she shouted at the walls; her voice bouncing back in a substantiating series of dying echoes.

They sat in silence until the walls were quiet again.

He smiled at her. 'That's my girl. So what were they studying?'

'Law, same uni as us, L.S.E. They wanted to save the world, you know? Defenders of the people and all that.'

'Why the move to Cornwall then? I'd have thought London would have been more active.'

'Ugly things still happen in beautiful places, you know? Their quality of life was important to them.

34

Being down here kept them sane, they said. They'd travel about a lot. Mum in particular. She was always off doing pro bono stuff for people. But they had enough money and weren't interested in making more so they'd pick and choose. Human rights stuff mainly, and latterly lots of deportations, repatriations.' She paused, shook her head. 'It's relentless. Why the fuck? I mean, just how? Just how? How did it all slip into this shit? This mindless selfish shit! You know? Yeah, course you do. So, anyway, they aren't too popular with the establishment right now. I guess they never have been.'

'Wow. I had no idea.'

'Yes, well...' She stroked Yoko's damp head which was now resting on her lap. The dog's eyes fixed on her face. 'Good girl,' she smiled, fighting back tears again. She wondered what Yoko had seen? Why had she run? Left John, her parents, her home? She hoped that it was just out of the need to protect. The bond between Suze and Yoko had always been a special one. But even so it didn't bode well. She knew that she couldn't afford to think about it right now.

They waited until night fell and the tide had receded far enough to allow their exit. The sky was clear and the moon bright enough to light their way over the rocks, made even more treacherous by water and seaweed. They continued heading east along the coast, slowly and in silence, edging their way as far away from it all as possible.

Jake was going over everything in his head, trying to work it out. Sure, they'd had to move before, but that was always precautionary, an odd word, a stranger paying too much attention, something unusual on their site, a warning. Brian would pick something up, warn

35

them. They'd change servers, change proxies, start all over again. But it hadn't felt personal. Nothing like this. He'd imagined doing time for it. That was okay. He could handle that. It went with the territory, and they all knew that; even joked about it sometimes. This was a whole different ball game. This was their lives that were on the line and he couldn't fathom it. As the miles passed, nothing sprang to mind. None of this made sense.

Suze was desperately trying to force images of the farm out of her head, trying to focus on the here and now, trying to stay in control of what she could cling to. Dawn was beginning to break and a place to hide becoming urgent. This was no longer familiar territory and she didn't know what lay ahead along the coast. They warily headed back inland, skirting farmers' fields, clinging to hedges, avoiding roads.

'Wait here,' Jake said, 'I'm gonna check out the house there. It looks empty. For sale sign and shit. Okay?'

The place would once have been called quaint. A little cottage in the country with views of open terrain, a garden, but now it was something else. It was dark and destitute. A feeling. A sense of foreboding clung to it. But it was shelter.

'Okay,' she replied. She sat crouched behind the hedge, watching him make his way furtively across the road and on through the tangle of grasses and weeds which used to be someone's garden.

He was back in a couple of minutes. 'Yeah, it's good. The back door was already open. Place has been vandalised a bit but not too bad. Come on.' He held his hand out to help her up, half expecting chastisement, but she smiled weakly, accepted.

7

The house looked like it had been sitting vacant for quite a while. Tattered curtains hung limply from the windows, with cobwebs appearing to hold them in place, making the half light they allowed in almost ineffectual. Furniture, modern and little used, had been left behind; the scribblings of a child on one of the arms of the leather settee, stuffing protruding from the random slashes. Ornaments and pictures still attempted to decorate the shelves and tables, coated in a heavy, unforgiving dust. The walls had been daubed with graffiti, swastikas in black, 'England for the English' and 'Fuck of home fuckers', in red, mock dripping blood.

'Charming,' Suze muttered under her breath. 'Your spelling sucks by the way. Wankers,' she hissed.

They checked each of the downstairs rooms. More of the same. Graffiti, vandalism, mindless destruction.

'We should check upstairs too.'

They crept, hesitantly, up the creaking stairs. Yoko was leading, sniffing intently, her hackles down, her tail low but not tucked. It seemed that she was less anxious than they were. She stopped as the stairs turned a corner and looked back. Suze pointed ahead, instructing the dog to lead on. She did, albeit more cautiously now. Three doors led off the upstairs hallway. The door to the bathroom stood ajar. Suze tapped it wide open with her boot. It was relatively unscarred. Someone's toiletries sat on the shelf above the sink. A razor, toothbrushes and paste, deodorant. Shampoo, conditioner and soap were still lined up alongside the bath, a scum ring near the top, a bath mat hanging over the edge. A dead houseplant lay forlorn and crumbled on the windowsill, little more than dust.

Suze stared at Jake, as they stood outside one of the closed doors, asking the question. He nodded. She turned the wooden handle. The door crept open. A staleness wafted out making Suze wince. Another room that, if it hadn't been vandalised, covered in dirt and grime, could be mistaken for being lived in. The double bed had sheets, pillows, a duvet. The mirror of the dressing table had been flung to the floor, smashing into shards that lay amongst perfume bottles, a hairbrush, trinkets.

'This is so creepy,' Suze whispered.

'Isn't it!' Jake replied, shaking his head, biting his lip. 'So sad.'

Suze picked up a small picture which was lying amongst the debris. It was black and white, turned sepia with age. She wiped the cracked glass with the sleeve of her hoodie. A mother and child smiling at the photographer, dressed formally in lace collars and tight buttons. She carefully removed the broken frame and turned the picture over. On the back was written in a delicate script, Poznan, 1954, Irenka i Krystyna.

'Wow!' she whispered.

'What is it?'

'Look.' She held the photograph out for him to see. 'A little piece of someone's history.'

'So sad,' he repeated. 'I wonder if they had to run or

were taken?'

'I'm thinking the latter. I mean you don't just leave all of this stuff behind, do you? Not if you've got time. I mean, some of it must be precious. This.' She held the photograph up. 'This must be precious.' She gently placed it in the inside pocket of her jacket. It felt right to care for it; take it away from here.

They carried on checking. The wardrobe was full of clothes. The cupboard likewise. Shoes lay scattered across the floor. The other bedroom had belonged to a child. Some baby clothes had been left, some children's books and toys. The cot was neatly made. Its tiny quilt and pillow hand embroidered with flowers and the name Katya. Scum had been scrawled across the walls in huge red letters.

'Fuck's sake,' Suze muttered, as she turned away and closed the door behind her.

A window at the end of the hall offered a decent view of what was around them. The road they had crossed and beyond. It all seemed very still and quiet. Unthreatening.

Satisfied that they had no unwanted company inside or out, they went back downstairs and moved through to the kitchen. Nevertheless they kept their voices low, tones hushed.

'Look,' Suze exclaimed, as she opened one of the cupboards. 'There are cans, packets, all kinds of stuff.' She picked up a packet of biscuits and studied them. 'Long past their sell by date. Ah well.'

'Edible? Any of it?' Jake asked hopefully.

'I'm pretty sure the cans will be fine. We've got baked beans, peas, ham, peaches...not bad. All we need now is a can opener.' She continued to rummage through the drawers and cupboards, feeling strangely intrusive. 'Shit!' she said, as a swarm of bluebottles buzzed out from under the sink. 'Disgusting. Something must have died under there. Bloody stinks.'

'Of what?'

'I have no idea. Something dead!' she said, pushing the door tightly shut again. 'If you want to investigate further be my guest.'

'Nah, you're all right.'

'Oh brilliant! They had a dog too,' she said, as she opened a door to a large sack of dried dog food.

Yoko knew instantly what it was, her tail wagging happily as she sniffed at the sack.

Suze found a couple of bowls and filled one with water, the other with food.

'Here you go, Yoko,' she said, putting them on the floor for her. It was gone in seconds.

One of the drawers held cutlery, including a can opener. She wiped the dust from the lids of the cans, opened them, sniffed. Satisfied that it was edible, she spooned their contents into bowls for her and Jake.

'Jake,' she called.

There was no reply. She called again, louder, then wished she hadn't. *Stupid, stupid, stupid!* Perhaps the idiots that scrawled their hate on the walls were frequent visitors. Perhaps they were on their way here. Or New Dawn were close by. Or. Christ, there could be any number of dangers and there she was calling for Jake as if this was normal. As if everything was okay.

Yoko had finished her food and was contentedly licking her lips. She would know. She would smell trouble, strangers. Surely? Of course she would. Yoko was the smartest dog Suze had ever known. Always one step ahead. Always reading the situation. Footsteps echoed in the room above her. One set. Casual. It must

40

be Jake.

'Come on girl,' she called, patting her thigh, as she made her way tentatively towards the stairs. She paused at the bottom. Yoko trotted up, wagging her tail. Suze followed.

Jake was looking out of the upstairs window. He turned and smiled when he heard them approaching.

'You scared the crap out of me! I was calling you.'

'Sorry. Wasn't thinking. Or rather, I was thinking. About all of this, you know? Lost lives.'

'I've scraped enough food together for a scran. You coming?'

'Yeah. Sure.'

Everyone's hunger sated, they made their way back upstairs, cleaned up the broken glass and curled up on the double bed. Suze's head on Jake's shoulder, his other arm around her. Yoko across Suze's legs. Nightmares filled her head. She could see her parents' house being trashed. She was hiding under a table, then behind a door, watching, screaming, but making no sound. She watched as her father burned; as her mother was shot. She saw it all and did nothing.

When Suze awoke she was dripping with sweat. She felt sick. A faint memory of her nightmare clung on to her consciousness; the terror still there, the images thankfully fading. It took her a few seconds to remember where she was. She looked across at Jake lying beside her. 'Are you awake?' she asked.

'Yeah. Have been for a while but didn't want to wake you. Just glad you managed to drop off eventually. Sounded like you were having some pretty evil dreams.'

'Sorry. Did I disturb you?'

'Don't be silly. It's nothing.'

She sat up and twisted her head from side to side. 'Shit, my neck's stiff.' It clicked. 'Oh,' she complained, as she reached behind her head and tried to rub the pain away.

'Here.' Jake positioned his legs either side of her and gently massaged her. He could feel the knots in her neck, the tension in her shoulders. He worked at them until his fingers ached. 'Better?'

'Oh, that's brilliant. Thanks.' She turned and smiled at him.

He stroked the side of her face, searching her eyes, trying to read her. 'I would do anything to ease the pain you must be feeling right now. To make things right again.'

'I know,' she said, as she kissed him gently on the cheek. 'I know you would.' She glanced out of the window at the evening sky, the sun submitting to its demise. 'It'll be getting dark again soon. I think we should get moving fairly quickly.'

'You don't want to hang on here for a bit? Get ourselves together?' Jake asked. 'I dunno. Rest?'

'Nope. It's too close and too obvious. If they are looking for us I'm pretty sure empty houses in the area will be high up on their list.'

'Yeah. Yeah, you're right. Let's get organised then. We could do with a change of appearance, couldn't we? Some different clothes. We should have a rummage. There's plenty there.'

'Oh God, wearing dead people's clothes.'

'You don't know that. They might be fine.'

'You and I both know that fine is far from what they are.'

'Point taken. But needs must. It's not as if they have any use for them now, is it?'

They checked through the wardrobes, feeling awful about it but persevering.

'Well, what d'you know, a couple of Barbour jackets. Nice and respectable. And a flat cap. What d'you reckon?' Jake said, throwing one jacket at her and donning the other. He ran his fingers over his limp Mohican. 'Hmm.' He flattened it down and pulled on the cap.

She laughed. 'I can cope with that. We could almost pass for a couple of respectable country folk,' she said. 'A change of hair would help too. I wonder...' She checked the bathroom cupboard and returned brandishing scissors and peroxide. 'Brilliant. Seems somebody else was changing their appearance. Can you chop it all off for me?'

'Oh no...I'll do something horrible. I can't.'

'Don't be stupid. It's either that or I do it myself.' She held out a chunk of her hair and moved the scissors towards it.

'Okay. Come here then,' he said, sighing. 'Fuck.'

'You might find it easier if you can stop your hands from shaking,' she said.

'It's your fault. I'm terrified of what you might do to me if I screw up.' The truth was he hated watching her trademark long black hair falling to the floor.

'Idiot!' she said with a smile.

He began, tentatively snip, snipping, inch by inch.

'Give me them!' she demanded, her arm outstretched. She snatched at the scissors and hacked off a handful to just above her shoulders. 'There! Does that make it a bit easier for you?'

'Shit. If you insist, then...'

*

She looked at her reflection in the bathroom mirror

and barely recognised herself. A short blond bob, no face jewellery. 'Wow!'

'You know, it suits you.'

'Yeah, yeah,' she said sarcastically, running her fingers through her hair and ruffling it. 'Still, I don't look like me any more, so that's good.'

'That you don't.'

Yoko started barking.

'Shhh. Yoko. No!' Suze whispered urgently. 'Here!'

Yoko padded into the bathroom. Her hackles raised, her tail tight and low.

'What the fuck?' Jake mumbled. He tentatively peered out of the little window which opened onto the fields at the back of the house. He could see nothing but open countryside.

The back door opened with a clatter as it bounced off the wall. Several pairs of heavy feet tramped into the house. Suze and Jake froze, staring at each other. Eyes frightened wide.

'Woo hoo. Party!' a voice boomed from downstairs. The voice sounded young. Male. The words slurred and over excited.

'Fuckin' ace. Fuck. Yeah! Let's get to it!' another male.

'Get those fuckin' knickers fuckin' right off her,' a third male.

A muffled squeal. Kicking. A slap.

'Shut the fuck up!'

Another slap.

Suze and Jake stood ensnared by fear, disbelieving, hiding behind the door.

'Come fuckin' here ye fuckin' foreign tart ye.'

They could hear thumps and groans and heavy breathing, then grunts of ecstasy mixed with a concoction of obscenities. The smash of a bottle breaking. Laughter. Shouting. Stumbling. Swearing. The hiss of a spray can. Furniture being turned over.

Suze was crouched down beside Yoko stroking her, trying to keep her calm. 'It's okay girl,' she whispered repeatedly. 'Shhhh.'

'Gang bang! My fuckin' turn. Right. Oh yeah, oh yeah.'

No, no this isn't happening. No. I won't...

'Jake,' Suze whispered, 'we have to do something!'

He nodded.

She drew on every piece of hate that she held. New Dawn, her parents, this house and what it meant. All of it. It swelled in her and flew out of her. 'Bastards,' she screamed, as she charged down the stairs, scissors held high, like a woman insane, a dervish. Yoko ran barking at her side. 'Leave her alone. Leave her the fuck alone!' she shrieked as she lunged at the rapist on the girl, sticking the scissors into his back. A boot landed in her side. Yoko jumped at the leg above it, snarling and biting.

'Get your fuckin' dog off!'

Her teeth had sunk in and she wasn't letting go.

Jake had the leg of a chair clenched in his hands held high like a baseball bat. He swung at the closest youth, then the other, aiming for their heads. The third ran off.

'I'm fuckin' out of here! They're fuckin' mental!'

'You!' The second one pointed at Suze as he followed. 'You're fuckin' next!'

'Is that right, big man?' she called after him as he ran off, shouting and cursing, threatening his revenge.

*

Suze sat holding the girl, rocking her back and forth, stroking her greasy blonde hair. 'Oh God. Are you

45

okay?' she was asking through tears. The anger now drained, replaced with upset, with disgust, with an awful empathy for this girl.

Jake pulled back the curtains to check they had left.

'Ah shit, those bastards,' the girl said, wiping her nose on the back of her hand, looking at the floor. 'They do this like we just animal.' She spat on the floor. 'Nobody care. Nobody.'

Suze wrapped her arms around her, trying to offer strength, comfort, anything. The girl broke into deep lunging sobs.

'Shhh. It's okay. It's okay. They've gone,' Suze said, looking across at Jake for confirmation.

He nodded his head. 'Yeah, it's all clear.'

'I'm Suze. That's Jake. And you?'

The young woman looked up. Her face was bruised, her lip cut. The rip in her dress revealed older bruises, scratches and burns. She pulled at the faded material in an attempt to cover herself. 'Magda. I Magda.'

'Okay, Magda. Come on. Let's get you cleaned up,' Suze said, helping her up and leading her to the bathroom. She turned on the shower, undressed Magda and helped her in. The girl slumped to the ground and sat under the heavy stream of water, shaking. 'It's okay. Here,' Suze said, handing her a piece of cracked soap. 'Wash it all away.'

Jake knocked at the door and called through. 'Hey, sorry but we need to get out of here, like soon. They might come back with reinforcements, weapons, and, yeah we should move.'

'Right,' Suze called back. 'Magda. Come on love. Let's get you dressed, okay? Do you live near here?'

'I work for men at farm. Not far. Is just there.' She pointed back in the direction they had just come from.

46

'Is five, ten minutes.'

'Do you know those youths that attacked you?'

'Sure, I know. Is normal. They live farm also. They like crazy people. Shout and beat and rape. Is normal.'

'Why do you stay?' Suze asked.

'What I do? No papers. No money. I nothing. I no-one. If any leaves others punished. So we stay. What else we do, huh? What else we do?'

'But you can't just go back....to that? There must be something we can do. Something to help.'

'No. You go. You has problems many. I see this. You go.'

'Maybe, but, shit. We can't just leave you,' Jake said, as he threw some food into a couple of bags.

'You come? You help? They kill. Is their way. You go. I go. Is all,' Magda said, as she headed back towards the farm. 'You good people. God with you.'

They pulled what was left of the door behind them and ran out into the night.

'Why?' Suze asked.

'I dunno. People like that are...' He shook his head, 'I dunno.'

8

They kept to the hedgerows, high and protective, all night. The drone of a helicopter drew further into the distance leaving the gentle sounds of the night to reclaim their rightful place. They could again hear the rustles of the night creatures all around. The heavy beating of a large bird's wing. The call of an owl screeching its presence from a distant tree. The scurry of its prey at their feet. Dawn began to announce its arrival too early through the song of a plaintive bird, swelling within minutes to a choral cacophony.

'It's so beautiful,' Suze said. 'I used to love waking up to this. Dad would put the tent up in the back garden and I'd sleep out most of the summer. It was so cool,' she smiled. 'Like I had my own private domain.'

'For me, that was summers at our country house in Estonia,' Jake said in reply.

'You had a country house!'

'Yeah. Not like you have over here. Nothing posh. Most people had them. Little wooden houses in the middle of nowhere. No electricity, no running water. Just a glorified shed really, with a bit of land and a well. It was total freedom for a few weeks every year. Good times.'

'I was just thinking that, you know? We've been friends for what, five years now?'

'Must be, yeah. Since uni.'

He remembered it well and could have given her the precise day, the hour, but that might have seemed creepy. The first time he'd seen her he was struck by the air of confidence she seemed to exude. She didn't bother with make up or fashion. Her look was hers – casual, alternative and just a bit funky. She refused labels, disliked designers and took pleasure in undermining the establishment at every opportunity. She debated with the lecturers, questioned them, and was respected for it. He respected her for it. Hers wasn't a desire to be querulous, to appear smart, to cause offence, like it might have seemed. It was a need to know, to learn, to understand. Her comments were well thought out. Often important.

'And we've never really told each other much about our histories, have we? I mean, how much do we actually know about each other? It's all been study and politics, going out for a drink, a laugh, but where we come from? What made us, us? Not much.'

'Is this what the dawn chorus does to you then? Make you all philosophical?' he asked, teasingly.

'I'm serious!' she slapped his arm. 'I mean who are you? Jake the cool dude. Jake the party guy. Jake the political machine. I don't know, Jake. I just don't know,' she said, her voice beginning to break.

'I'm not trying to avoid anything, Suze, but it's getting light. Can we talk about this later?' he asked, putting his arm around her shoulders and giving her a squeeze. 'Right now we need to think about somewhere to disappear for the day. Any ideas?'

'I don't know. Last night has put me right off any empty houses. Maybe we should just try and make do with something in the woods over there?' she said, pointing across the field to a distant outline of trees.

'Okay. Might as well. Race you across,' he said, laughing and beginning to run. 'Last one there buys the round.'

'You idiot!' she laughed. 'And that's cheating. Injured woman here!'

Nevertheless she chased him across the field of grass, heavy with dew, trying really hard to rise above the discomfort. She hated losing. Cattle lazily turned their heads towards them, then continued grazing, sensing no danger. She caught up with him just before the woods began. She lunged at his ankles and brought him to the ground with a thud.

'Bitch!' he laughed.

'Cheat!' she said, pushing down on his back and running off into the agreeably dense woods, Yoko at her heels.

She sat against the melancholic trunk of a fallen tree. Its impressive girth announcing the great age it had reached prior to its demise. Running her fingers along its gnarly bark she picked at pieces of moss, enjoying the earthy smell it gave off. She remembered her father telling her how the moss on a tree could help you find your bearings if you were lost, but she had forgotten how. How many seemingly irrelevant moments had now become so very precious?

'Here's as good as anywhere, I reckon,' Jake said, walking around the roots and inspecting the cavernous hole they had left in the ground. 'We could cover all this with branches and leaves and we'll have a pretty cool lean-to.'

They collected a decent amount of wood from the forest floor, then gathered ivy, moss, and leaves. Jake instructed and Suze followed. It didn't take them long to finish their task, weaving ivy in and out of the branches to hold them in place and offer some camouflage. Some protection.

'Well done you. I'm impressed!' Suze said, as she climbed into the hiding place, settling herself into a niche he had lined with moss for them, on top of which she placed their sleeping bags. 'Quite the boy scout, aren't you?'

'Actually it was the Internet. This is the first time I've put theory into practice. It's been a long held ambition.'

'Really?'

'Really!'

'Well, I am truly impressed. Come. Sit,' she said, patting the space beside her.

He joined her, lifting his arm to make a rest for her head, which she accepted. She could feel his heart thumping, blood pulsing. It felt safe. It felt good.

'So, what would you like to know?' Jake asked. 'About the real me?'

'Your childhood. Family. Stuff like that.' She was thinking about the pictures she'd seen, the letter. She hated not knowing. It was what made her good at her job. Questions and more questions. Digging away like a badly behaved terrier.

'Okay, but you likewise, yeah?'

'Of course.'

'Well, Russian dad, English mum, you know already.'

'Yes, but there must be a story there. How did they meet?'

'Mum decided that she wanted to travel a bit after uni so she took a course in teaching English as a foreign language and went off to Tallinn.'

'Cool!'

'Yeah. Anyway she was teaching English to a group of programmers and Dad was one of her students. Apparently he was really annoying; always questioning her and going off on grammatical rights and wrongs. She couldn't stand him to begin with. Thought he was arrogant. After the course finished he asked her if she'd take him on as a private student, one to one. She was going to say no, but he was offering good money and she said he had a killer smile.'

Suze laughed, 'Yeah. I can see that.'

He blushed and played with the braided leather around his wrist. 'So, they started dating, moved in together pretty quickly and then my sister and I came along.'

'Sister? Ah. The girl in the pictures? In your lock-up?'

'Yeah. Ilona. She was two years older than me.'

'Was?'

'Yeah. She was killed by some drunken idiot behind a wheel.'

'Oh my God! I am so sorry. I had no idea.'

'She was the reason we moved over here. Mum was really struggling with it and Dad, well, he'd do anything for her and jobs in I.T. are mobile so we moved to London. That was, what, ten years ago now. I was brought up bilingual, well, trilingual actually, English, Russian and Estonian, so fitting in at school wasn't too difficult. Jakov became Jake and we took Mum's surname just to make it easier. Dad didn't like doing it, heritage and all that, but I guess he could sense what might be coming. Smart guy. Mum still struggled though. She'd started drinking after Ilona's death and it just got worse when we moved here. It was bad. I mean really bad. She'd become this unrecognisable nasty person, shouting and screaming at me and Dad. Saying stuff like she wished it had been one of us instead of Ilona, you know? Hard times.' He became silent and shook his head, biting his lip, chewing at it.

'I'm sorry, Jake. I shouldn't have asked.'

'Hey, it's all part of my history, you know? It's not something that'll ever go away. You just have to move on, don't you?'

'Yes, I guess so.'

'She still drinks. Dad just puts up with it and I try and avoid her, well, both of them to be honest. That was how I got the lock-up. Dad gave it to me so as I could get away when she was on a particularly bad binge, which was pretty often. One of her favourite taunts was to tell my dad that I'm not his. You can imagine how much that cut him. Poor guy.'

'What about you? Christ, that must hurt. So do you know for sure? I mean...hmm.' She fiddled awkwardly with her newly short hair, missing its old length.

'What?' he asked cocking his head at her, trying to pull her back.

'Ah, nothing.' She shook her head.

'C'mon,' he said, nudging her gently in the ribs. 'I thought we were doing an honesty thing here.'

'I was going to say I'd want to know, but I've never tried to find out about my natural parents so...,' she shrugged her shoulders in a resigned way.

'You're adopted? Wow! I had no idea. Shit. You guys just all look so, um, I dunno, natural together, I guess.' He suddenly remembered, felt an embarrassed flush creep up his face, pulled back. 'Sorry. I wasn't thinking. Are you okay talking about them?'

'The way I see it is as long as they're still being

talked about, they're still alive, you know? Keeps them here. Real,' she said, clearing her throat, looking up at him with the eyes of a hurt child.

'Yeah. I understand that. So, what do you know?'

'I was given up for adoption immediately after I was born. Apparently my mother was underage and her parents insisted. Anyway, as far as I am concerned they are my parents, Katherine and Geoffrey, nobody else. Just them. They've always made me feel like I was theirs. I love them.'

His T shirt became damp with her tears. He kissed her head and held her close. A wind was picking up. The sound of the trees being tossed about overhead by the impending storm was strangely soothing, mesmeric. The gentle patter of rain became more incessant. Thunder rumbled. He counted the seconds between it and the crash of lightning until they were simultaneous. Yoko hid her head under his jacket, shaking.

9

'I'm well impressed with your survival skills,' Suze said, smiling, as she peeled off her sleeping bag as if it were the skin of a chrysalis, and stretched. 'That was quite a storm and we're pretty dry. Well done!'

He laughed, 'Yeah, quite impressed with myself too. So, breakfast, or should I say dinner?'

'I reckon, as we've just woken up, it's breakfast. This must be what it's like to work nights, huh?'

'Yeah. Guess so. Let me see. We have beans, sardines...'

'Beans are fine. I'll be back in a sec. We girls need to go for a pee.'

Jake laughed.

'Come on, Yoko,' Suze said, pushing some of the branches aside to allow their exit. The ground was heavy with mud and mulched leaves giving it a rich earthy smell. Yoko squatted urgently then snuffled around contentedly, wagging her tail in appreciation. Suddenly her nose was up and she was sniffing, scanning, growling, running off towards the edge of the wood. 'Yoko! Here!' Suze called quietly, urgently. 'Shit!' She ran after her, not wanting to call any louder in the quiet of the late afternoon. Trees and heavy shrubbery were all that she could see. She stopped. Tuned her ears in to the quiet of the woods. Listened for sounds of dog, sounds of anything that didn't belong. Something running ahead and to her left. That must be Yoko. She called again, quietly, barely above a whisper, but she knew the dog could hear. The question was, could anyone else?

Christ Yoko. Of all the days you could choose to run off. Really!

She followed the noise, slower now, scanning every shadow, dissecting every sound. Everything could just as easily be innocent or a threat. Anxiety swathed around her, despite her attempts to keep it at bay. No, she was being foolish. If there was anyone out there they would have made a move by now. This was all okay. Normal. Wildlife.

At last she could see Yoko. She was jumping joyously up at the trunk of a tree where a squirrel sat twitching on one of the higher branches. Its tail flicking up and down like a taunt. Suze grabbed her collar.

'Yoko. That was bad,' she said, with as much reprimand as she could muster, stifling a laugh. Yoko lay down at her feet, submissive, chastised. 'You have to stay close, okay?' She ruffled the dog's neck and they turned back towards the camp. 'Find Jake,' she commanded, pointing in the general direction of where she thought the camp sat.

Yoko trotted off, this time understanding that she had a job to do. Suze could follow with certainty. Once in work mode Yoko was perfect.

'I was beginning to panic there. You were gone a while.' Jake said, as they appeared through the trees.

'This little monster ran off after a squirrel.'

'Oh did she indeed?' Jake asked, looking disapprovingly at her. 'You bad girl, you.'

Yoko slunk as far back under the branches as she

56

could, looking suitably ashamed, and curled into a ball, her sorrowful gaze fixed on Suze.

'So, what's the plan for today then?' Jake asked.

'Keep heading east, I guess. I think I'd feel safer, less conspicuous in a town, a city. Oh God, I don't know. The dangers of being amongst people, or struggling to get by out here. What do you reckon? I mean, we can't live in the woods for ever, can we?'

'Okay. I'm good with a town. We'd best sit tight till evening though. How are you holding up?'

'Oh, it's a blast!' she replied, with a sardonic laugh.

'Seriously.' He put his hand on her shoulder, stroking it encouragingly.

'What can I say? Stay positive, irrespective? It's worked for me to date. I don't think I've got much of a choice really, otherwise they've won haven't they and I'm not giving them that.'

'Yeah, I agree but sometimes...Well, just...yeah, just keep being you.'

*

When the light began to fade again they moved on, walking purposefully, silently. The soft light of dusk left a haze across everything. Features were indistinct. Trees a blur. The land seemed to shrink; wrap itself around them. Nightfall, and the landscape was beginning to change; roads becoming wider, traffic more frequent. Noises which startled them now came with disconcerting regularity. Something there, but not close enough to touch, to see. The darkness that kept them hidden also hid everything else. There was no moon, no starlight. The sky a heavy oppressive black. They trudged on, doing their best to ignore their fears, the anxiety that leapt out with every shadow, every sound. Carry on. Just carry on.

In the distance the sulphuric glow of a copious quantity of street lights lit up the night sky. It was a peculiar feeling, the combination of relief at the possible anonymity it offered, mixed with the anxiety of being noticed, reported. They decided to brazen it out and head on in. It was dawn by the time they finally reached the town's outskirts; just a couple out taking their dog for its morning walk. Curfew was from dusk till dawn. They could move about with a touch less caution now. Suze smiled as she pulled a couple of leaves out of Jake's hair and removed some smudges of dirt from his face with spit and her fingers.

'I feel like someone's mother,' she said.

'Thanks, Mum,' he laughed. 'Presentable?'

'Yes, you'll do. How about me?'

He ran his fingers through her hair, straightened her jacket and nodded. 'Beautiful.'

'Liar! Okay, let's do this,' she said, reaching for his hand.

'Will Yoko be okay?' he asked.

'Sure. She'll just stay at my heel. Won't you girl?' she said, stroking the dog's head. Yoko's tail wagging in agreement.

The street lights had dissolved into the liquid light of the morning sun. They were on a street of tidy bungalows with well tended lawns, manicured hedges, twitching security cameras and flashing burglar alarms. Most curtains remained drawn, windows dark; the predominant populace only awake in the individuality of their dreams and nightmares. A young man was unlocking the metal shutters of a local shop, which were clack, clack, clacking their way up the display of lottery posters, greetings cards, cigarettes and newspapers. He glanced across at them.

'Morning,' Jake smiled and waved politely. He was completely ignored. 'Oh well,' he shrugged.

'What did you do that for?' Suze whispered, with an accusatory frown and a tug at his arm.

'Just trying to be neighbourly,' he replied.

'I'm not so sure of the wisdom in that. Your accent is so patently not local.'

'What, you want me to go "oo ar" or something?'

She shook her head. 'Nope. Just be quiet is all.'

'Duly reprimanded,' he said, smiling at her and squeezing her hand.

The further shake of her head expressed chagrin.

The neat, sterile bungalows gave way to more compact, less affluent, red brick, terraced houses. Then on to blocks of flats. Suze and Jake felt less conspicuous amongst the chipped render and peeling paintwork. The people who lived here had more to concern themselves with than a couple of strangers walking by. There was another day to be got through. Mouths to feed. Another soul-destroying attempt at finding work, even for a day. Queues formed on street corners where employers looking for labour would come, choose what they wanted, and drive off again. A struggle. It was all a struggle.

Suze and Jake didn't look, didn't stare, pretended not to notice, to be intent on each other, on their dog, because that was what you did. You didn't look at a man or a woman when they were down unless you could help them up. A smile, a confirmation of shared humanity, were currency they couldn't afford to spend right now, and they hated themselves for it.

Then at last they reached the anonymity of the city centre, where life seemed to carry on pretty much as normal. Well stocked shops with fancy displays, luxury goods, things and more things, layer upon layer of apparent necessities. People ignoring each other, bustling their way to work, to the shops, heads down, purposeful. Don't look around. Don't look up. Don't draw attention to yourself. Join in. Be like everyone else, and it will all be okay. CCTV scrutinising, a dangerous voyeurism.

Not far from the centre was a well tended park with a small river running through it. There were neat little flower beds connected by a gravel path dotted with wrought iron benches. It was all very clean and pretty, and to them, somehow alien. They chose a bench next to the rose garden and sat, exhausted.

'So what now?' Jake asked.

'Some bread would be good. Something fresh.'

'Yeah sure. I was thinking more about the bigger picture, like where to sleep, what to do next, that sort of thing. But, yeah, why don't you wait here with her.' He bent down to stroke Yoko's head. 'And I'll pick up some supplies at the market we passed back there. Bound to be some cash operators.'

Hard cash was only used by the black market, the underground, the right shops. Everything was bought via ID Cards. Another layer of control.

'Okay, cool.'

'See you in about ten, okay?'

'Yes, okay.'

She let her head fall back and closed her eyes, exhaling deeply; blowing it all away. *Help me, Mum. A bit of wisdom please.* The crunch of several feet stomping arrogantly along the gravel pathway drew closer. She tried to ignore it, focussing on her dog, stroking her. Keeping herself calm.

'Oi, oi, oi, wot 'ave we got 'ere then boys, eh?'

Fuck. There were three of them. All wearing khaki bomber jackets, tight jeans, braces, Doc Martens. Heads shaven, sneers lewd and licentious, danger imminent.

'Allo darlin'. You don't mind if I sit 'ere now do ye? Course ye don't.' He perched himself beside her on the back of the bench. His feet on the seat. He breathed alcohol on her and something sharp, chemical. Glue, she guessed.

Yoko bared her teeth, snarling. Suze didn't stop her.

'Actually, I do. Now, if you don't mind, I'd rather you just fuck off, all right?' she replied, not taking her eyes off the dog.

'Oo...posh bitch with a dirty mouth on 'er. Gets me all 'ot an bothered, that do.' He stood up and cupped his crotch with both hands, thrusting his hips. 'Now, I knows a way of gettin' me all calm an' happy like,' he leered at her to the approving laughs and depraved sneers of his mates. He jumped off the bench, slid down beside her and put his arm round her squeezing hard.

'I said fuck off!' she hissed at him, recoiling, elbowing him in the ribs. Yoko now barking and snapping at their feet.

'Oh, now that weren't right clever now, were it? What you wanna go an' get me all angry for now then, eh?'

'All right boys, I think the lady would prefer to be left alone. That's enough now,' came a voice with a soft American twang from somewhere behind.

She turned to see two older men approaching. They were dressed in tatty clothes; dirty jeans and faded T shirts, their boots caked in mud. They confidently gripped the heavy wooden handles of their spades. *Oh, thank God!*

'We was just bein' friendly like. No harm done, eh

61

lads?' he said, flicking his cigarette on the ground. Spitting. 'Come on. Let's get out of 'ere. Tara, girlie. Nice chattin' weren't it? See ya,' he added pointedly, threateningly. He swaggered off with his pals, exaggerated laughter trailing behind them like a bad odour. A siren began to screech. They whooped and ran.

'You okay love?'

'Yes. Thanks.'

'Nasty bunch that lot. Always causing bother.'

'I can imagine. So, so you work here?'

'Nah, we started a community vegetable garden just up yonder. Been keeping an eye on it, weeding and the like.'

'Cool. Very civil minded of you.'

'We try. Roger, by the way. I'd offer a hand but they're filthy,' he laughed, scratching his dread-locked blonde hair, 'And that's Pete.'

'Likewise,' Pete said with a smile and a shrug of his shoulders.

'Suze. Hi.'

'Thought as much,' said Roger.

'Excuse me?' Suze said, with more than a hint of alarm. Her hands started to sweat. She looked around. *Jake, where are you?*

'Hey, don't stress yourself. It's kinda obvious on which side of the fence we sit no? It's probably a good idea if you come with us. You're a god-damned sitting duck out here.'

'I have no idea what you're talking about. Thanks and all that, but I'm just waiting for my friend then we'll be off.'

'They're out looking for you already. That's what the siren's for.'

'No. I can't just....how do you? Ah shit!'

She was cursing herself for her choice of words, her lack of caution. It was obvious that she had given herself away and there was little point in trying to pretend otherwise. How much did they know? They could be anyone. Undercover infiltrators. She'd read plenty of reports about them. Warned others about them. How they would sneak into your trust, into your cell, and you'd be gone. All of you. Swept up in a dawn raid. Re-educated. Gone. She knew better than this, better than to let her guard down, but she wasn't herself. She was lost. Her thoughts scrambling. *Keep it together Suze. Keep it together.*

'Exactly who are you two?' she asked. Not that there was much point. If they were infiltrators they would lie anyway, but she was trying to stretch out time. Calm herself down. Allow more reasoned thought. Hold out for Jake.

'Who we are doesn't matter right now, but you're Suzannah Bateman and your friend's Jake O'Connor. According to the papers you're a couple of drug crazed junkies who wrecked your parents' place, shot your own mother, set the place alight and ran off with everything of value you could carry. They say you're armed and dangerous and should be called in if you're spotted. We know otherwise. You need to trust us.'

Inside she crumpled like a piece of discarded clothing. Yoko nuzzled her and licked her hand as if in encouragement. She wrapped herself around the dog, clinging on to her as if she were her only lifeline. *What do I do now? What in Christ's name do I do?*

'Sweetheart, you – '

She cut him off. 'Don't fucking call me sweetheart,' she hissed at him, pulling herself together, drawing on her anger. 'Don't fucking call me sweetheart!'

10

They led Suze along a deceptive trail of alleyways, over some waste ground – rubble, a discarded pram, a boot, an old oil drum blackened with fire, broken chairs, a scattering of rusted syringes, a crumpled newspaper – through a small copse, more alleyways. She tried to store the route in her memory, but it was totally confusing. Her thoughts flew off to her parents, to Magda, to Jake, and now what? What was she doing?

Finally they turned up a narrow, unpaved path, bordered by rough, ivy clad, stone walls. The stonework crumbled into fine sand against the touch of her hand. Set into the wall was an arch shaped doorway which came to a point at its top. The curve was lined with narrow, old, red brick, speckled with moss. The tenacious roots of weeds and grasses gouged a precarious living from the spaces left by fallen mortar. Peeling blue paintwork had faded and worn away to insignificance, barely discernible from the raw wood. What looked like holes made by nails marked out a double X across the door, making her wonder if it had once been boarded up. Her mind swarmed with possibilities. A black metal handle turned and clicked the latch open.

She was now in the garden of a somewhat dilapidated Georgian house. It was totally enclosed by stone walls which stood at least three metres high. Vegetable plots boasted, amongst other things, beans, peas, garlic and salad. Bushes hung heavy, laden with fruit, and off to the back a large greenhouse packed with tomatoes, peppers, cucumber, and chillies. Nearer the back door was a herb garden, filling the air with the heady scent of the Mediterranean. This all set her more at ease. They lived the lifestyle of who they were purporting to be. They followed a path of rustic grey stone slabs which led to the back door. Surely this was genuine. These were people who believed in something else. Something better. They had to be!

Inside, huge house plants took pride of place. Suze sat on a chunky old settee of well worn, burnt orange velvet, looking around, taking stock of her new surroundings. Her fingers played against the gentle rub of the fabric. The floors were sanded, the woodwork stripped. Windows, huge, with wooden frames and sash openers, shook themselves at the lightest of winds. Hand made scatter rugs and assorted floor cushions added warmth and colour. Someone's rather good artwork adorned the walls; portraits of faces that felt somehow familiar.

Yoko sniffed around contentedly – that in itself a reassurance she would trust – then stopped to look up at a tortoiseshell cat who sat on a Welsh dresser preening herself, well out of reach, licking her paws, wiping her face, eyes surreptitiously keeping tabs on the intruders. A second cat, grey and sleek, jumped up beside Suze, purring and kneading her leg, rubbing its head against her arm.

'Hello there,' she said, as she stroked its arched back.

Yoko barked and darted to her rightful place behind Suze's legs. The unimpressed cat continued its purring and kneading.

'Just push her off if she's bothering you,' said Pete. 'She's a little terrorist, that one.'

Suze smiled. 'No, no. I'm an animal person. She's cool. Yoko's well used to cats too, from the farm...' Her thoughts were jolted back to that morning. She struggled to hang on to her composure, to fight the images which tried to force their way back out again. She pushed them aside. Held on.

'After John and?' Pete asked

'I'm sorry?'

'Your dog, Yoko?'

'Indeed.' She managed a forced laugh, not wanting to explain further.

'There's a crazy old dog hanging around here somewhere too. I'm sure he'll let himself be known as soon as he realises you're here,' Roger added, with a grin.

'Here. Some tea,' Pete's partner Dana said, smiling softly, reassuringly. 'It's just camomile and honey. Always good in times of stress.' Her face was warm, friendly, with soft hazel eyes, a full mouth which smiled easily, forcing dimples into her ruddy cheeks wrapped in shoulder length brown curls.

'Thank you,' Suze smiled in return, a shaky hand carefully accepting the delicate porcelain mug. She blew on her tea, her thoughts drifting off amongst the steam. Visions of her mum danced out of her memory. Picking herbs on hot sunny afternoons; the kitchen laden with bunches of them left hanging upside down to dry. The shelves of earthenware pots boasting home made concoctions and remedies. Being tucked up in bed with tea and honey, cold compresses, stories and cuddles. She breathed an inadvertently heavy sigh.

66

'You okay?' Dana asked, sitting down beside her, placing a hand on her arm. Gently stroking her.

'Yes, just reminiscing. You remind me a bit of my mum. Took me back...hmm.' She shook her head and drew a deep breath, trying to return her focus to the present. 'I'm sorry.'

'Don't be. After what you've been through?' Dana's voice rose, accentuating the confirmation of understanding; of caring. 'You're doing remarkably well. I can't imagine how you must be feeling.'

'Thanks, I'm worried about Jake too, you know?'

'Of course you are,' Dana added.

'We've got people out looking,' Pete said. 'They'll do their best to find him before curfew's in full effect. There's been nothing from the force about him so far so, fingers crossed.' His words said as encouragingly as the situation allowed.

'From the force?' Suze asked, nerves tingling again. Caution.

'Yeah, we'd hear about it if they'd caught him,' Pete replied.

'What, you've got an interception thing going on here?' Suze asked, incredulously.

'We've got insiders, yeah. Not in New Dawn but there's a few coppers who don't like what's gone down recently. They're not all bastards, thank God!' Roger added, putting his hands together as if in prayer, and looking skywards.

'No, no, of course not. That is so cool. So, how much do you know then?'

'Well, the local force was told to keep an eye out for you two after the whole farm fiasco. You really pissed New Dawn off by getting away. I mean really pissed them off man! Your pictures have been on the front

67

page of the local papers,' said Roger, almost gleefully.

'The hair's good by the way. You look really different,' Dana interjected.

Suze smiled and shrugged her shoulders, 'Yes, well. Needs must. But it didn't fool you though, so...'

'I could tidy it up for you later if you like,' Dana offered.

'Sure. Thanks. Jake's got many skills but hairdressing...'

She wanted to say, "No, it's fine. I like it how it is." She wanted to stop this; to get up and leave. She wanted to go back two days. Just two days. That was all.

'No, really he's done a not bad job,' Dana smiled.

'Drug crazed killers on the rampage, was the headline. Have you seen it?' Roger asked.

'Drug crazed what!?' Suze said with revulsion, 'No, no I haven't.'

'You want to? There's a copy here somewhere,' Pete said, rummaging through the papers in the wicker magazine rack. 'We didn't believe it – knew who you were,' he added. 'There you go.' He handed her the paper.

And there they were, staring back at her from the front page. The photographs were fairly recent, from a bar they'd been at not that long ago. She shook her head and mumbled, 'How on earth?' and read on. Every last contemptible, shameful word. She felt sick, violated. 'How dare they? Bastards!' she said, as she threw the paper down. 'Complete and utter bastards!'

'I know. Vile isn't it?' Dana said, taking her hand and giving it a squeeze. 'We were big fans of your site, by the way,' she added in an attempt to alleviate the mood, change direction, reassure. 'A bit of truth amongst all of the madness.'

'We tried.'

'Hey, you succeeded, big time,' Roger said.

'Do you know if they know we're here, I mean, in town?' Suze asked.

'Afraid so. Well, at least they got a call from some cretinous "good citizen" this morning about a possible sighting. They must have been pretty sure or they wouldn't have gone to the lengths of the sirens. There have been what, two maybe three street-clear curfews called in total,' Dana replied in a tone of disdain.

'So what are his chances? Jake's?'

'I'll be honest with you, unless he's managed to hole up somewhere really safe, they're slim. They're stomping about out there relentlessly and they won't give up easily. It'll be door to door the lot,' said Roger.

'Shit. So, I've put you guys in danger then?' She met each of their eyes in turn. A silent apology.

'No, not at all. Don't worry. You're not the first "refugee" we've had in here, and you probably won't be the last. The basement's like our guest quarters and it can only be seen from the garden, and even then, if you didn't know it was there you wouldn't know it was there! So, yeah, safe.'

'Cool. I am so indebted to you. Thank you,' she said. 'Oh, and sorry for swearing at you earlier. It was just...ahh, sorry,' she added, directing her apology towards Roger.

'Hey, no worries. We're all part of the same whole now aren't we?'

*

After dinner they sat talking about the parts they'd played in the dissension. They told Suze about the fake IDs they'd printed; the network of people across the country who also helped in moving, resettling, adopting. The successes and failures. Their hopes for the future. Suze tried to listen; tried to focus on these people and their stories, but it was difficult. Her mind kept churning over the past few days and the enormity of what had happened to her, to them. She tried to remember what she had actually seen at the farm; what had really happened, but it was so confused. A nightmare which she couldn't quite piece together. Then there was the shut down: Brian, Jake. It bothered her and she couldn't shake it.

'Roger?' she said.

'Yeah,' he replied.

'A while ago you said you knew who we were. How come? I mean how did you put me and Jake with Utell, then with the whole farm thing? How did you know that? How did anyone know who we were?'

'It was all over the Web when Utell went off,' he answered, playing with the beads on his dreadlocks as he locked eyes with her. 'Everyone questioning; coming up with their own theories. Some of them were wild man. I mean – out there! Even going so far as to say that you guys were working for New Dawn. A fact finding deal.'

'Are you serious?' she asked, disgust dripping from her face.

'Sure am. Of course, that could have been New Dawn muck-spreading! Who do you trust eh? Who do you trust? The general thinking was that you'd been hacked; IP traced the lot. You know the rest.'

'Yeah, but we were on a floating Proxy, Brian had installed a barrage of fire walls, alerts. When it happened before, as soon as we were breached the alert would go off, we'd shut down, move along and fire up again with a new computer, a new base, everything.

This time there was no warning and they knew exactly where we were.'

'I don't reckon there's any way of staying hidden for long when you do what you do. Drones zipping about all over the place. And you can bet your bottom dollar that they know way more than we do. Must do, yeah? You take one step, they take two.'

'Yes, I must admit, we were thinking something along those lines too, but how come we've been identified? Me Suze, him Jake. How come?'

'That I can't tell you.' He held his hands up. 'We knew through one of our sources in the force. How he knew? No clue man, no clue.'

'And finding me in the park?'

'Pure coincidence. Pete and I go up most days just to check on the plants and stuff, then those nasty little thugs caught our eye. We had no clue as to who you were till we were right up close.'

'Hmm...I see.'

11

A set of stone steps, worn away by the feet of ghosts long past, took her down to a large basement. There was only one window, which was well below the level of the back garden and barred with black wrought iron, as was the glass panel of the door. It opened into a low ceilinged room made deceptively bright by the lemon yellow walls. A couple of settees sat in one half of the room with a table and chairs at the other. Under the window was an old-fashioned, heavy porcelain sink, a couple of kitchen cupboards and a small two-ring cooker. The bedroom was at the front of the basement, completely subterranean, no windows. They had asked her to avoid the back, just in case.

'Shit girl, I hope you're feeling better than me about this,' Suze said, as she sat on the bed, untying her boots. Places of confinement always made her feel uncomfortable; claustrophobia a regular unwelcome guest. Yoko wagged her tail, perhaps enjoying the attention, perhaps in encouragement. Suze sniffed at her clothes as she placed them over the back of the small faded brocade chair. 'God, I stink,' she said. She walked across the narrow hallway to the bathroom and indulgently accepted the blast of hot water on her face as she stepped into the shower. *Oh, so good.* She scrubbed at herself, as if that could somehow erase the feelings of trepidation which swathed themselves around her, like a pestilential parasite. Defiant. Relentless.

She climbed into bed, patting the covers as a signal to Yoko to join her, who needed no second invitation. The darkness held such a totality she felt she could touch it, feel its imagined solidity. Despite her overwhelming exhaustion, she couldn't switch her thoughts off as they churned the day's events over and over, spinning like a blizzard through the snow storm of her mind, screeching incessantly, searching for some form of understanding, of reason. The walls began to close in on her; sweat clung to her; her legs ached with an infuriating intensity which seemed to be clawing at her bones. She felt dizzy and disorientated. 'Aaagh,' she cried, almost inaudibly, kicking out her legs in frustration. She stretched her arms, her fingers, feeling for the lamp. 'Shit, shit, shit.' She fumbled, knocked something over. 'Okay, deep breaths, deep breaths.' The reassuring feel of the switch. 'Okay.' Yoko sat up at the foot of the bed, her soft brown eyes blinking at the sudden brightness of the lamp. She yawned, stretched and crept on her stomach towards the top of the bed, her front and back legs flattened as if that would make her less conspicuous. Suze stroked her head, 'You daft dog. Come here,' she said, happy to have had a smile brought to her face.

She sat up and plumped the pillows, punching a hollow for her head, using more force than was necessary. 'Oh, this is ridiculous. Come on Suze. Sleep, for Christ's sake!' She began with her toes, stretching and relaxing, inhaling, exhaling, moving slowly up through her body, finishing with her head. Blowing out all the pent up energy with a final exhalation, she

73

focused on the light in her mind. Trying to switch off. Trying to reject the barrage; the assault of words and images. Perhaps if she followed them; took them to a conclusion? She tried.

Suze was suddenly alerted by Yoko jumping off the bed. Turning on the lamp she saw her sniffing at the door, her tail wagging timidly between her hind legs, as if she were scared of something. She barked softly.

'Shhh, Yoko. It's okay,' Suze said, patting the mattress. 'Come here.' Yoko padded gently across. 'I know. You don't like it down here either, do you? But it'll be okay. You'll see,' she said soothingly, rubbing Yoko's chest, trying her best to believe it herself. Pass the positivity on to Yoko. 'Good girl.'

Yoko's ears pricked; her head cocked to one side, her hackles raised. Something was up.

'Quiet. Quiet!' Suze whispered, her voice firm, authoritarian. She could hear the insistent clatter of an old fashioned doorbell. Once, twice, three times. Each press longer and heavier than the last had been. Then muffled voices? Footsteps? Reality had begun confusing itself with imagined fears. She cursed the quality of the building, the thickness of its walls, the depth of the flooring above her. The very things which were keeping her safe, hidden, had become an annoyance. *Shit. What's happening up there?* No, no it was footsteps. Heavy ones. She panicked and turned the light back off, then crept on tiptoes across the hallway into the shower room. Yoko instinctively followed like a welcome shadow. *Christ.* Crouched behind the shower curtain with Yoko wrapped around her legs she tried to calm herself; tried to rationalise things. There was an incessant drip, drip, drip, from the shower head which seemed peculiarly in rhythm with the pounding in her

74

chest.

She had no idea of how long she'd been sitting there for, but her back was getting sore; her legs were stiff. Straining to hear, it seemed that silence had returned to the house upstairs.

'What do you reckon, Yoko? Shall we move?'

Gingerly, she opened the door and made her way to the back of the basement, tiptoeing, listening intently. She wanted to catch a glimpse of the outside. Everything seemed quiet; nothing but the breathless silver moonlight lit up the back garden. It's gentle light drifting in and out of feathery clouds, at once illuminating the shadowy night, bringing it suddenly to life like the touch of an artists brush on a dark canvas. Next rendering it back into black emptiness. Reassured, as much as was possible from her vantage point, she and Yoko retreated into the bedroom.

'Where are you Jake?' she whispered into the night, not wanting to think about it, but unable to let it go. The guilt she felt as she pulled the covers over herself and let her arm fall across Yoko's back was monumental. She would know, wouldn't she, if something awful had happened to him? She would feel it. When he'd come off his bike a couple of months ago, she'd known. There was this attachment, like they were brother and sister. They felt things, knew things, were connected. She felt horribly alone without him.

She lay there, knowing that sleep wasn't going to come. Her internal clock was so messed up and she was far too anxious now. Should she admit defeat? Get up? No. She would stay there until morning. Try to adjust back to some form of normality. Try to settle herself. She tossed and turned, despite her best efforts to switch off again.

Footsteps. She could hear footsteps again. This time they were making their way down the stone steps. She was sure. The back door opened and someone came in. No time to move. Not this time. *Shit.* She sat on the bed, her eyes transfixed on the door. Yoko ran across to it. Her tail was wagging. She threw her head back and barked. This was no warning. This was joyous. A greeting.

'Suze?'

Suze bolted up and clattered the door open, running down the hall in her T shirt, boxers, and bare feet. He was standing there with this huge big grin on his face, his arms open.

'Jake! Where have you been? Where the hell have you been?' She leapt at him, wrapping her legs around his waist, her arms around his neck. 'Don't do that to me again. Don't ever–' He smelled of dirt and sweat and...Jake.

'Hey, I'll leave you two to get reacquainted,' Pete said, smiling, as he closed the door behind him.

Jake slumped onto the settee, throwing his head back with a heavy sigh, running his fingers through his hair. Yoko jumped up beside him, nuzzling his arm, demanding a stroke. 'So,' he asked. 'How come you end up here and I'm left skulking around in ditches and dirt?'

'Oh, pure skill,' she replied laughing. 'Look, just give me a sec while I get some clothes on, okay?'

'Don't bother on my account,' he said with an exaggeratedly lascivious grin.

'Idiot!' she replied, slapping his arm and walking off to the bedroom.

'Is there somewhere I can get myself cleaned up a bit?' he called from the hall.

'Yes. The door opposite is the bathroom.'

'Cool.'

*

He sat beside her as he towelled his hair dry, his muscles rippling beneath the tattoo which stretched from his stomach up across his chest, down his left arm and back. It was a cross between a Celtic and Aboriginal design, swirls and angles in black, snaking their way around his body. She caught herself staring at it.

'That's really cool. I've never seen it all before,' she said admiringly.

'Well, thank you. It's a work in progress. Not too sure where it's going though.'

'Your own design?'

'Yeah. Well, I sketched it and the tattooist did the real deal.'

'Hmm. I like it,' she said, smiling at him.

He walked back to the bathroom, hung the towel on its rail and returned, pulling his T shirt on, messing his hair. 'So, how did you end up here?' he asked, stressing the did.

She told her story. He winced at the part with the skinheads.

'Good timing on Pete and Roger's parts then.'

'Yes, indeed. Extraordinarily so.' Her expression said more.

'What, are you dubious about it?'

'Oh, I don't know. I just don't know who to trust any more, you know? At first I was wary, sure, but they seemed like really decent people. They'd just come back from working on this community garden they've started, which is cool, and, well, it wasn't like I had a whole lot of choice at the time. I'm guessing they, or their friends found you so...'

'Yeah. Yeah they did.'

'As conveniently as they came across me?'

'No actually. It was me who found them. You know that feeling you get when you just know someone's watching you?'

'Sure.'

'Well, I got that feeling big time in the market and felt really uncomfortable, so I made a hasty retreat. Then the siren started and I thought, *oh shit* and tried to find a less conspicuous way back to you. By the time I got to the park you'd gone; I couldn't see you anywhere. I knew you'd wait unless you had no option so I went to look for some place safe to hide. I found this huge oak tree in the park and climbed up as high as I could just praying no-one had seen me.'

'You hid up a tree?' her voice rose in incredulity. 'No!'

'Yes!'

'You are, you're a bloody boy scout!' she said, grinning.

He raised his eyebrows and smiled. 'They were milling around down there, New Dawn. I just held my breath, making deals with gods I don't believe in, you know?'

She smiled at him, 'Yes. Yes I do.'

'Anyway, I hadn't seen any uniforms for a while. I actually managed to nod off for a bit.'

'Without falling out?' she asked with a giggle.

'Without falling out!' he confirmed, giving her a look of mock contempt. 'A couple of guys came along and I could hear them talking about you and me. How you were safe, but they were having no luck finding me. I decided to take my chances and climb down. They got a bit of a shock when I appeared out of nowhere.'

'I can imagine,' she said, laughing at the imagined scenario.

'They seem to have quite a network here. It's cool.'

'Yes. They were telling me about it yesterday. This basement has apparently been a refuge for quite a few immigrants and the like. They've even got insiders in the force.'

'For real?'

'Yes. That's how they manage to pick people up before New Dawn or immigration get them.'

'Wow.'

There was a gentle knock at the door.

'Would you guys like some breakfast? If you come on up we're about to eat,' Dana said.

'Cheers. That would be great. We'll be up in five,' Suze called back. She smiled up at Jake. 'Okay?'

'Sure.'

Breakfast was an abundance of fresh fruit, yoghurt, home made bread and jams, eggs and coffee. The couple who'd brought Jake back were there too, as well as two other people neither of them recognised. They were all seated around a huge oak kitchen table, scratched and scarred by more than one generation. The chairs were an eclectic mix, wood and wicker, some padded, others bare. After eating, the others made their farewells and left.

'Was it my imagination or did you get a visit last night?' Suze asked Dana.

'Yes, well, we knew we would at some point. They just had a little nose around up here. Nothing too serious. It does mean that we'll be left alone now, so you can relax a bit,' Dana replied, smiling.

'I was having a major panic down there!'

'Oh, I'm sorry. Did you manage to get some sleep at least?'

'Yes thanks, a little.'

'Good, good. So, do you two have any plans?'

Suze looked at Jake with a shrug. 'Not yet. We need to have a good think. Weigh up our options.' She laughed. 'Yes, like we have a whole bunch of those!'

'We do need to find out what's happened back home. Get in touch with family and friends somehow,' said Jake. 'The sat phone's got a signal scrambler, but after what happened with the computer I'm not sure I'd trust it. Certainly not in your house anyway.'

'No, of course not, but we can easily help there. Why don't I nip down to the shops and pick you up a couple of throwaway mobiles?' suggested Pete.

'That would be excellent. Cheers mate,' Jake replied. 'We need to find out what happened to Brian, if anyone's been visited, stuff like that.'

'Brian?' Pete asked.

'Yeah, he was with us when we found out we'd been taken down. We left the old safe house together, but he got lost somewhere along the way,' Jake said.

'We haven't heard anything about a Brian,' Pete said, looking at Dana and Roger for confirmation. They both shook their heads. 'You got doubts about this guy?'

'As in can we trust him?'

'Yeah.'

'No doubts at all. He and I have been friends since we were at primary school. He's been in on this from the start. I'd trust him with my life. Probably have a few times!'

'Right, right,' Roger added, nodding his head.

'So how much will you need?' Jake asked, reaching down into his jeans' pocket for some cash.

'No, no, you're all right there. My treat. You're gonna need all the cash you have and they'll be like 99p each. No biggie! I'm guessing you run ID free?'

'Yeah. We've got a couple of fakes that do if we need to flash them, but nothing's on them. Close scrutiny would be very bad!'

'Right. I guess they know though. If you're not using your official IDs you must be using something, right? Anyway, the amount of fuss they're making about you two, they're gonna make life as hard as they can and no mistaking. Is there anything else I can get for you guys while I'm out?'

'No. We're good. Thanks,' Suze replied, wishing she could have asked for a change of clothes. Ah well.

*

Pete handed across the flimsy silicone mobiles.

'Brilliant,' said Jake, as he turned his over in his hands. He keyed in Brian's number first.

'Hello,' a voice said at the other end.

Jake hung up straight away. 'That wasn't him. Shit. This is bad.' He tried his father.

He threw a look to Suze. She bit her lip, took a deep breath.

'Mr O'Connor?'

'Uh-huh.'

'This is just a quick courtesy call to let you know you're one of the lucky people who's been selected for our prize draw.'

'Oh, am I now. Well, I'll not be interested in that. Thanks all the same. Goodbye now,' his father said, with just the hint of an accent betraying his Russian origins.'

'Ah fuck. He's got unwelcome company.'

'Are you sure?' Suze asked.

81

'Yeah. We've got this code thing. My dad's big on conspiracy theories. He reckons it's part of his genetic imprint, the KGB and all that. I used to think it was just paranoia, until recently.'

'That's clever of him. Are you okay?' Suze asked, reaching out to touch his arm.

'Yeah, yeah. It's not as if I wasn't expecting it. Are you going to try someone?'

'I don't know. I've caused enough problems already by not thinking things through, you know?'

'There's no way you could have known what was going to happen, Suze. Don't beat yourself up about this, any of it. Okay? It wasn't your fault,' Jake said, holding her gaze, fixing his words. 'None of it.'

She would love to have been able to believe him.

12

'I've been wondering,' Suze said.

'Oh, oh,' Jake cut in. 'Ominous.'

'No, seriously. Why the big deal about us? They got the site, closed it down. They must know that someone else will fill the gap. I mean, it's not as if we were the only source of alternative news or information, is it?'

'Okay. With you so far.'

'There must be something else, something we're missing. For sure they'd enjoy locking us up, using us as a deterrent, trying to find out what we know, but to go to all of this trouble? New Dawn after us, calling a curfew, door to door, and then there's that piece of shit in the papers. All for us? For Utell. Really?'

'What in the papers?' Jake's expression held more than a hint of disquiet.

'Oh right, you haven't had the pleasure have you?' Suze replied, standing up to fetch the paper from the rack and thrusting it at him. 'This piece of evil shit.'

His expression turned to one of consternation as he saw first the headline, then the photos of the two of them enjoying a beer at La Mexicana street cafe. It was a quiet little place in the back streets, and, they had thought, safe. As he read on he covered his mouth with his hand, shaking his head in silent repugnance.

'Unbelievable,' he said, looking across at Suze.

'How can they...Ah fuck yeah, we know only too damned well how they can, don't we?'

'See what I mean? All this just for the site? I don't think so. We're missing something here,' said Suze, her pale blue eyes searching his, questioning.

'Have you guys been working on anything yourselves? I mean, you're both journalists, right?' Roger asked. 'Is there something you've happened upon that someone really doesn't want out there?'

'Shit, there's so much,' Suze said. 'Anything spring to mind, Jake?'

'I don't know,' he answered, visibly trying to connect synapses in his brain. 'We'd need to sit down, go over our notes, check back. And there's the photographic stuff too.'

'Have you got access to all of that without using your computer?' Roger asked.

'Yeah. Brian's a tech genius. He made sure we were all secure and backed up. Everything's copied on portable hard drives,' Jake replied.

'Your hard drive's good though, secure?'

'Absolutely. Encrypted, mobile passwords, the lot.'

'Good, good.'

'Have you got it on you?'

'Look, it's getting late. How about we crack open some beers and let you two just relax for a bit? You can go over this tomorrow after a decent night's sleep,' Dana offered.

'I must admit, I'd kill for a beer right now,' said Suze, 'Oh, that's so not funny any more is it?'

Dana laughed as she handed her a cold bottle. 'There you go. Cheers.'

They clinked bottles and tried to keep the conversation to idle chit chat, though it was difficult.

After a few drinks, pleasant conversation and much needed laughter, Jake and Suze excused themselves and retired to the basement. As they stood in the back garden waiting for Yoko to relieve herself they looked up at the night sky. It was a beautiful night; the moon glowed a fierce orange, tingeing the few clouds with an ethereal golden hue.

Jake put his arm around Suze's shoulder and pulled her close. 'Hard to believe that that same moon shone down on us not so long ago when things were just, well, normal, isn't it?' he said.

'Yes, I know what you mean. The coup was bad enough but this...Jesus! I can't imagine how this is all going to end, you know? What the hell are we going to do, Jake?'

'I'm clueless, Suze. Completely clueless.'

They stood, silent for a while longer, just breathing.

'Come on, Yoko,' Suze called quietly across at the dog who was contentedly nuzzling around in the bushes. 'Let's go.'

'Is there just the one bedroom then?' Jake asked, as they walked down the stone steps, their footsteps echoing softly in the velvet night.

'Yes, I'm afraid so.'

'Do you want me to take the settee?'

'No. I'd sleep better with you beside me,' she said, feeling a bit pathetic and mistrustful of this unaccustomed desire to share her bed. 'If that's okay?'

'Of course it's okay.'

He held her close, forcing the protectiveness he felt towards her to the fore until they both fell asleep.

*

When she awoke he was already up, showered and dressed.

85

'Hey, morning,' she said, stretching and yawning. 'Have you been up long?'

'No, half an hour or so. That's the best sleep I've had since we left London.'

'Me too,' she said, smiling at him. 'Have you any idea what time it is?'

'Half nine. Dana popped down with clean clothes for both of us,' he said. 'She's lovely isn't she?'

'She is. I can't believe how lucky we were. I'm going to have a quick shower then we'll go on up, okay?' she said, as she picked her freshly laundered clothes up off the chair and headed to the bathroom. 'Oh and thanks for being such a gentleman last night,' she said over her shoulder. 'You're a good friend.'

His rueful smile was unseen; his heavy sigh unheard. He looked down at the floor and kicked at nothing. *Ah shit!*

When they went up to the main house Dana was alone in the kitchen. Roger and Pete had gone on their regular trip to the community garden. The old dog lay contentedly in his basket. He lifted his eyes for a quick look when they came in, flicked his tail so gently it remained on the blanket, then fell back into his snore filled sleep. Yoko appeared somewhat miffed at being ignored and decided to steal the food from his big earthenware bowl.

'Yoko!' Suze reprimanded.

'Oh, don't worry. The old guy hardly eats these days. Well, not dog food anyway. I leave it down for him just in case, but unless it's fresh meat he's really not interested and even then I have to hand feed him. Not long left for this world I'm afraid,' Dana said, looking affectionately across at the straggly brown and white mutt.

'Oh, I'm sorry. It's a tough one that,' Suze said, as she pulled a chair from under the kitchen table.

'Yeah, I'm not looking forward to it, but he's had a good life. He was well loved before we took him in.'

'Is he a rescue dog then?' Jake asked.

'Sort of. He belonged to a Polish family who were repatriated. It was bloody awful. They were harassed and bullied then finally taken to the camp. Poor old Bilbo here had to be left behind so I said I'd take him. What can you do? I'd known the mother for years. She helped organise a centre for families with autistic kids. You know, like a support group where the kids could play and the parents relax. Such a good person and yet, apparently an "undesirable" one. Foreigners stealing our jobs and destroying our culture. What a load of bullshit! It just makes me so angry...' She caught herself mid rant. 'Ah, preaching to the converted aren't I? Sorry!'

'No, no. It's so important to keep it alive, keep the anger, don't you think?' Suze said. 'We can't allow this to settle into normality. Staying quiet, giving in. No, no way.'

'I totally agree with you,' Dana said. 'It was what happened to them that made us start to be more active. I couldn't bear standing back and letting it all happen again without at least trying.'

'Good on you,' Suze said. 'Have you had much success?'

'Short term, yes. Long term? Well, it's so hard. There is this huge network and we can move people around, hide them but...' she sighed heavily. 'Honestly I think most end up repatriated eventually. It's just not quite so awful if we can keep them out of the camps, you know? Those places are just so inhumane. People treated like animals because they're from Eastern Europe, or Africa. Or just not here. Unbelievable.' She shook her head. 'You can't help but draw historic comparisons, can you?'

'No, you can't. We met this girl, Magda, a couple of nights back. Christ, I say met! We interrupted a bloody gang bang in this empty house we'd taken refuge in.'

Dana turned quickly, her eyes wide with concern.

'I guess it was what, twenty miles west of here, or thereabouts?' She looked to Jake for confirmation.

'Yeah, about that.'

'She said there was a farm where a whole bunch of immigrants are being used as slave labour; that rapes and beatings were commonplace and they were too scared to try and escape. We asked her to come with us but she refused. It was heartbreaking. It felt so shit just not doing anything to help, you know? Just walking away, but she insisted.'

'Do you think you could find it on a map?' Dana asked.

'Probably. What do you reckon Jake?'

'For sure, yeah. What can you do though?'

'It depends who's running it. If it's an official camp, probably nothing, but if it's some jerks taking advantage, that's a different ball game. The least we can do is find out.'

'How can you do that?'

'Oh, there are ways,' she smiled, as she clicked on Open Maps and turned the keyboard over to Suze and Jake. They retraced their steps using close view, managing, finally, to find the empty house.

'Here. It was here we met her,' Suze said, unsettled by the imagery happening in her head. 'She headed off that way,' she pointed with the cursor, 'and said it was about five or ten minutes away.'

'Which would be...' Jake scrolled the screen up, 'about there.' Their eyes were drawn to a collection of abysmal looking huts, surrounded by high chicken-wire fencing, interspersed by spotlights standing tall like sentries. Outside the fence stood a large farmhouse emanating a completely contrasting, well-to-do, aura.

'Wow. Do you believe in fate, or that there's no such thing as coincidence?' Dana asked.

'It used to be the former, nowadays the latter. Why?' Suze replied.

'The empty house you stayed in, it was Krystyna's, the Polish woman I was telling you about. She always said there was something dodgy about Crannock Rise. That place.' She gestured at the buildings on the screen. 'But she never alluded to what it might be. Well, well, well.'

'Oh my God! Would she have been sent there?' Suze asked.

'No. They never send you to a local camp and, as far as I know, that's not a legit one.'

'So is that good or bad? For Magda, the girl?'

'It's good, in so far as we can try and get them out, if we can convince them to come with us, that is. Sometimes the Devil you know and all that.'

'For sure,' Jake said.

'At least they'll have an option now. Leave it with me. I'll get word out, feelers spread,' she smiled reassuringly.

'Can I ask you something?' said Suze.

'Of course. Fire away.'

'Last night when we were talking about hard drives and the like, did you deliberately change the subject?'

'Oh dear, was it that obvious?' Dana replied, guiltily.

'No, no, I'm just hyper sensitive these days.'

'I just think the less people that know your secrets the more likely they are to stay that way. Safer.'

'So it's not because you don't trust Roger? He is full of questions isn't he?'

'Oh, don't worry about him, it's just the American in him. He needs to know everything,' she smiled. 'No. No, I'd trust him with my life. Anyway, what about you? What do you guys want to do? Any plans?'

'I reckon we need to try and get back to London,' Jake replied, 'Find out what's really going on.' He looked across at Suze, his raised eyebrows asking the question.

'Yes. I think bolting like we did was unwise,' she said, nodding. 'We need to face this and get it sorted.'

'I thought that might be the case,' Dana said. 'I'd do the same in your shoes. They'll be focussing their efforts on here for a while, I guess, since you've been spotted and all.'

'Uh-huh. That would be logical,' Jake confirmed. 'The problem is how, and where to stay when we get there?'

'We can ask Roger when he gets back. He's the expert in moving people and hiding them.'

'Oh really? That's cool,' Suze said.

'It won't be the most comfortable ride, but it'll get you there,' Dana answered. 'It's a well travelled route.'

'Brilliant,' Jake added.

13

'Dana, Pete, thanks for everything and good luck,' Suze said, giving them both a warm hug.

'Yeah, you've been brilliant. Cheers,' Jake added, shaking their hands.

'Hey, it's been a pleasure. You two take care now and keep us posted, yeah?'

'Will do. Take care.'

They made their way out through the back garden. More mixed emotions. Leaving behind something that had felt safe – at least as safe as the times warranted – and going towards what? Danger? Definitely. Answers? There had to be answers.

At the end of the lane a blue removals truck was waiting. They clambered in to the back, manoeuvring around furniture, packing boxes, and rolls of carpet, until they reached a secret panel between the driver's cab and the back of the van.

'Not the most comfortable space, but it should serve its purpose,' Roger said as he pulled the panelling across in front of them and screwed it securely in place. He thumped the panel. 'That's you guys. Sit tight now. We'll get you there.'

They sat, knees pulled up against their bodies, facing each other. The sound of boxes being pushed back against the panel, furniture scraping on the metal floor added to their seclusion. It was hot and sticky with a bare minimum of air, but this was of little consequence compared to the feeling of security it offered. Even Suze's claustrophobia, which sat nagging at the back of her head, reminding her that it was there, waiting, was worth it. These people knew what they were doing. It was a relief to have someone else take the reins, if only for a few hours. What lay ahead was an absolute unknown, but for now they could do nothing but wait. Wait and trust. Neither of which came naturally to them at the best of times. Question and move was their norm. Even before the riots, that had been what made them tick. Question everything. Don't sit still, settle, and let complacency creep in.

Suze flapped her hand across her face like a fan, in a futile attempt to alleviate the heat. She looked across at Jake. 'Phew...fun huh?'

'Bundle of laughs,' he joked back at her, tilting his head to one side, imitating Yoko. The dog wagged her tail, appearing to appreciate the gesture. 'This poor little mutt here must be so confused,' he said, scratching the top of her head. 'Don't you worry girl, it'll all be fine,' he added, unsure of whether the comment was directed more at Yoko or Suze.

The truck trundled on for a couple of hours. Three knocks sounded on the panel between them and the driver's cab. The signal that they had reached a checkpoint. Suze called Yoko to her and told her to lie down and be quiet.

'You movin' another fool up to the big smoke then are you, Roger?' asked the guard in a very friendly manner.

Suze raised her eyebrows at Jake and gave him the thumbs up.

'Darned fools if you ask me, but yeah. Keeps me in business though, doesn't it?' Roger replied with a chortle.

'You don't mind if I 'ave a little look, do you? Regulations an all. Wouldn't be the first time I'd caught some sneaky illegals who'd crept in unnoticed.' He shook his head and grimaced. 'Cheeky bastards, so they are.'

'Sure, sure. It's just the usual; furniture, bits an bobs,' Roger replied, as he jumped out of the cab and walked around the side of the truck. He unlocked the back door and pulled it open.

They could hear the guard climb up; feel the swing of the van with the addition of his weight; hear the squeak of the boxes and furniture as they scraped once more on the metal base. It went quiet. The guard had paused. They held their breath.

'Right you are then, mate.' The van jumped up again with the release of the guard. 'You back through tomorrow then?'

'I ain't sure yet. Hopin' to fix up a return pick-up. Pay for both journeys is best.'

'Good luck with that then. See ya,' the guard said, thumping his fist on the van as he turned to walk away. Yoko let out a gentle growl. The guard stopped in his tracks. Listened. Looked back. Shook his head. 'Could 'ave sworn I heard a dog,' he called back at Roger.

Jake and Suze froze. Held their breath. Stared at each other. Hearts pounding. Sweat dripping.

Roger laughed. 'No dog here, mate.'

'Must be losing it.' He laughed back and walked on.

The truck pulled off the gravel slip road and back onto the motorway. The slightest of breezes crept through the four holes which had been drilled on the roof to allow ventilation.

'Thank fuck!' Jake muttered beneath the breath he was fighting for.

Suze was still staring, exhaling heavily, calming herself back down.

'Suze? You okay?'

'Yes. I think. Jesus! I thought we were done for.' She turned her gaze to Yoko, stroked her. 'You!' she gently chastised.

Yoko was panting, also stressed, also unsure, looking up at Suze for some reassurance.

'Good girl,' she said. 'It's okay.'

'That's us one step closer to London then. I'm not sure how I feel. It's usually good going home, but this time – hmmm,' Jake said.

'Yeah. I know what you mean. It's lost that whole safety factor thing, hasn't it?'

As the day wore on the heat became oppressive; they could feel the force of the sun, smell the melting tarmac mingling with diesel fumes. A glint of light broke through the ventilation holes and stretched through the darkness and across the compartment. Specks of dust danced and flickered their way through the beams of light, snatched for a few fleeting seconds from their invisibility. Suze stretched her hand up to play with the light, casting shadows on the metal panelling.

'Dad used to make these shapes for me when I was a kid. You know, rabbits, birds and the like. We'd spend hours making up stories to go with them. It was like I had my own little shadow puppet theatre. I loved it. It was so cool.'

'Cute.'

'He likes to take credit for me ending up in journalism. A love of words and stories.'

94

She remembered how proud he had been when her first piece got published. How he had framed it and stuck it up on his study wall, alongside a whole lifetime of her scribblings and writing. Her mother had done the same with her pictures, imagining a shared artistic talent, despite them not being blood relatives. The stairway of the farm held photographic evidence of her life from when she was a baby, through school and on to university, each step a different year of her life. Everything she had done had been celebrated, treasured, stuck up on the walls for the world to see. She imagined it all being sent crashing to the floor by New Dawn; splintering into tiny pieces, being trampled, burned, destroyed. It was all gone. Her life up until now was gone. She closed her eyes against the pain and pretended she had fallen asleep.

Jake sat and watched her, not wanting to imagine how she must be feeling but doing it anyway. That strength she had. That feistiness. She was clinging on to it, but he wondered how close to breaking she really was. He would do anything to make her feel better; to alleviate her pain, but he didn't know how and felt so inadequate.

There was a sudden jolt. That awful, unmistakable thud and scrape of metal against metal. The van was spinning then rolling over and over. Tumbling. Another crunch of metal, splintering glass. The compartment had collapsed on one side, Jake's side. Suze had no idea which way was up. Her head felt sticky. She put her hand to it and smelled it, as if she didn't know already. The sharp metallic smell of blood made its way up her nose and into her mouth so that she could taste it. Her ankle screamed at her. She could feel the softness of Yoko's body beside her. The dog whimpered feebly and made an attempt to slither closer to her. 'Oh thank God, Yoko girl. Good girl,' she whispered stroking her head, trying to calm her. 'Jake?' she cried out in a voice like sand on steel. 'Jake. Are you okay? Jake?' She fumbled around, her trembling hands working their way up his legs, his torso, his head. 'Please, please, please God, let him be okay.' His body lay limp, offering no response to her pleadings.

She spun around and lay on her back, kicking and kicking at the twisted metal. The agony of her ankle becoming more intense with each kick. It didn't matter. She had to break through this. She had to get them out. Finally the panel gave way and clattered to the ground allowing their exit. She turned back to Jake and strained to adjust his body so that she could pull it through the gap. He came to and opened his eyes.

'Suze, you need to–run. I–I can't move. You need–to run.' His voice, barely audible, spoke the pain he felt.

'No way. I'm not leaving you like this, Jake. We can do this. Me and you. Come on.'

'Go Suze. The police–' He was drifting back out of consciousness. His eyes closed.

'No, no, no, no, no. Jake! Shit!' She limped around to the front of the truck. Roger was trapped in the mangled mess of the cab, his head split open. His eyes wide, staring, empty. She scanned around. They were on a motorway. It was quiet. Behind the safety barrier was a deep ditch, beyond which were trees, dense enough to offer a place to hide. *The computer, the hard drive. Shit!* She went back to where Jake lay and twisted his satchel over his limp head and shoulder. A blue Audi was pulling over. She knew she had to move.

'I am so sorry, Jake. Christ,' she whispered, and stroked his face. 'Yoko, come on girl.'

They clambered down the grassy verge and into the ditch. She lay on her stomach, pulling Yoko down beside her. Both of them frightened, both of them breathless, both of them confused. Suze lifted her head slowly, painfully and peered over the brow of the hill. Her vision was blurred, hazy, as if she were watching a poor quality download. She rubbed her eyes and reopened them but to no avail. She could just make out the bleary image of a woman, who appeared to be making a call on her mobile, as she hurried out of the car. The woman looked up and down the motorway as she ran to the truck.

Suze slithered up the other side of the ditch and into the shadows of the woods. She sat and watched for a minute, no more, then with a wince, she turned her back on it all and limped further into the woods, tears streaming down her face, Yoko at her heel. It would appear no-one had noticed her.

She kept going for as long as she could, forcing herself through the pain, using the trees for support, at times resorting to crawling on all fours. Anything to keep moving. The woods soon came to an end and in front of her lay a gentle decline with a stream at the foot of it. She sat down and pulled herself with her good leg, sliding on her backside. When she reached the stream she rolled on to her front and allowed her head to fall into the cool water. Yoko lapped furiously beside her then lowered herself into the running water, paddling, swimming in circles.

When Suze lifted her head she could see a trail of red flowing downstream, drifting amongst the reeds and bull rushes, gently twisting its way into eventual nothingness. A panic. Yoko! But as she focused on the dog it became apparent that the blood was her own.

That was okay. She could cope with that. Losing Yoko? No. That would be the end of it all.

Dragonflies of a blue so very pale it was hardly a colour at all danced their jerky dance, hovering, flitting, resting. Their little gossamer wings beating such an irrational rhythm. A crow sat on the bank opposite, its feathers that inky black, so black it was blue. It cawed and bobbed its head up and down, up and down, staring with its fierce little orange eyes. Suze eased herself out of the water, lay back on the mossy bank, and drifted off, Yoko's wet head across her stomach, her hand on the dog's damp neck.

When she came to everything was blank. Her memory had left her. She didn't know why she felt so scared. Didn't know what she had done. Didn't know what it was that was making her feel so very bad. The physical pain she could overcome, work through. But the mental anguish? The brutal blade of betrayal which carved its way through every insignificant scrap of her was something else, something else entirely.

14

Suze was woken by the tender voice of an elderly woman. 'What should we do, love?' the voice was saying. 'She's in a bit of a pickle isn't she?'

Yoko still lay across Suze, teeth bared, snarling her warning. An elderly man was crouching beside her. 'It's all right. We only want to help, there's a good dog,' he said gently. 'Can you sit up, dear?' he asked. His face was friendly, his eyes concerned, his air confident.

'I..I think so,' Suze replied, holding her arm out for assistance. She was on auto-pilot, functioning somehow out of necessity, unable to process what was happening, but understanding she had to move. She had to get herself away from here.

'Right you are, take it nice and easy. That's it,' he said. He checked her pulse and stared in her eyes. 'Good, good. Now we need to get you to your feet. Lizzie, can you take the other side?'

'Yes, of course,' Lizzie replied, wrapping Suze's right arm around her shoulder.

Everything was spinning, Suze felt little beads of perspiration building up on her forehead. She swayed as she bit against the pain which seared up her leg, and the pounding in her head.

'There now,' he said. 'You just take your time. That's it. Nice and slowly.'

99

Lizzie smiled and said, 'What a clever little dog you've got there. She wasn't keen on letting us near, you know. Made sure you were safe. That we were friendly. What's her name? Look at her just trotting along at your heel. What a sweetheart. How on earth did the two of you end up out here in the middle of nowhere?'

'Lizzie,' George said in a gently reprimanding tone. 'Let's just get the girl home shall we? I don't think she really wants to chat right now, eh?'

'Of course, of course. Sorry dear. I am such a chatterbox. Deary me. We were just out for our evening walk, you see. We do this every day, rain or shine. Walk along the river. It's so nice isn't it? Just to walk in the countryside. We're so fortunate, George and I. Aren't we, love?'

'Lizzie!'

'Oh,' she mumbled. 'Silly me.'

They walked for about half an hour following the path of the river as it twisted its way through pleasant meadowland where cows and sheep grazed. The meadow was interspersed with the occasional copse. Starlings and crows rose, shrieking, as the humans approached, swooping above them in alarm, in warning; settling down again as they passed. Lizzie and George paused regularly to check how Suze was coping. She was in pain. She knew that she had injured herself somehow. She knew that she was in some kind of trouble. What that trouble was, or how she'd ended up here, she still couldn't remember. Pictures drifted in and out, words, warnings. *Be careful Suze. Be careful.*

'Here we are, dear. Safe and sound.'

It really was the quintessential English country cottage with roses climbing up whitewashed walls, interspersed with black wooden beams. The neatly trimmed thatched roof draped itself over the building, like a much loved, well worn cloak. Window boxes and hanging baskets trailed lobelia, ivy, and geraniums. Tubs of herbs adorned the gently curving, crazy paving path which led to a wooden door nestled beneath a heavy semi circle of thatch.

As they led her inside she felt a warmth. The ceiling was low, with black beams which looked original. Lace covered the backs of the two large armchairs which stood either side of the open fireplace. In the recess of the bay window was a sumptuous cream settee adorned with an assortment of Turkish killim cushions in rusts, reds, and browns. It all felt loved and cared for.

'You just sit yourself down. Here, give me your jacket,' Lizzie said, holding one hand out and pointing at the settee with the other. Her skin was weathered and tanned, with liver spots betraying her age. Her nails were beautifully manicured and her fingers boasted a selection of fine gold rings. The white hair which framed her soft face was short and neat. Her brown eyes twinkled with warmth, and her smile with compassion. 'Would you like a nice cup of tea while we wait for the doctor?'

'If I could just freshen up a bit? Use your bathroom?'

'Of course dear, of course. Let me help you. Here,' she said, offering her arm and leading her down the hall. Yoko stuck close to her heels.

Suze locked the bathroom door behind them, relieved herself and washed her face and hands. She stared at her reflection in the mirror, trying to bring something back, to trigger a memory. Nothing. There was a nasty gash, running about three inches along her forehead, which still looked fresh, giving her some idea

101

of a time frame. Whatever had happened, had happened recently. Her left eye was heavily swollen and beginning to discolour. 'Shit!' she whispered to herself, dabbing at the cut with some soap and cotton wool she'd found in the bathroom cabinet, wincing at the sting of it.

When she hobbled back into the living room George and Lizzie were in quiet conversation, their heads close together. They jerked apart and smiled towards her. Was she even safe here?

'There you are, dear. A nice cup of tea,' Lizzie said, gesticulating at the ornate cane coffee table. 'There's nothing quite like it to pick you up, I always think.'

George patted the settee. 'Come and sit down. Let me have a look at you,' he said, as he opened the clip on his black doctor's bag.

'Oh,' Suze managed the semblance of a smile. 'So you're the doctor?' stressing the you're.

'Retired, but yes I still do bits and pieces when required,' he replied, smiling back reassuringly. 'Sorry, this might sting a bit,' he added, as he began cleaning the wound on her forehead. 'You look familiar. Do you live hereabouts?'

'No, no I don't.' She paused and thought for a bit. 'I don't think so at least.'

'Hmm. So, you have a memory lapse, do you? What can you remember?' He applied an anaesthetic and began stitching the torn flesh together.

'I–I don't know. The last thing I remember is you two at the stream. Before that–I honestly don't know.'

He smiled at his handiwork before putting a dressing on top. 'That should heal up nicely soon enough. You'll have a scar but nothing too serious.'

'Thank you. This is so kind of you.'

'Don't mention it, my dear. Hippocratic Oath and all that.'

'Can you remember your name at least, dear?' Lizzie asked.

She shook her head. The only thing she knew for sure was that something bad had happened. Something about which she felt horribly guilty and very, very afraid.

'It's probably just a touch of concussion,' George said, reassuringly. 'Quite normal after a trauma, my dear. The best thing you can do right now is relax. These sorts of things usually clear up quickly enough. Once you settle a bit. Give it time.'

'What about your dog?' asked Lizzie. 'Do you remember anything about her?'

Suze reached out and stroked the dog's silky ear. The dog turned and licked her hand, nuzzled against it, snuffled against her face. Suze put her arms around the dog, her fingers disappearing in the thick coat. That smell. That beautiful smell. She smiled. 'Yoko. Yoko, my girl,' she said, a tear escaping, trickling down, and landing on Yoko's coat. More of them. 'Oh, Yoko!'

Yoko licked at the tears, her tail tucked slightly.

'Oh, how splendid!' Lizzie exclaimed.

'Good, good. I'm sure the rest will come back to you soon enough. In the meantime we need to get you to hospital. Just to be on the safe side. Concussion can be a nasty old beast if not taken proper care of.'

'No. No hospital,' she said, with an unquestionable firmness.

George's eyes stared in surprise, his white eyebrows rising in an arc.

'I don't know why but I can't go to a hospital,' Suze said slowly.

A glance swept between George and Lizzie.

'Whatever else has happened, it is imperative that you look after your health. Without that you have nothing. I really must insist!' George strode across to the telephone.

'Please. No! Don't!'

'What about your bag, dear? Perhaps there's something in there?' Lizzie asked, handing her Jake's computer bag.

Suze reached out with trepidation. There was a feeling to this. One she didn't like. The moment she felt it in her hands images came flashing back as if somehow transmitted by the fabric. She clutched it tightly. The crash, Jake, Roger...It began coming back in sickening waves; one building upon the other, each one a punch to her stomach. The memories were working backwards in peculiar flashes until they came to that morning at the farm. Her parents. She hung her head. 'Oh God, I can't stay here. They'll be looking for me–'

'Who'll be looking for you?' George asked.

'Are you in some kind of trouble, dear?' Lizzie added.

'I need to go.'

'Really. You can't. You're in no fit state to go anywhere by yourself right now,' he said firmly. Doctor to patient. 'If nothing else, you need to rest.'

She stood up. The strapping of her ankle, combined with the pain killers she'd been given, left her able to walk, albeit slowly.

'Please, give me an hour or so before you call the police. Give me a chance?'

'Good God girl, why would we call the police? What on earth has happened to you?' George asked, his face a tangle of questions.

She smiled a half smile which held only hurt. 'You know, I wish I knew. I only know it's bad and the people who get close to me end up dying. Just know that if you see something, or hear something about me it's not true, okay? You did not help a bad person. I am not a bad person.'

With that she limped across to the front door, Lizzie staring, unusually quiet, not at all sure what was going on.

'You're really in no fit state–'

'I'm sorry,' she said, over her shoulder as she walked out through the front door and closed it behind her. Her head was spinning; she felt sick. Good sense told her she shouldn't be moving, but she also knew that she had no choice. No-one else could be put in danger because of her. As she made her way towards the fields, some already harvested, with bales of hay awaiting collection, others boasting heavy golden crops, part of her hoped that George and Lizzie would give her that head start. Another part hoped that they wouldn't. That this would all come to an end. That she could give up. What was the point any more?

The whir of a helicopter would normally make her run for cover. She didn't. It shouted at her. She obeyed. The weapons told her to drop to her knees. She did.

'Go Yoko,' she screeched, pointing back at the cottage. 'Go!'

Yoko paused. Stared. Hunched down and slithered towards Suze, her body trembling.

'Go!' Suze commanded, crying now. 'Go!'

Yoko turned and ran, glancing back and checking as she did as she was instructed. This went against everything that was instinctive to her. To stay with her owner. To comfort. To protect. But above all, she knew to obey.

As Suze lay on her knees, her hands outstretched before her, her face on the ground, the whirring blades above drew closer. She considered standing, allowing them to take their toll. Two men in uniform jumped out and landed beside her, their guns pointing at her head. They cuffed her hands with nylon thread which was far too tight. They hoisted her up and dragged her into their machine. Staring out of the helicopter she could see Yoko being led into the cottage by George.

'Oh thank you,' she whispered, with the back of her hands pressed flat against the sticky, acrylic window.

'Oi! You! Not a word! Shut it!' one of the faceless hissed at her through his uniform, as a black hood was pulled over her head.

Goodbye girl.

Part II

15

She was in a cell. Despite the oppressive darkness she could sense the walls that surrounded her, feel their unwelcome intimacy. There appeared to be no windows. Her clothing had been removed and she was dressed in a loose polyester shift. The foetid air was oppressive and dank. It smelled of a noxious combination of disinfectant and mould. A hospital left to its cankerous demise. She tried to move but found she was strapped to the bed at her wrists and ankles with unforgiving leather. *Shit!* She summoned all of her energy and tried to break the ties, pulling at them, kicking, screaming, punching. Again and again, aware of the futility, but unwilling to submit.

'They'll untie you soon if you settle down,' came a voice from somewhere behind her. She arched her neck, straining to see who was there. Nothing but black.

'When you settle down.' The voice was female and strangely surreal, almost chimerical.

'Who's there?' Suze asked anxiously.

'When you settle down.'

'Where am I? Who the hell are you?' she cried in a frenetic whisper.

'No, no, no. That's not right. When you settle down,' the voice whispered. 'Shh...'

Suze closed her eyes in frustration. Her heart thumped furiously as it pumped anxiety through her veins, pummelling at her thoughts. Beads of sweat dripped off her forehead. Nausea snaked its way around her insides. She began to shake uncontrollably. Claustrophobia clung to her limbs, demanding that she move. It thrust itself upon her like a rapist. She knew there was nothing, absolutely nothing that she could do. The voice behind her continued with its mantra, telling her to settle down, telling her that what she was doing wasn't right.

*

Time had passed. How long? she had no way of telling. The rasp of something metal sliding drew her attention to the door. A lock clicked and it swung open. The light breaking through it forced her eyes to close for an instant. When she reopened them she saw two men in white coats come in with a metal trolley which squeaked gratingly with each rotation of its wheels. They wore surgical masks over their noses and mouths.

'She's been good, look. Settled down, good,' the voice from behind her said with a strange triumphant giggle.

'Right 27, you know the drill.'

27 accepted the small, white, plastic cup in one hand and the pills in the other. She swallowed them, opened her mouth and stuck out her tongue. A wooden spatula explored her mouth. A nod confirming that the pills had been swallowed.

'42, just a little prick.' A needle was stabbed unceremoniously into her buttock. 'There we go. Now, if I undo these are you going to behave yourself?'

Suze nodded as first her legs, *thank God,* then her arms, were released. She sat up slowly, studying the imprints left where the restraints had been, her skin raw and red. She tentatively spun her numb legs, which felt strangely detached from her body, over the edge of the bed. Her bare feet touched cold concrete. The men backed out, closing the door behind them, but leaving the hatch open, allowing a beam of light to force its way through the darkness of the dingy cell. She could now make out the woman who had been standing behind her. Her red hair had been crudely cropped. Green eyes shaped like almonds stood out in a hollowed face which was remarkably beautiful. She was tall and elegant with long limbs which moved with a strange languorous fluidity. Her white shift only accentuated the ethereal quality of this strange woman.

'Hi, I'm Suze.' She tried a smile.

'No. No, that's not right. You're 42. I'm 27. Hello 42.'

'The hell I am! What in God's name is this place?' Suze asked.

'The education centre. You have to behave,' she said, with the smile of an innocent.

'You're kidding me, right?'

Of course she knew about these places. She had heard the stories. Written about them often enough, decrying their use, their necessity. People went in defiant and argumentative and, if they came out at all, were subdued, unwilling to talk, to go on record. Something else entirely. Others simply disappeared. Officially they were being held. Too dangerous to society to be released. But rumours amongst certain circles suggested that they had somehow been got rid of. "Ludicrous conspiracy theories," the press announced, publishing dated photographs as evidence.

27 tapped her finger to her mouth and frowned.

'You'll see. Sleep now. The medicine. Sleep now.' She tiptoed her way across the concrete floor to the other bed and curled up like a cat.

She's fucking purring. Christ, they've put me in a mental asylum. Her head began to spin as the drugs took their effect, forcing her to lie back down, despite her unwillingness, and she was soon asleep. She was woken by a soothingly gentle voice from the tiny speaker mounted in the ceiling.

'Today is going to be a great day. You are part of something great. England. Our country. Our birthright. We live for it. We'd die for it. Our great, great country. God save the King.'

'God save the King,' 27 replied. 'You too,' she said to Suze, pointing with the grace of a ballet dancer, tilting her head, smiling. 'You must.'

'Fuck that!'

'No. You must. You must love the King.'

Suze's eyes stared in disgust.

'Say it. You must.'

'I'll do no such thing.'

'You will, or they'll make you. You'll see. Just say it,' 27 whispered at her, as she crouched beside the bed and picked up something which wasn't there. She held it up to the light between thumb and forefinger and carefully examined it, her head cocking from side to side. Then with measured precision she released it, blew on her fingers and smiled as if she had achieved something of great importance. Suze couldn't help but stare. The woman was fascinating.

The guards brought a plastic tray of breakfast for 27 and placed it on the floor by her bed.

'Follow the rules and you get fed. It's that simple,' one of the guards said to Suze, as he left the cell and locked them in again.

'Aargh!' Suze shook her head in repugnance, thumping her clenched fist on the thin foam mattress.

'You mustn't do that. You must be good. You'll see. Be good,' 27 said in a voice so soft, so gentle, it was childlike. 27 picked at her breakfast of bread and cheese, humming along to the music which was now playing over the intercom, swaying back and forth in time to the mesmeric rhythm.

The men in white coats came back in with medication; oral for 27 and hypodermic for Suze. This time it wasn't a sleeping draft, however. She felt intoxicated, confused, as she was led out of the cell, her legs resisting the request to walk. It felt almost pleasant, almost as if she were floating. They led her along a stark corridor painted an army green. The flooring was highly polished grey linoleum. The extent of its cleanliness was evident in its clinical smell and the way in which it squeaked with every footstep. Her feet were bare and made a gentle padding sound. She thought she could hear voices, quiet voices whispering behind the rows of locked doors onto which numbers had been posted. Mostly there were two numbers to a room, but some stood out in their solitude.

At the end of the hallway were double doors. The first were metal, prison like, the second, wooden with reinforced glass panels. Both were locked. Beyond these was an office. It was in total contrast to everything else. The furniture looked antique, certainly expensive. The walls displayed pictures of the royal family, the leaders of the coup and their political allies. Sitting on a leather chair behind the intimidating oak desk was a middle aged man dressed in an officer's uniform. Suze was made to sit in a wooden chair facing him.

'42,' he said, with slow, exaggerated precision, in a voice exuding authority. His plastic smile perfectly matching the coldness of his steely blue eyes. 'Stand when you're being spoken to,' he barked.

'But they...'

'Stand!'

She stood, finding it difficult to balance in her state of drug induction.

'God save the King,' he said, as he rose from his chair and saluted to the picture on the wall, clicking his heels as he did so.

She shuddered. 'God save the King,' she mimicked, in a voice which didn't feel as though it were hers.

'Right. The rules are simple. Do as you're told, when you're told. Respect authority. Don't argue. Don't question. Got it?'

'Yes.'

'Yes, sir!'

'Yes, sir,' she replied meekly, hating herself for it, but unable to do anything else.

'You do not want to see me again. Do you understand?'

'Yes, sir,' she answered, with a bowed head.

'Take 42 to the classroom,' he instructed the guards, with a dismissive wave of his hand.

'Sir!'

She was led back past her cell and into a blacked-out room with screens covering three of the walls. They sat her in a large chair in its centre which looked and felt like one from a dental surgery. Her wrists were strapped to the arms, her ankles to the legs and her neck to the headrest. Her head was locked into some machine type thing. Cold, metallic. She couldn't move at all. They placed a skull cap on her head. She could feel something like pins, only not sharp. Her eyes were clipped open with metal pincers, claws. She couldn't look away. A terror grabbed hold of her. What the hell were they going to do to her? She felt the humiliation of a warm, wet flow of urine. It crept up her back and sat in a puddle under her body.

Images flashed across the screens surrounding her, enveloping her, spinning and spinning, destabilising. They closed in on her, suffocating, overpowering. They didn't make any sense. Random words, faces, parades, bodies, happy families, looting, rioting, dancing, singing, marching. Then some she did recognise. Her parents. Was that really them? There and gone. Too quick to be sure. *Shit! Come back. Come back!* Then Jake. Smiling. Gone. YOUR FAULT. More happy families, smiling politicians, cheering crowds. She fought back tears. *No. Enough of that shit. You will not beat me. I will not be broken. Bastards. Fucking bastards.* She dug her nails into her hands, drawing blood, forcing the pain to take control of her mind, refuting the barrage of brainwashing they were bombarding her with. It seemed interminable as she fought for control. Fought to hang on. Finally the screen went black.

'Would you look at that, Jenkins, she's only gone and wet herself,' the guard untying her said mockingly to his compatriot, allowing his hands to rest on her breast as he reached across her. She spat at him in her mind but kept control. If she was going to survive this she would have to hide herself. Become someone else.

'Yep, we'll have this one tamed in no time. Won't we sweetheart?' the second guard grunted, through his licentious leer, his hands rubbing his crotch. 'No time at all.'

115

Will you fuck!

16

Nigel Richardson stood at five foot eleven, although, when asked, he declared himself to be six feet tall. He was an impressive man, always impeccably dressed and coiffed. His aristocratic good looks, silver tongue, and dazzling smile had served him well during his rise through the corridors of political power. Like his father before him he was used to getting his own way. He gave orders, they were followed, unquestioningly.

'What do you mean, she's been processed?' Nigel bellowed down the telephone, his face flushed a furious red, the veins in his neck bulging. 'The instructions were quite clear, were they not?' This was not how it was supposed to be. After everything! The months of meticulous planning. The strings pulled. The favours called. And now this? Just when he thought it was all over. Taken care of. Unbelievable!

'I'm sorry, sir, they were simply following procedure,' the voice at the other end replied with due deference.

'Procedure? You damned, incompetent fools! You know full well my orders supersede any bloody procedures! For Christ's sake, I...' He shook his head in disbelief, as he paced up and down the Persian carpet.

'Should I have her brought to you now then, sir?'

'No, no, it's too bloody late, man. Have her thrown

117

in with the rest of the dogs. Just make damned sure you keep a close eye on her. No more bloody cock-ups. Do I make myself clear?'

'Yes, sir. Very clear, sir.'

'Good. I'll be in touch with final instructions.' He terminated his secure connection and walked across to the burr walnut drinks cabinet. His perfectly manicured hands reached for a Riedel Vinum whisky glass, into which he poured a generous amount of forty year old Laphroaig. He felt himself begin to calm as he took the time to allow all of his senses to appreciate his favourite single malt whisky. The gentle glug of the deep amber liquid spilling into the fine lead crystal. The peaty aroma followed by the smoky, salty, seaweed flavours set his taste buds alight. Finally the warmth trickled down his throat and gently worked its magic throughout his body. 'Ah!' he sighed.

He walked across to the French windows and took in all that was his. The sweep of the gravel path which curved its way around lawns stretching down to the lake. Walled gardens housing roses and exotic plants. The much admired Edwardian greenhouses in which his fine collection of orchids took pride of place. This was his England. He pulled the tasselled velvet cord which summoned his butler.

A gallop across the fields was always a good way of clearing one's mind, making the right choices, coming to important decisions. This one had to be dealt with promptly and precisely. He would not allow any of this to disturb the path he had so carefully created. He had done it. Risen to the very top. His word was sacrosanct. His public life had to appear likewise.

'Yes, sir?' the butler asked.

'Tell the stable boy to saddle up Excalibur.'

118

'Very well, sir. Will that be all, sir?'

'Yes, yes. Off you go,' he said, with an imperious wave of his hand. At the sound of footsteps descending the grand wooden staircase, he turned around to see his wife, Annabel. Confound the woman. She was always there when he didn't want her to be. When he had no need of her.

'Ah, Nigel, there you are. Might I have a word?' she asked nervously. She had been beautiful, some might say she still was. Those who could see beyond the hunch of her shoulders, the fearful sunken eyes. Her timidity, he told others, was menopausal, bloody infuriating. She knew otherwise. Deep down she did. This had been creeping up on her year upon year, derision upon derision, blow upon blow.

'Not now, woman, I'm busy.'

'Oh, I'm sorry, dear. Later perhaps?'

'Good God. I'm surrounded by blithering idiots!' he barked at her without looking in her direction, as he strode across the black and white chequered marble entrance hall, his highly polished riding boots squeaking their quality. He donned his riding hat and slashed the air with his crop.

Annabel turned, inhaled deeply and closed her eyes before retreating into the confines of her drawing room. Her hands were shaking as she opened her laptop and clicked play. Beethoven's seventh stole the silence. She reached into her tapestry basket and set the piece she was working on beside her on the arm of her chair. Next she lifted up the tray of threads which were lined up in order of colour, rather pretty really, each one only slightly different from its neighbour, the full spectrum. Under this were some pictures whose edges evinced the frequency of them having been fondled. She picked

119

them up with great care and sat them on her lap, placing them in the same order as always. Seven precious photographs. All she had left of her daughter, Sophie. There were a couple of letters too, but they had stopped writing to each other. It was too dangerous. She had also cut out some clippings. Places she knew her daughter had been to. Places she could imagine they had visited together. There was one of her playing for some orchestra, but which one? Ah, yes. The London Philharmonic. Yes, that was it; she was sure now. How could she forget such a thing? But then, forgetting was something she had learned to use, something which helped her get from day to day. She sat for a while, allowing memories and emotions to escape out of the pictures.

'I am so sorry,' she whispered, as she stroked the well fingered photograph of Sophie, aged thirteen. 'So very sorry.' She stared at those eyes. Sad, betrayed eyes that belonged to her daughter and yet, she hadn't known. Hadn't seen it at the time. How could a mother not see that? She hated herself for it.

She picked the pictures up, one at a time, pausing at each for a few seconds, then replaced them with such tenderness, as if she were giving a newborn kitten back to its mother, and closed the lid.

Portraits of the other children – their children – smiled serenely out of their gold frames. These were the smiles of confident young people who were sure of their place in the world. She loved them all. Of course she did. But Sophie was the one who pulled hardest at her heart strings. The one who gave her sleepless nights and fraught filled days. The one who was supposedly forgotten. "How can you stay with him Mum?" Sophie had asked, with eyes that held the anguish of a stolen childhood. How indeed? she'd thought, but things are never quite that simple, are they?

Her mind cast back to the early days. She, a young widow; Sophie her only child; Nigel her handsome suitor. They'd met on holiday in Greece. She remembered him playing with Sophie, making her giggle. It was so sweet, she had thought. Here was this gorgeous man playing with a little three year old girl on a beach, as if they were so close. As if he truly cared. As if there was nothing else of any importance. Just her. Just them. He had taken them for dinner, dividing his time equally between mother and daughter, charming them both with stories and compliments, smiles and presents. He was perhaps a little self absorbed, but then he was on one of the, "One hundred most eligible bachelors" lists, so she could forgive him that. And he had chosen to spend his time with her. She felt like a princess! They had swapped phone numbers and she had thought that would be that. A holiday romance which was lovely but would never amount to anything more. Only it had.

A whirlwind romance was followed by a sumptuous wedding. Both families had been surprised but supportive. Nigel's parents delighted that at last their playboy son was settling down, albeit with someone far beneath his station. At least she meant security, an heir, and she seemed pleasant enough; polite and charming. She could pass for something she wasn't. Annabel's parents were relieved that a decent man with a healthy bank balance had been willing to take a single mother on board. She would have a secure future ahead of her.

They had three children in quick succession, two boys and a girl. All of them were sent to boarding school despite Annabel's protestations. This was the way of things in the Richardson family and so it would continue.

Annabel hated the hollowness of the impressive stately home during term time. Nigel had forbidden her from working, from volunteering, from having any form of a social life outside of his. The long disconsolate days elapsed through approved, gentile pastimes. She would count the hours until the school holidays, which were wonderful. Full of children and noise and laughter. They would take trips to the beach, picnic on the lawns, go riding, play tennis, but mostly just have simple fun; mostly without Nigel.

When Sophie was nine or ten Annabel had begun to notice a change in the child. She had become quieter, somewhat sullen, avoiding the company of others, preferring to be alone. She had taken up playing the violin, practising for hour upon hour in the solitude of her room. Her school work had begun to suffer and friends had drifted away. Annabel was worried, as were Sophie's teachers. Whenever she tried to bring the subject up with Nigel he would dismiss it with hurtful comments about Sophie's background. After all, she wasn't one of his. What did she expect? He too had changed, becoming bad tempered and aggressive, belittling her at every opportunity, hurting her, although only in private.

It all came to its awful conclusion when Sophie was fourteen.

'Oh wonderful!' Nigel shouted, sarcasm dripping off his tongue. 'So, that little trollop of a daughter of yours has gone and got herself pregnant has she? And do we know who the father is?'

'She won't say,' Annabel replied. 'She's really upset, Nigel.'

'Damned bloody right she is, the little whore! Does anyone else know?'

'Not as far as I know, no.'

'You had better make damned sure it stays that way,' he hissed at her, as he slapped her face with the back of his hand.

She fell to the floor. 'No, Nigel please. Not again. Please, please don't hurt me,' she cried, barely audibly, as she scrambled backwards trying to get away from him, her shoes slipping on the marble floor, her legs forsaking her. He picked her up by the throat and slammed her against the kitchen counter. She winced at the pain and hated herself for the tears which now fell down her face. His eyes held that look she'd seen so many times before. The loss of control. The hatred. The savagery. Had it always been there, just well hidden? Or had it all been her fault? She wasn't good enough. She didn't offer the stimulation he required mentally, or physically, and this was how he showed his frustration. His disappointment.

'Get her to a clinic and abort the little bastard. Then have her sent away. I don't want to hear any more about it, or her. Do you hear?' he hissed, as he threw her back on the floor.

She curled herself into a ball, again. Winced at the blows, again. Vowed she would leave, again.

Nothing was said the following morning because, of course, nothing untoward had happened, had it? Heavy make up and sunglasses, forced smiles and polite conversation, were a common breakfast. He would complain about her regular "hangovers" with the staff and children. "The bloody woman's been at the sherry again!" he would say with a dismissive laugh.

After he had been driven off to the House, by the

state chauffeur, Annabel and Sophie headed north in the Audi.

'I'm not going to kill my baby, Mum,' Sophie said.

'I know darling. It's all right, I know.'

17

27 might have been insane, but at least she was human company of a sort. Any form of discussion, however, was nigh on impossible. Suze had tried on several occasions but to little effect. The woman seemed to have absolutely nothing to say that made even the slightest bit of sense. The distraction of her inane ramblings did help time to pass, days to blend. It felt like daytime, but she couldn't be sure. Everything had been done in an attempt to confuse. There was no pattern to her time here; sleep, when it came, was disturbed before she was rested. Meals were sporadic. Lights were turned on and off at unpredicatable times.

Sessions in the classroom were frequent, happening, she thought, daily, or thereabouts. They had bandaged her hands in order to prevent her from creating the diversion of her self mutilation. The images from the screen had begun to slither into her mind like maggots squirming and writhing their hideous way through the decaying body of a corpse. She tried to force them out; to replace them with memories of her own, times of happiness. Her parents, Jake, but not as they showed them to her. No. Her own pictures. Her own memories. It became more and more difficult; the fight seeming endless in its futility.

Weeks had passed and today she was being led

somewhere new, down a different corridor with a different smell. Nothing had been said, but that was normal. Confusion. Not knowing. She had learnt simply to accept it. To do what she had to do, at least on the outside. Her brain however, she fought for. Every minute of every day she reminded herself of where she came from; what she believed in. This, though was different. This smell was somehow so enticing. Suddenly she found herself outside. The unexpected blast of fresh air, the rustle of nearby trees, the sound of birdsong were all so intoxicating she was almost moved to tears. She inhaled deeply and closed her eyes, imagining something else, somewhere else.

The concrete courtyard appeared to be part of an institutional building, a borstal or something military, she guessed. She was one of perhaps fifty people, most dressed in blue, like her. A few in the white of her cell mate, 27. They walked around the perimeter like automatons; dreamlike creatures with nothing to say. Twice around a two hundred metre perimeter and back inside. That was it. It felt more like torture than reward. A tiny glimpse of another world, then bang, darkness, loudspeakers, flashing images, confinement, terror. She tried to focus, to search for something, anything, to keep the darkness out.

Her obsession now was the next stint in the exercise yard. It worried her, wanting something so much. It gave them a power over her and she knew that was its purpose. She had found a song playing in the distant recesses of her desecrated mind. Rage Against the Machine, "Killing in the Name of." She sang it in her head, feeling the pound of the rhythm pulsing through her body. *Some of those that work forces, are the same that burn crosses. Killing in the name of. Killing in the name of...* The anger of it fed her, strengthened her, focused her, reminded her. Jake and his band thrashing it out at the illegal anti-fascism gig last year (Was it really only a year ago?). The words had been changed slightly to fit with the time and the place, but the feeling was the same. The crowd had gone mental, refusing to let them stop. Encore after encore. Then the forces came. Brutality. Dispersal.

Her parents had been at, "Rock Against Racism" rallies in their youth, thinking that they too would change the world. Dancing and singing in protest against injustice. Something's Gotta Change. Then it had been about colour; now it was also about nationality. The same songs with the same message generations apart.

She remembered Richardson and his infamous speech which was the tinder under the fanatical fire of fascism. The reason for their protest gigs. "They are tearing away the very fabric of our Britishness, slowly but surely, taking our jobs, taking our culture, diluting us. This must stop! We demand a return to our values! We demand they return to their homelands! We demand repatriation!" The crowds had chanted his words in reply; marched along the streets shouting his name. People raised a glass to him, confirming their approval. And so it began. Repatriations, protests, battles, riots, the army, the coup, New Dawn.

Finally the next exercise session came. She could sense it. An expectant buzz slipped along the corridors. The smell was different this time. It was raining, but softly and there was a hint of snow. It felt more like walking through a fine mist which clung relentlessly to her clothes, saturating them. It was beautiful to her, cleansing and refreshing. She held her head up allowing

127

it to bathe her face with its steely cold grace as she paced around the quadrangle, keeping in time with everyone else; the regulatory distance apart; the regulatory deportment. She'd always had that urge to fight regulations. This was different though; this she had to control; this was about survival.

'Hey, 42. You can't fight this, you know? It's a done deal,' said a woman's voice from behind her. 'Just toe the line. Do what they tell you. They are right, you know.'

She ignored it.

'We all start off like you, thinking we know best, but they do. They really do.'

Some of those that work forces, are the same that burn crosses.

Just like the last time, after two circuits, they were marched back indoors. Suze was cold and shivering but at least in touch with just a tiny piece of that place where life, in whatever form, continued. Her senses heightened, her skin prickled. It was time to dull it all down again; to switch off.

'I don't like wet, no, no, no, no,' 27 mewed, as she paced the cell on tiptoes, shaking her languid limbs, pawing at her drenched clothing which clung defiantly to the sensuous curves of her body. 'No, no, no, no. Go away, away, away!' The voice had become a shrill screech which bounced off the walls. She began to claw frantically at her face as if something abhorrent were clinging to it.

'Here. It's okay,' Suze said, as she tentatively dabbed at 27's hair with the sheet from her bed. 'It's only water. It's okay.'

Their eyes met and held a fleeting contact which seemed to go so much deeper. Suze couldn't place it. A commonality? An understanding? Empathy?

'Can we get some help in here please? A towel? Dry clothes? Please? She's cracking up. Come on! You can hear it!' Suze called with exasperation. 'I know that you can!' Every sound was transmitted from their cell to the guards' station. They couldn't so much as cough without it being heard. There was no need to torture 27 like this.

After too long an officer came in. A new one, or at least one Suze hadn't seen before.

'All right, 27. No need for this.' She bent down to lay two piles of dry clothes and towels on the small wooden table which sat between the inmates' beds.

'Get it off me,' 27 screamed. 'Off me, off me!' Her arms were flailing around the guard, hitting her like the wings of a wounded bird trying to escape its predator.

Something fell onto the floor at Suze's feet and she kicked it under her bed. Her heart skipped a beat, her thoughts ran wild as she tried to maintain a look of normality.

'Meds! Now!' the guard called.

'She doesn't need that. Just let me get her dry,' Suze said. 'Really!'

'Your place is not to interfere. Sit down and be quiet or you'll get one too,' the guard replied in a voice so devoid of any feeling it could easily have been a robot, or perhaps it was? Suze wondered at the possibility. She knew they existed. Humanoids.

One of the men in white coats was there in a matter of seconds. 'Here,' he said, as he jabbed a needle into the translucent white skin of 27's arm. 'That'll do it.'

A speck of scarlet blood escaped from her vein and trickled down her arm. 27 slithered onto her bed as her legs slowly gave way under her. The guard rolled 27

129

around like a slab of meat on a butcher's counter as she changed her wet shift for a clean, dry one. She left and the door clunked firmly as the automatic lock once more secured their confinement.

Suze was biding her time, thinking that soon the soothing music, which signified time for sleep, would drift out of the speakers. It did. She lay down and waited for what she thought was long enough then felt, surreptitiously, under her bed, fumbling, patting the dusty concrete, inch by inch, her breath quickening, thoughts racing. An unfamiliar sensation, somewhere between fear and ecstasy, hit her in swathes of gauze. A web of emotions which dared to whisper something of hope. She felt a small plastic prism and wrapped her fingers around it. *Dear God, let this be something.* She pushed it under the thick cotton of her regulation underpants, hoping that there wasn't going to be a full body search any time soon, and lay back down. The incessant flickering of the eyes in the ceiling tormented her with their treachery. Had she been careful enough, discreet enough? She was sure that she had been, but – There was always a but in places like this.

The prisoners were taken to the bathroom in one's or two's and forbidden from any communication with other inmates or staff. When it was time for their next toilet break, Suze pushed the key into her vagina and walked to the latrines trying desperately not to look any different from normal. Its edges were sharp and dug into her tender flesh. The pain was almost enjoyable. It reminded her that she was alive, that she could rise above the present. She prayed. In the security of the stall she only just managed to fish the key out using finger and thumb, groping like the first fumbling of a nervous teenager. She examined it, turning it over in her

130

hands. It was an electronic key, but there was nothing to signify what it might be for. There also appeared to be some sort of code; a sequence in which buttons had to be pressed. She wondered, now what?

'42. Out of there! Now!' the guard called from the other side of the stall, thumping her truncheon on the door.

'Sorry. Stomach ache,' she replied, slipping the key back inside herself.

'Quiet. You know the rules.'

The flush was pulled. She left the cubicle and headed to the door.

'Hands!' the guard bellowed.

Shit! Stupid mistake. She walked back to the wash-hand basins and scrubbed at her fingers with carbolic soap and cold water. No glance was shared between inmate and guard, as the rules demanded. As they headed back to her cell, she kept her head down, as ordered, concentrating on each step, dismissing the present, focussing on the way ahead. Experience had taught her not to raise her hopes, not to expect. That could be dangerous. But she couldn't suppress the "what if?" that was spinning all kinds of scenarios around in her head. No! Put them away. Put them away. *Some of those that work forces, are the same that burn crosses.* The song sang in her head; the rhythm did its job. Again.

18

Everything was quiet. The "sleep music" had played some time ago. The inmates were asleep. The guards relaxed, only paying attention to their duties when it was patrol time. On the hour, every hour, irrespective, a patrol was carried out.

'Let me see. Let me see,' 27 whispered through the darkness. 'I know you have something. Let me see.'

'Shh,' Suze whispered in reply, barely a sound at all. She sat up slowly, assuming that it was too dark for the camera to pick anything up. She listened intently. Nothing. She reached into the innards of her mattress with her fingers, fumbling between the sponge and the rubber cover until she felt the key. She slid it out of its hiding place in the slit of the seam she'd carefully unpicked stitch by stitch, and handed it to 27.

There was a sharp intake of breath as 27 turned it over in her hands, feeling its contour. Her fingers ran across every centimetre, over and over again. 'You have the key. We can play,' she squeaked. Her eyes became huge, staring, as she clasped her hands over her mouth.

'Shhhh,' Suze urged. 'This is our big secret okay?'

'Yes, yes. Shhhh,' she mimicked, with the smile of a child on Christmas morning, her elegant fingers clapping silently in excitement.

'Have you seen them use this? Do you know how it

works?' Suze mouthed, the words barely a breath. She allowed a minuscule moment of hope to flit, unchallenged, around that dormant section of her mind.

'Yes, yes. I watch everything. I see everything. I know,' came the triumphant reply, as she stretched onto her tiptoes and twirled around.

'Okay, cool, 27, but we need to stay calm, keep quiet, yes?' Suze mouthed. She took hold of 27's hands and held them tight. 'Which doors does it open?' she asked, hardly daring to imagine the reply.

'All of them. One key, different numbers,' 27 answered, impishly.

'Do you know the numbers? Any of them?'

'Yes, yes, I know. I watch like a cat. I watch. They are easy with me. They think I am crazy cat girl.'

'And you're not so crazy, right?'

'Not so crazy,' she replied, with the giggle of a mischievous schoolgirl.

'Okay, so when shall we do this?'

'Now. We go now.'

'Are you sure?'

'Yes. Very. It is a good night. New year. Not many guards. Probably drinking. We go now. Yes.'

'Wow, I had no idea. Talk about timing! Okay. Ready?'

Suze hesitated. *What am I doing? Ah, fuck it!* She took 27's hand in both of hers. 'You go, girl,' she whispered, as she squeezed them. 'Do your magic.'

27's face glowed with pride. She pressed three digits and the cell door clicked open. She turned back with a triumphant smile, her eyebrows raised. Suze returned the look then took a deep breath and held it as she pushed the door far enough open to see the length of the corridor. It was silent and seemingly deserted.

Flickering strip lighting on its lowest setting left an ominous, deceptive hue clinging to the ceiling, sliding down the walls. They crept out, holding hands, 27 leading the way, and sneaked along the corridor. They stopped at the door of the guards' room, which was normally wide open. It was closed. Music was playing and they could hear laughter, glasses clinking. They exchanged encouraging glances and carried on, crouching below the panel of reinforced glass. No-one seemed to have noticed them, despite the security cameras winking in the ceiling. They ran to the double doors which led to the office. Three more digits and...nothing. *Shit!* Suze stared at 27 with a look of alarm.

'Sorry,' 27 whispered. 'Wrong ones, wrong ones. Ahhh.'

'It's okay. Try again. Come on,' Suze replied, giving her a reassuring pat, scanning the corridor. Their whispers sounded irrationally loud. She imagined she could hear them echoing their way down the corridor and into the guards' office. Keeping her eyes fixed on the path they had just crept along, she waited. Waited breathless and desperate as 27 tried again.

Three more digits and they were through. Jesus! This was happening! Next, the private entrance for high-ranking staff; three more digits and the shock of cold night air. The sky was clear, the ground alive with tiny sparkles of frost dancing under the overhead lights. As they ran along the path their last barrier, the main gate, duly clicked open.

'Oh wow, 27... I don't believe it.'

'Donna,' she smiled, 'Donna. Now run!'

'Okay, Donna.' Her heart swelled with the whisper of that name. Everything had suddenly changed. Life had begun again.

They ran, still holding hands, but Suze leading now. Despite the cold they could feel sweat building up between their palms. Their breath drifted up in icy plumes, disappearing into the anonymity of the night. As they ran through the gate, spotlights that had been roaming back and forth froze, screeching stop. They didn't. It was only about ten metres to the curve of the road with trees and hedges; places to hide. They could make it. They rounded the corner to momentary safety. Suze looked to the forest on their left and the road ahead. *Which way?* She had no idea where she was, nor what lay beyond either choice, neither did she have time to think.

'This way,' she called as she tugged Donna towards the forest, relying purely on instinct. Donna looked back towards the place which had held her for so long. 'No,' Suze urged. 'Don't look back. Run!'

Donna was crying then laughing, crying then laughing as the trees began to surround them, hide them. There was the unmistakable crack of a gun. She dropped Suze's hand and fell, face first on to the ground. Her body had become leaden. Suze didn't stop to look. She knew. *Killing in the name of...Killing in the name of...*

She powered on, her legs and arms pumping, working, pumping, in the ruthless harmony of prey running for its life. Any thoughts other than escape were pushed away. The bullet hole in Donna's body. Away. Dead eyes. Away. Another life. Away. There was no time for anything other than the way ahead. Escape. No time for the pain she felt. Away.

She was now deep in the trees. More shots rang out pinging off wood and bark. The shouts of her predators became muffled by the ever thickening forest. The siren fired up, drowning out all other sound. She ran, relentlessly twisting her way around the myriad trees, ignoring the branches that whipped at her face, the thorns that scratched at her bare legs, feeling like a thing possessed, a wild animal. Night creatures fled in alarm. She felt at one with them.

She thanked the God she didn't believe in for the clear sky and the brightness of the moon flickering through the foliage above her. It allowed her to run without checking, run without looking back, run with the knowledge that it was leading her away from the camp and on to something else. It didn't matter what. She ran. Her chest burned, her lungs screamed for her to stop. She began to stumble, to flounder, to become careless.

The whir of a helicopter. Its light flashing through the woods. She stopped, clung to the trunk of a tree, held her breath as it crept towards her. Was it slowing down? Had it picked her out? She couldn't look. Wouldn't look. It would pass on by. It had to. She wouldn't allow Donna's death to be in vain. Jake. Her parents. None of it could be in vain. The helicopter flew over her, swept back again and off. She waited until she was sure it was far enough away so that she wouldn't be seen, picked out amongst the trees.

When she opened her eyes there was nothing. The sound had become distant. She exhaled deeply. Allowing herself a minute's rest she leaned back against the reassuring strength of the towering pine tree. Its scent danced through her, invigorated her, gave her that one last push.

'Come on, Suze. Come on,' she said, as she focused on the silver orb of the moon shimmering in the dark, night sky. Her guide now had wisps of cloud flitting across it, making her progress more difficult. One minute she could see, the next it was pitch black and she had to stop. Finally, as if a candle snuffed out by the pinch of her assailants' fingers, it was gone; smothered by a cloud which held a feeling of permanence. *Shit!* She didn't want to stop, partly due to the cold, but also because she was afraid of losing her way, perhaps doubling back, getting caught. 'Come on Dad. You and your moss. What was it?' she whispered, as she wrapped her arms around a tree. She could feel the contrast of the rough, gnarly bark and soft, delicate moss. 'Okay, the mossy side is facing away from where I've come from. Okay. That'll do it. That's enough. Thank you, Dad.' She walked on with a sense of achievement, of purpose, slowly and carefully, but onwards. She felt as if her father were with her, guiding her.

She had travelled a good distance. How far, she had no idea, but it felt considerable, even in this terrain. There must be several miles between them now. The sirens were no longer audible. Neither the helicopter. She could only hear the sounds of the forest, the scramblings and scurryings, rustlings and crackles. The ancient trees creaked as they bent with the strengthening wind, which brought with it a flurry of snow. She felt the cold now that she had stopped running. It nibbled at her toes and her fingers. Her nose began to run. *Keep moving. Keep moving.* She swung her arms around her body in an attempt to warm herself up. The snow became heavier; bewitching swirls of white butterflies which danced around her, settled on her, played with her. It lay its carpet down, defying the darkness, illuminating the forest so that she could see more easily. Silver linings, eh?

It had been hours now. She was sure of that. Her progress had become a slow, stumbling walk. Her hands, feet and knees were cut and scratched raw from the many times she had lost her footing. The snow was falling heavily, covering her tracks almost as soon as she had laid them. She had that feeling. That feeling that tells you something or someone is watching you. Eyes upon you. Fear took hold of her in its irrational vice. It toyed with her, forcing her to stop and look around. The density of the trees forbade reassurance. *You're being stupid Suze, there's nothing there. Come on.* She was shivering, uncontrollably and violently, as she walked on; now more tentative, looking around, checking. Something was moving to her left. She could see it now, its shadowy form inching silently along, its eyes on her. It looked like a dog but was too big for that, surely? As quickly as it had come it was gone. A picture of Yoko flitted into her mind, punching the wind out of her. She stumbled. Bit back a cry. Almost fell to the ground. So much guilt.

Another creature appeared to her right. Then more. They seemed to be surrounding her. They floated, spinning around her. Their teeth snapping, jowls drooling, eyes, red and demonic, penetrating.

She shook her head and stumbled on, trying, unsuccessfully, to shake reality back. Her hands and feet had become numb. So numb that she could barely feel them; her breathing slow and shallow. Waves of dizziness became stronger, forcing her to reach her hands out to gain support from the trees. She had forgotten where she was and what she was trying to escape from. Her legs buckled and she slumped down, collapsing on the snow covered ground like fallen prey.

138

Scarlet blood crept its way across the white, like paint spilled on a blank canvas. She curled into a ball and giggled, then was still.

19

Richardson's sleep was broken by the shrill beep of his mobile. He reached across to his bedside table and fumbled for the phone. The icon informing him that a message had been sent flickered on the screen.

'What the devil?' he mumbled, opening the drawer, pulling out his spectacles and putting them on.

The message, from an unidentified phone, simply read "publicity". It was a coded message meaning that he should call this number from his secure line. It could only mean trouble, although quite what, he couldn't fathom. A man in his position had to be ready for all possibilities. Times were unpredictable. Despite his best efforts there were still too many troublemakers, those who didn't follow the rules; didn't see all that was being achieved, and had to be taught a lesson. Silenced one way or another. Curfews had helped calm the situation. New Dawn had added another layer of security. The riots had been sentenced to history. This new order, his new order, would rise above everything. It was all so close.

Disgruntled at being woken up in the middle of the night he threw the covers aside, donned his bespoke dressing gown – he would only wear clothing made especially for him by his tailor – and walked across the heated flooring to his study.

He punched in the number which answered his call immediately.

'Something of a problem, sir.'

'Which is?' he answered impatiently. He loathed squirming hesitance, but also thoroughly enjoyed the fact that most felt the need to grovel before him. Something of a predicament.

'There's been a breakout, sir. The girl. She's –'

'How the hell is that even possible?'

'She –'

'No. Don't answer. I assume this is recent and that you are on her tail.'

'Yes, sir.'

'She can not escape the boundaries. It is simply not possible.' He spoke slowly and clearly, as if to an imbecile. 'Use whatever force is necessary and put an end to this once and for all. Understood?'

'Yes, sir. Of course, sir.'

Richardson could almost hear the click of the man's heels, see his salute.

'Bloody fools!'

He checked his watch. Three thirty. An ungodly hour. Too early to rise, yet too late to offer a substantial sleep. He sighed, returning to bed anyway. As he sunk back into his pillows an uncomfortable feeling washed through him. He was not in control of this. It should never have been allowed to happen, to get this far. His guard had been let down and that could only mean trouble. Something of this magnitude should have been stopped at the outset. Kept close. Finished. He should have done it himself.

20

Daylight was fading when, at last, they came to a stop. He lay Suze down on a deerskin inside his hut and covered her with another. He called his dogs and had them lie beside her while he lit a fire. When she came to she was caught in a terrifying deja vu. Her legs wouldn't move and there was a weight across her body. She felt that same panic beginning to work its way through her and was afraid to look; afraid of seeing she was a prisoner once more. She took deep breaths, trying to calm herself, trying to rationalise things. Something nudged her arm.

When she opened her eyes they were staring into the face of a dog. It was immense with a head bigger than hers, its eyes staring, its huge legs across her body. Another lay across her feet, two more to her left. She laughed at herself and mumbled, 'What on earth?' under her breath.

Providing shelter above her was a frame made out of branches, intricately woven together to form an igloo shape. Over this was a sheet of canvas patterned with forest camouflage. The ground was carpeted with deer skins, barely visible under the pack of dogs panting beside her. She felt somehow reassured by being in their company. From outside she could hear the snapping of twigs, the scratch of matches and the crackle of flames.

142

The evocative smell of a camp fire drifted into the tent. She had been undressed by someone and was completely naked. *Where in hell am I?*

She slowly, gently, worked herself free of the dogs and with the deerskin wrapped tightly around her, crawled tentatively past them. They didn't move but eyed her carefully as she flipped open the canvas door. There, leaning over the fire, was a giant of a man who stood well over six foot tall. The clothing he wore was home-made, leather and hide, topped with a shaggy fur affair which didn't look dissimilar to the dogs. His hair was shoulder length, braided and unkempt with an assortment of tiny animal skulls and feathers attached to it. A long beard and moustache were similarly decorated. Around his neck were the teeth of some creature, threaded onto a leather thong. Slung over his back was a rifle. Strapped around his midriff a belt boasted an assortment of knives. She watched, part mesmerized, part terrified, as he tended the fire, building it up, stepping back, admiring it, as if it were a work of art. He balanced a battered old kettle, that was blackened with age, over the flames. To the kettle he added a handful of something which looked like crushed leaves, but she couldn't be sure.

'Ah, it lives,' he said, with a warm smile and a thick Scottish accent, as he turned round to face her. His brown eyes twinkled amidst a splendid array of laughter lines. 'They dugs bin keepin the cauld aff ye aw right, huv they?'

'I'm sorry?' she replied, 'I have no idea what you just said.'

'Acht,' he shook his head, 'I was asking if the dogs were keeping you warm,' he said with exaggerated precision and a softer accent.

143

'Sorry,' she replied, with more than a hint of embarrassment. 'Yes. Thanks.' Her mind was spinning. Thoughts racing. How had she ended up here? Where was she? Who was this man? Most importantly, was she safe? Despite his appearance, she didn't feel any threat from him. He was peculiarly reassuring.

The kettle sat steaming on its bed of burning wood nestled in stone. The man reached over with a gloved hand and swung it on to the ground where it let off a long, slow hiss. Rummaging into a canvas knapsack he took out a tin mug and wiped it with some snow and the edge of his sleeve, then shrugged his shoulders in a dismissive kind of a way. He poured some of whatever he'd brewed into the cup.

'Get that down you. It'll help you feel better. Mind now, it's still a wee bit warm,' he said, as he crouched in front of her at the entrance to the tent, the exterior of which was covered with netting thick with leaves and twigs, leaving it barely recognisable as any sort of man-made structure. 'Ranulf, by the way. My name.'

'Suze.' She smiled in return, the feeling of at last speaking her own name a powerful reminder of who she was; that she was somewhere else; that she was, or at least appeared to be, free. Whoever this man was, he certainly wasn't New Dawn, or any of their ilk. He was his own force of unconventional nature. Albeit a formidable, perhaps even frightening one. For now she would trust. It wasn't as if she had much choice anyway. She wrapped her hands, now tingling with pins and needles as they came back to life, around the battered tin cup. The steam ran around her face as she blew on the hot infusion. She had no idea what it was, but it felt, and tasted good, in an earthy, smoky kind of a way.

'Better?'

'Getting there. Thanks,' she replied feebly.

'You almost died out there, lass. Lucky the dogs there found you, so you are.'

'Thanks guys,' she said, rubbing the nearest head.

'Not scared then?'

'What?' she asked.

'Are you not scared of them,' he repeated. 'Most folk that don't know them are.'

'No, they're gorgeous.' To her they were less frightening than the man. 'What are they, breed wise, I mean?' she asked.

'Ovcharkas. Caucasian Shepherd dogs,' he said proudly. 'Safe as houses with them on you're side and no mistaking, aye.'

'I can imagine. I can't say as I've ever seen one, let alone a whole pack of them. But then again, I've never come across anyone quite like you before so...yes. It kind of fits.' She smiled somewhat quizzically in his direction.

'Aye well.' He smiled back.

'So how come you're out here in the middle of nowhere, in a blizzard, with a pack of monster dogs? It's a bit weird, really, isn't it?'

'No half as weird as a wee lassie running about in her nightie!'

'Touché!'

'So, Suze, I'm guessing from your fashionable outfit you escaped from the prison place back there. Aye?' he asked.

She was about to speak, then faltered. 'You know, I can't stay here. I'll just get warm if that's okay and move on.'

'Ocht, don't be daft. Where would you be heading

off to, like? You've no idea where you are. You've no clothes, no food.'

'Speaking of which, what happened to them?'

'Don't you be worrying about that right now. Who is it you're running from anyway? No just the prison, like. I mean, is there more to it than that?'

She paused, looking Ranulf in the eye. Trying to read his intentions. She would tell him. What point was there in not doing so? He had saved her life after all.

'New Dawn.'

'New Dawn is it, aye?' Cannae stand those bastards. Thank Christ we got our independence when we did, eh? Otherwise they'd be trampling all over us as well, so they would.'

'Are we not in England then?'

'Naw, you're in Scotland, lassie. You'd just about got to the border when you passed out. I carried you over, like.'

'How far away from the centre are we then?'

'Ocht, the border's eight mile or so an you must've got yourself, ten, twelve miles away on your lonesome, or thereabouts. Far enough, I reckon. Don't worry.'

'You carried me all that way? Wow, thanks. Thanks a million.'

'Nae bother, lass. Asides from which, what was I meant to do? Leave you to die? Don't think so, eh? And if they had managed to follow you that far all there is from then on is a mass of dog tracks going off in all kinds of directions. They bastards won't have a clue,' he laughed. 'Aye, I'd get a right good giggle watching them run around in circles, so I would. And then there's the border. No allowed up here. No legally anyhow.'

'You're sure I'm safe then?'

'Aye, lassie. Safe as houses, as they say, eh?'

So, if you don't mind my asking, how come? How come you're away out here with these guys?' she asked, stroking the nuzzler.

'Acht, I've always wandered about with my dogs. He's Volki, by the way. Taken a liking to you, but! I run up and down all the time following the deer and that. Plenty of them hereabouts, aye.'

'Hey Volki,' she said, rubbing his chest. 'And you live out here?' she asked, with more than a modicum of incredulity.

'Naw, I just come for a few days at a time. Do a bit of hunting, that's all.'

'So you're a professional poacher then?'

'If that's the way you choose to look at it. I don't!' he bristled.

'Hey, no, no offence meant at all,' she said, as she felt the heat of a red blush creep up her face. 'I mean, yes, why not, you know?'

'Right, so we've got that sorted then!' he said, dusting his hands. 'Now, it's getting late. Best get some shut eye afore we head off, aye?'

She was tired and glad of the escape from her embarrassment so was more than happy to comply. He put the fire out with handfuls of snow. Smoke and steam combined in a cacophony of hissing and spitting, ending with a final phtt, as the last ember turned from orange to grey. The sudden quiet wrapped itself around her.

Unsurprisingly, sleep didn't come easily. She lay amongst the dogs with this strange man on the other side of them. Questions kept spinning around and refused to settle themselves. Who was this man? How come he can just cross the border with an unconscious girl on his back? Then there was her escape. Donna

147

being shot down like that. Left lying there. She tried to push the images away, the questions away. Every time she thought she'd done it – that sleep was coming – something else crept in and gnawed away.

21

Richardson was reading over his notes. He had a speech to give to the Collective next week and he trusted it would secure him leadership. At last, his rightful place. He had, of course, been pulling the strings for quite some time now. The military was in his pocket. He could sway things any which way he pleased and whilst that was rewarding, useful, it wasn't quite enough. He had always had that quest for ultimate power. He stood in front of the mirror, securing the correct smile, the most appropriate gestures, the pauses, the questions.

The rude interruption of his phone irritated him, but it was his "special" line. Best to answer it. He picked up the direct line and answered with a brusque, 'This had better be good news!'

'Indeed it is, sir,' a confident voice replied. 'We got her.'

'All to plan?'

'Not exactly, sir, but she is dead.'

'What do you mean by *not exactly*?' Richardson asked with more than a hint of displeasure.

There was a moment's silence at the other end.

'Spit it out man. For God's sake! Do you at least have evidence?' he hissed, as he strode across to his desk and flicked the cigarette box open. He took out a Sobranie and lit it up, drawing the smoke deep into his lungs.

'Ah, well, not exactly. Um, we don't have the body, sir, but we do know she's dead. Eaten by wild dogs, wolves of some sort, it would appear.'

'What?' he bellowed. 'Wild dogs?! It would appear?!' His face becoming that furious shade of crimson once again; his pulse racing. 'What the bloody hell does that mean?'

'They ran into the forest– '

Richardson cut in abruptly. His words sliced the tension like a razor, slowly, precisely. 'They? What do you mean they? For Christ's sake!'

'Her cell mate, the crazy cat girl, she went with her.'

'How the bloody hell did that happen? I was led to believe that she was a trustee. A blithering idiot, but a trustee, nevertheless!'

'She was, yes sir. We don't know exactly what happened; why she ran, but she's dead. Shot at the forest's edge.'

'And?'

'42, Suzanna, ran off into the trees and seemingly disappeared. Our forces followed, of course, and searched relentlessly. There was a blizzard and–'

'I dont want pretty pictures. I want to know that she is dead, how she died and where her body is.'

'Sir, yes. My apologies. The search party came upon a piece of her uniform, one of her shoes chewed almost beyond recognition and a large splattering of blood. This was amidst a mass of animal prints which trailed off further into the woods. There was the mark of something being hauled. A body, trailing blood. She's dead, sir.'

'You are absolutely sure?' he asked, calming down somewhat.

'Yes, sir. DNA checks confirm it was her blood.'

'Very well. We'll speak no more of this. Do you understand?' He forcefully stubbed his cigarette out, twisting it into the crystal ashtray.

'Yes, sir. Of course, sir.'

He disconnected the call and sat back in his leather chair, his feet up on the desk, his hands behind his head. 'At last,' he said to no-one, with a self congratulatory smirk. 'The little runt is no more. Aaahhh.' He picked up his sat phone and keyed in a number.

'Executive planners. How may I help you?'

'Miss Knightly please?'

'Yes, sir. One moment.'

'Knightly here.'

'Ah, dear Miss Knightly, I feel in need of a rather special celebration. I thought perhaps the hunting lodge? Might it be available?'

'Mr. Davis. How lovely to hear from you. The lodge is indeed available. We have some rather special game, fresh in, if you're interested.'

'Dear Miss Knightly, you are a treasure. I'll be with you within the hour.'

'Very well. And are you with company today, or should we expect just you?'

'With company. Myself and one other.'

'As you wish, Mr Davis. I look forward to your visit, as always.'

'Splendid, splendid,' he said, as he clicked end call and dialled another number. 'Charles, my man, what say you to a spot of hunting? I'm heading off to the lodge as we speak.'

'Bloody good idea, old man. I can get there by, hmm, seven?'

'Excellent! I shall see you there.'

He was humming to himself as he strode out to his Jaguar and ran his fingers along its sleek contour. 'Ahh,' he sighed with appreciation. 'Life is bloody good.' The sumptuous leather welcomed him. The computer greeted him. He checked for any delays, possible problems, then, satisfied, turned it off. There could be no record of these forays. It wasn't wise. He revved up the engine with unnecessary force and sped along the gravelled drive, spitting stones and dust in his wake.

'Tosser,' the armed guard at the gate muttered under his breath, as he doffed his cap and smiled at his departing employer.

Mahler filled the car as Richardson headed south. He allowed the music to flow through him, swelling the immense feeling of satisfaction that had engulfed him. Thirty minutes later and he was there. He identified himself and the electronic gates swung open in greeting. He drove along the drive and pulled up at the front door of the lodge. Knightly, dressed immaculately in her definitive leather, was there to meet him.

'Mr Davis,' she said with a smile, mock kissing his cheeks with exaggerated sound effects.

'Knightly, my dear lady. There's a nice big bonus for you today,' he said with a wink, passing a brown envelope into her gloved hand.

'Why, thank you, Mr Davis. I am sure you're going to enjoy this. It is a bit special.'

'You've yet to let me down, my dear.'

'I've left staff for you. Use her. Send her home. It's up to you. Usual rules. It's all yours until tomorrow then,' she said, as she handed him a set of keys. 'Enjoy!'

The lodge stood in five acres of private land which were enclosed within three metre high walls. There were some wooded areas, a small lake and gently undulating grassland. Roaming the grounds was a herd of deer. The house itself was fairly modest with three bedrooms, two reception rooms, a kitchen, bathroom and sauna. Its décor was so overtly sumptuous that it was verging on tacky. Not to Richardson's taste but then, that was part of the fun.

He sat down on the leather settee which squeaked the acceptance of his weight. A smiling, buxom, blond welcomed him. She tottered across the glossy parquet floor on five inch, red stilettos, her long legs coated with silk stockings. Suspenders glinted underneath her black satin mini skirt. Through full lips brushed heavily with scarlet she purred, 'Good evening, sir. My name is Ruby. How can I help you?'

Despite this being a regular event, she had to pretend otherwise and formally introduce herself on each occasion. Familiarity on her side was not allowed. Each event had to hold the pretence of being fresh and exciting. She would rather that someone else be offered the Davis nights. She couldn't bear the man, nor his behaviour. But she was trusted. Her discretion dependable. Her looks sublime. Knightley insisted that she be his hostess, just as Davis requested. He is not someone to be refused.

'Ruby,' he said slowly, twirling the name around in his mouth. 'How delightful. Come a little closer, Ruby.' He took her naked breasts, one in each hand, as if weighing them. 'Very nice. Mmhhmm.' He licked his lips. 'Very nice indeed.' He bit one of her nipples.

She held back a wince and smiled. 'Now, now, sir. I am just waiting staff and that was very naughty,' she chastised him, with an accent which almost hid her true origins, but not quite. 'Would you like to see what we

153

have on the menu this evening, for your pleasure?'

'Indeed, I would, but I'm expecting company. I think a drink for now and the menu later. I am sure you can keep me amused until his arrival, my dear girl.' He appraised her again, cocked his head and smiled in approval. 'Ruby.'

'Very well. A single malt, sir?'

'A single malt.'

He slapped her buttock as she left, with enough force to make her yelp. She frowned as she walked away from him, but kept her head high, her step steady, her wiggle perfectly suggestive. Nothing could be shown, but she hated this. Every last bit of it. To her family, to those who had lost everything, she was lucky. She had a place of relative safety. She had shelter. She had food. As long as she held on to her looks, to her composure, she would be looked after. After all, she was a valuable asset. They had spotted her at the repatriation centre. A quiet word, a palm greased, and she was bought. She became one of the unregistered, which meant she could do nothing other than their bidding. With no ID card, no money, she had no choice.

She returned with a bottle of Laphroaig and a crystal glass on a silver tray which she placed on the coffee table in front of him. He patted the settee beside him and smiled at her. An intimidating smile. Predatory.

'Come, my dear, keep me company. There's a good girl.'

He slid his fingers up the inside of her thigh as she poured the drinks.

The intercom buzzed. Ruby, relieved by the interruption, withdrew politely and opened the door for his guest.

'Good evening, sir,' Ruby smiled professionally.

'How nice to see you. Whisky?' she asked, as she removed his jacket and hung it on a black velvet hanger.

'Ruby, my darling. How delightful you look tonight. Please, yes, a wee dram would be just grand.' Charles replied with a painfully bad Scottish accent. He made his way to the settee and sat himself down beside Geoffrey. 'Celebrating, old chap?' he asked.

'Indeed, my man, indeed!' The smile and toss of the head indicated his state of mind.

'Should I ask?'

'Best not!' he replied, with a knowing smirk. 'Right. Ruby. The lovely Ruby! The menu, I think.'

She clicked on the 106 inch screen and the menu duly appeared. 'Shall I stay and operate the remote for you?'

'No, no. Off you run. We can manage from here.'

She forced a smile and wished for a reprieve, a different life, a way out.

'Now, let's see. What do we have?...hmm... room one is a poor little Russian orphan girl. I do like these Eastern Europeans, don't you? Always so bloody willing yet with a certain feisty touch to them. So much fun!'

'Indeed. At least they're good for something, what!' he laughed

'And room two, oh my, gypsy twins! A little starter, I think.' He turned on the intercom to the room with the twins. 'Speak English, do you?'

'Little,' the boy replied, turning to face the camera. He looked to be about ten. His dark eyes were wide, staring, frightened, but he was strangely placid.

'Good, good. Now what you're going to do is take off your clothes. All of them. That's it.' Richardson began to salivate, licking his lips. 'Now, your sister's,

155

but leave her skirt on. Yes. Good. Open her legs. More. More! Turn her round. That's it. Lovely.'

'Bloody hell, Nigel, I don't know about you but I'm getting a trifle excited here.'

'A bloody genius, old Knightly. Oh, yes! What shall we have them do now, hmmm?'

Ruby sat in her room in the annex. It was soundproofed. The windows and doors were locked, barred and blacked out. She could neither see nor hear anything from the house, but she knew. She knew and she hated herself for doing nothing. For sitting in the dark and not even crying. Not any more.

22

At first light they were up. Suze was relieved, and surprised, that no move had been made on her. It seemed she had met another decent man and she felt safe. Peculiarly safe. Ranulf had fashioned shoes, of a sort, out of one of the skins, and tied them on her feet with strands of ivy. One more skin was wrapped around her waist, as a skirt, and another over her shoulders as a jacket. This man, whoever he was, was certainly resourceful. She laughed at herself, imagining what she must look like, dressed for all intents and purposes, like an extra out of some pre-historic movie. Ranulf nodded and grunted his approval. The remaining skins, venison and supplies were loaded into backpacks which had been custom made for the dogs. All signs of their having been there had been disguised or removed.

They headed north with the dogs initially yelping and scampering excitedly around them, then, with a click of Ranulf's fingers, following obediently in line. She was impressed. Intuitively she could sense that silence was the order of the day. It was a struggle for her to comprehend what was happening here. Everything was at such a wild tangent to what had become her norm. As they travelled on to the sound of feet crunching through snow, wind whistling through trees, crows cawing in alarm, she spun the last twenty four hours around in her head, over and over, thinking. Trying to make sense of it; to piece it together, but it was difficult to keep track of her thoughts, to focus. She pushed herself against the programming she'd undergone. Against the dehumanising. Against the torture. She would beat them, whoever they might be, whatever they had done to her, she would rise above it.

The majesty of the pine forests were soon deposed by layer upon layer of the bleak, solemn hills of the borders. She felt laid open, naked, as she scrutinised the exposure that lay ahead of her, with the frightened eyes of a hunted deer. Her instincts told her to stop, to take cover somewhere, but she followed in the tracks of this unbelievable man who appeared to be her saviour, and for now, it seemed as though he might well be an ally. He looked like one, acted like one, spoke like one. There was certainly nothing conventional about him. Nothing from him felt threatening. Could this really be happening? Good luck? Something decent and trustworthy finally coming her way?

Snow continued to fall heavily, making what lay ahead of them appear blurred and indistinct, but also covering their tracks in no time at all. After a couple of hours of trudging on, struggling through deep snow, they stopped at a waterfall. It tumbled out of the sky, down the almost sheer face it had stubbornly carved out for itself over the centuries. Grey rock, resplendent with jagged icicles, echoed to the scream of the torrent of water.

'Amazing eh?' Ranulf called above the tumult.

'Stunning, just stunning!' she replied, the vulnerability she felt in the desolate hills momentarily put to rest.

'No far now, lass. You holding up okay?'

'Yes. I'm good thanks,' she lied. Her body was aching for her to stop. The months of confinement having taken more of a toll than she had thought.

'Right then. Just over the next hill. No far.'

The dogs were greedily lapping at the pool of water at the foot of the falls, their paws cracking the delicate tentacles of ice encrusting its edge.

'Right you lot. Come on,' he called to them and clicked his fingers. They stopped immediately and fell into line behind him once more.

The last hill was seemingly endless and so steep that it was almost vertical, and treacherous with it. She found it difficult to keep going, but pride and determination pushed her on to its summit. The blizzard had finally stopped and the sky cleared. All around lay a crisp, white landscape which appeared flawless and pristine. In front of her gentle waves of snow-covered hills wove themselves against the pale, pale blue of the afternoon sky. Wisps of clouds in reds and pinks danced across the winter sun. Suze made her way down this last hill, slowly and carefully, being aware of the precision required in each footstep, tentatively crunching through the snow and waiting until she could feel solid ground, something stable beneath her feet, before allowing the transfer of her full weight.

When they eventually reached the safety of the valley they came to a small, wooden bridge which spanned a fast flowing burn. The bridge was narrow and there was no handrail. She hesitated as it creaked in protest at the weight of Ranulf crossing in front of her.

'Don't worry, it'll hold you no bother. Just mind your step,' he said, as he offered a waiting hand from the other side.

She cautiously put one foot, then the other, on the

159

creaking wood until she was close enough for Ranulf to grab a hold of her.

'Thank you,' she said, embarrassed at having needed help, but grateful for it nonetheless.

'There you go,' he laughed, as she exhaled with relief on touching solid ground again.

Across the narrow valley, dry stone walls separated a small piece of land from the surrounding wilderness. A couple of barren trees, south facing and still catching the angry winter sun, silhouetted themselves artistically against the hillside.

'Here we are then,' he said contentedly.

23

'Oh my God! I don't believe it!' Suze cried out, as her eyes focused on the small dwelling built into the hill in front of her. 'A Hobbit house. You live in a Hobbit house. This is so cool!' Her voice had become childlike in its excitement.

'Like it then, eh?' he asked, as he stood proudly, hands on hips, his face broken up by an expectant grin.

'I love it!' she replied, her arms open wide as if ready to embrace it.

'Come away in then, why don't you?' he said, as he led the way under an archway made from the trunk of a fallen tree. It supported a canopy of smaller branches which twisted their way back into the hill and were covered with turf. He opened the heavy wooden door, gesturing for Suze to go in first. The dogs followed, making a bee line to the kitchen area, where they sat, wagging their tails, expectantly.

'Just you behave yourselves an wait nicely,' Ranulf instructed.

As she stood in the centre of the main room her eyes followed the twist of the spiral roof which spun its way up like a wooden spider's web, supported by an assortment of tree trunks, logs and branches. Two staircases twirled up to a couple of sleeping platforms. At the top of it all was a large skylight, which was defying the last tinges of pink sunset with its dense covering of fallen snow. The ground floor was open plan with an area for cooking, eating, and relaxing. Everything appeared to be hand made, evoking a sense of timelessness.

She ran her fingers along a bulky cabinet whose drawers were made from hollowed out logs, enjoying the fleeting memories of her father it sparked up in her. It all seemed such a long time ago. A different person in another life. An imposing mirror stood above the cabinet, its frame a tangle of twisted, small branches which appeared to have been chosen for the quantity of their knots and gnarls. The sickly face reflected in the glass in front of her filled her with dismay. She hardly recognised the sallow skin, the bags under her eyes, the lank, greasy hair, peroxide blond, with black roots. The eyes were those of a stranger with no sign of the familiar vitality. Even their colour seemed to have changed, dulled, faded. 'Shit,' she mumbled under her breath.

'You all right, lass? Come and have a wee seat. Here you are,' he said, pulling up a chair for her, brushing dust off with his hands and wiping them on his trousers. 'I'll just get the fire going. Warm the place up a wee bit, aye? Won't be a minute.'

She watched as he carried logs through from a shed attached to the house and stacked them up beside the fireplace in the sitting area and then repeated the process at the kitchen range. He filled bowls with fresh venison for the dogs who obediently sat and waited until they were called to eat. Sated, they flopped themselves down in front of the fire and fell into dreams of whimpers, twitches and growls. It was comforting. She smiled. Then she cried. Softly. Secretly.

'Right, that's them sorted, now us, eh? Bloody starving so I am!' he called from the kitchen area. 'You all right with deer stew?'

She composed herself, breathed in and out, swiped at her tears. She had to do better. Pull herself together. Tears would get her nowhere. 'That would be brilliant,' she answered, hoping that her voice was clear, her pain hidden. 'I don't remember the last time I had something decent to eat.'

'I'm no a chef like, but I'll do my best. I'm sure it'll be better than what that lot fed you, aye?'

After they'd eaten he rummaged through the larder, picking up a peculiar assortment of bottles of different shapes and colours, reading the hand written labels then putting them back, until finally holding one up triumphantly. 'That'll do nicely! Good vintage this. Château de pretty-good-crop-o-elderberries 2019. Fancy a wee tipple?'

'Yes. That would be lovely, thanks.' Alcohol! My God! How long had it been? Oh yes. Back then. Her parents' house. Push it away. Bury it.

She tried, unsuccessfully, to suppress a laugh when he brought across two rather grand wine glasses with the bottle and set them on the log table.

'What's so funny, like?' he asked.

'Sorry, it's just I wasn't expecting the wine glasses. I thought they would be, I don't know, something carved out of wood or recycled jam jars or the likes.'

'Oh did you now?' he said, feigning hurt, hiding his accent. 'Well, these were a house-warming present from my daughter, Margot. She's quite civilised you know.' His eyes twinkled with an amused warmth. 'Aye, she wouldn't let me be the complete heathen.'

'So you've got family then?'

'I have that, aye, up in Edinburgh. Two lassies. All grown up now.'

'And their mother?'

'She died....' he paused. 'A while back. It was...an accident,' he said, gesturing with his head to the hills beyond the back of the house. 'Hmmm, aye, a while back,' he repeated, as he picked at a loose thread in his sweater.

'I'm sorry. I didn't mean to...sorry.'

They sat in silence for a while, drifting off in the flicker of the flames, travelling their own private journeys.

The wine was strong and after drinking one glassful she felt herself relaxing into a pleasant state of mild intoxication.

'Strong stuff,' she said, smiling, lifting her glass up so that the light of the flames danced around it. 'The wine.'

He smiled in return. 'Aye well, that's its purpose, eh? A wee bit relaxation.'

The effect of the wine loosened her tongue sufficiently for her to have the courage to ask what had been on her mind since their first meeting. 'The whole skulls and feathers and, em, teeth thing. What's the reasoning?'

'Ach, I just like them. Bits an pieces I've picked up. And you know what?' he said, with a mischievous twinkle in his eyes.

'No.' She raised her eyebrows in question. 'What?'

'Nobody, and I mean nobody bothers me!'

'Ha, I'll bet they don't!' she said with a laugh. 'So they don't signify anything then? All the things?'

'Naw. Just that I'm a total nutter who's best left alone, is all!'

164

She laughed again. 'Yes, I can see that working. And the teeth? Dare I ask what they're from?'

'Ah, these,' he said, fondling one of the impressive incisors between thumb and middle finger. 'These were from my first dog, Lexi, beautiful dog, so she was. Volki's mate an mother to two of these three,' he added, pointing to the pile of dogs lying at his feet. 'Aye, she got sick. Horrible, so it was. An Volki, Christ, he took it worse than me. Heartbroken, so he was. He's never been quite the same since, poor lad.'

'Oh, I'm sorry. Put my foot in it again,' she said, whilst thoughts of how he must have taken the teeth out of the dead dog made her shiver. She guessed her suspicion as to the origins of his fur jacket was also correct, which didn't help the unwelcome, gory images of skinning a dog that flitted amongst the conversation.

'Well, lass, don't know about you, but I could do with my bed,' Ranulf said, with a sigh and a yawn.

'Yes, me too.'

'Right, well, follow me then,' he said, as he stood up and stretched, making his impressive body seem even more so. He led her up one of two stairways. This one led to a platform which had been cut back into the hillside. There were two beds on it, a chunky wardrobe and a chest of drawers. A door led to a small en suite shower and toilet. He explained how to use it, told her to help herself to clothes and drew the heavy curtains around the platform, which entirely separated it from the rest of the house.

'Sleep well, lass,' he called behind him, as footsteps seeming far too gentle for his stature, made their way down the stairs.

'Yes, thanks. You too.'

She had showered, put on the T-shirt that had been

165

left out for her and was lying in a comfortable bed with proper bed linen. This was unreal. She couldn't believe her good fortune. It was now pitch black outside and the little house as dark as anywhere she had ever been. But this was a comforting dark. A dark that held no fear. A dark which seemed to wrap her up, envelop her in its serenity. Tonight, she hoped, she could sleep, uninterrupted, until daybreak smiled through the sky light.

24

Suze sat up with a start. She was sure that she could hear footsteps on the roof. Slow, heavy footsteps, followed by a sliding and thumping. It came again, and again. What the hell was going on? Terror grabbed hold of her as she stared, disbelievingly, at the roof above her, her heart thumping, her breath struggling. New Dawn had found her again. They were on the roof. They must have surrounded the place already. Any minute now and they would strike. Come crashing through the door, the roof. She leapt out of bed, wrapped the cover around herself, pulled the curtain aside and leaned over the balcony. There was no sign of Ranulf. No sign of the dogs. They would have barked, surely? Ranulf would have heard. Alerted her. Done something. Her head was spinning. She felt faint. *Keep it together, Suze. Keep it together.*

Suddenly light began to tumble in through the skylight above her. She could see snow being pushed off the glass with a broom type thing. It slid across the glass, down the roof, landing with a thwump on the ground below. One of the dogs barked. Not a warning bark though, a playful one. She let out a laugh. Bit her lip. Shook her head. It was all okay. She had no idea of what the time might be, but Ranulf was already up and busy.

Despite being told to help herself, it felt invasive rummaging through someone else's clothes, however she had little choice. It was that or deerskin! In the first drawer she opened she found a pair of jeans. They were slightly too big, but there was a belt to hold them up. In the drawer below was a well worn, luxuriously thick Arran sweater; hand made, she guessed. She couldn't help but wonder about the girl whose clothes these were. Was she an ardent non-conformist like her father? There was little here to explain either of the girls' characters. The lack of personal touches made her think his daughters didn't visit often. Curiosity, as usual, began to get the better of her.

She showered, marvelling at the effective workings of the plumbing, at the en-suite in a Hobbit house, which must, she assumed, be well off-grid. Unbelievable! She dressed and padded down the wooden stairs. The feeling of non-confinement, of freedom, felt alien to her and she couldn't quite get her head around it, understand it. Sleeping for as long as she needed, showering in privacy, dressing in normal clothes, seeing daylight. It was almost overwhelming. Almost too much.

Leaning on the window ledge she looked out at the dogs playing, lunging at each other, rolling in the snow, catching snowballs. Ranulf ran at them and threw himself on Volki, wrestling with him, laughing. He lay on his back; the big dog licking at his face. She took a deep breath, smiled and reminded herself that, yes, she was safe. This wasn't a dream. In the distance, beyond the house, rolling hills coated with pure fresh snow stood proudly, brightly, against the heavy grey clouds that were building in the distance. Such a dramatic scene. Such isolation. Such beauty.

168

'Morning, Ranulf,' she said, as the front door swung open, a gust of icy cold air accompanying it. She turned from the kettle she had just put on to boil. 'I hope you don't mind?' she asked, gesturing at the stove.

'Naw, course not. There's one of those wee espresso thingies somewhere that my daughters use, if you fancy. Me, I can't be doing with those tiny wee cups. A big old-fashioned mug's more to my liking,' he said, smiling up at her as he removed his boots and thumped the snow off them. 'Oh, morning back,' he added, after a couple of minutes. 'Sorry, my social skills aren't the best these days.'

The dogs padded in behind him, panting heavily, clumps of snow clinging to their paws which clinked along the wooden floor like icy castanets. Little puddles of water trailed in their wake.

'Bed,' Ranulf instructed, pointing to the alcove which was their domain. They skulked off obediently, if unhappily, and lay with their eyes trained on Suze in the kitchen.

'Do I smell baking bread?' she asked.

'Oh Christ, aye!' he exclaimed, as he grabbed a dish towel and swung the heavy handle of the wood-burning stove up. A deep squeak, almost a groan, announced the opening of the heavy oven door. 'Phew, just as well you reminded me there, lass. I'd forgotten clean about it, so I had.' He slid the bread out and placed it on a wire rack, then tapped at the crust with his fingertips. The hollow sound it made led to a satisfied nod. 'Why don't you go an sit yourself down and I'll get breakfast on the table, aye?'

'Are you sure I can't help?'

'Naw, naw. Away an sit. You still need to be taking it easy. A wee bit of convalescing, aye?'

169

She sat watching the approaching clouds grow, stretching their way across the landscape, smothering out the sun, as it grew increasingly dark. A storm was beckoning. It wasn't long before the snow began to fall. A few flakes became a flurry, then a full on blizzard. Everything had disappeared.

Ranulf bent down and glanced out of the window. 'Aye, that'll be on for the day then.' He flicked a light on. 'Aye.'

The window was quirky and irregularly shaped, neither square nor round. The walls were perhaps a metre thick, leaving a large window ledge which held an assortment of stones, pebbles, and sticks, carefully placed to show them at their best.

'Do you collect these?' she asked, twirling a piece of quartz in her hand.

'Aye, I do that. Just things that take my fancy, like,' he answered, as he came to join her at the table. 'From all over, they are. Wee mementoes of places an people, aye.'

'This one?' she asked, holding up the quartz.

'From the beach at Eyemouth. Holiday wi the girls when they were wee, like.'

'Hmm. And there's a story behind each of them?' she asked, as she carefully replaced the quartz.

'Aye, there is that. Now...' He placed the warm bread on the table with some butter and home-made bramble jam. The plates were wooden, as was the cutlery. The smell of fresh timber still clung to them. 'Tuck in, lass,' he said, as he tore a chunk off the bread and handed it to her. 'Fresh bread's best torn, no cut, eh?'

'I guess I'm about to find out,' she replied with a smile, as she watched the butter turn from yellow to gold and dissolve into the bread. 'Yes,' she said, smiling

170

across at him after her first mouthful. 'You're right, it is. Delicious!' she enthused. Simple pleasures, like warm bread, were now spectacular. Every single experience a re-birth which she relished.

'So, Suze, what's your story?' he asked, as he cleared the table. 'How come a nice wee lass like you has ended up on the run from that shower?'

For some reason she felt complete trust in this man and it all just blurted out. Everything that had happened. The site, her parents, Jake, the Centre and Donna. She paused every now and then to haul back her composure, which threatened to walk out on her at each turn of events. At each death. It all sounded so unbelievable – ridiculous – as the words tumbled out. A far-fetched tale from a deluded mind. She wondered what he was thinking as the story unfolded. He allowed her to finish uninterrupted, apart from the occasional breathy whistle or incredulous, 'Naw!'

'So, let me get this straight. You don't rightly know who's after you, who's behind it all, or why?'

'Correct.'

He sat for a while, tugging at his beard as if it held the key, the answers. 'Seems to me we need to do a wee bit of investigating, aye?'

'We?' she asked with scrutinising eyes.

'Aye, we. I cannae be saving your life and no find out what it's all about now, can I?'

'That's really decent of you but, I can't have you doing that, putting your life at risk, you know? Everyone who gets involved with me...dies.' Her voice cracked and she hung her head; the weight of the memories becoming too heavy. The table became smudged with a tear that had escaped her resolve. 'Shit,' she mumbled, wiping her face with the sleeve of her

171

jumper.

'Aw, come on now,' he said, as he reached across the table for her hand. 'Let's do something, eh? Best way to get over bad shit is to do something about it. Get busy. Start our own, wee, private investigation.'

'I can't. I have to go,' she said with resignation, getting up and heading for the door. 'Thank you for everything but–'

'Dinnae be daft,' he said with gentle admonishment, as if he were addressing a misguided child. 'You're going nowhere, lass. Now sit back down an behave yourself. Volki!' he commanded, pointing to the door. Volki trotted over and sat obediently, blocking her exit.

'Oh bloody hell! You're a hard man to argue with.'

'Aye, an that's been said before. Sit.'

'Are you talking to me or the dog?'

He laughed. 'Bit of spirit left in you. That's grand, so it is. Sit,' he repeated, pointing at the chair. 'There's a good girl.'

She shrugged her shoulders and returned to her seat, feeling foolish, feeling humiliated. 'So?'

'So. Let's be having names, dates of birth, addresses, last knowns, and anything else you can think of, aye?' He made his way to wooden shelving which stretched its way around the entire house. It was alive with what appeared to be random piles of books, maps, magazines, papers and other paraphernalia that you seldom saw any more. He pulled a small metal case from behind a pile of National Geographics, set it on the table and clicked it open. Inside was a rugged laptop.

'Impressive piece of hardware,' Suze said. 'It looks – military,' she added, unable to hide her consternation.

'Aye, it is that,' he confirmed, as he connected the

172

satellite.

'You're not...?'

'Naw, no any more, but I still have contacts, like,' he added, as he selected encryption mode.

'So, what were you?'

'Special ops.'

'No shit!' she said, with a laugh that was part nervous, part disbelief. Her mind was reeling; warning signals going off in all directions. Sparking. 'Youre winding me up, right?'

'Naw, straight up.' He was chatting to someone online.

'Till when? Where?'

'Ocht, it was a while back now. Russia, the Middle East. Covert stuff,' he said casually, as if it were common; your everyday nine to five.

'So, you were a spy? Is that what you're saying here?

'Sort of, I suppose, if that's how you want to look at it.'

'So, you speak, what, Arabic? Russian?'

'Aye, and a few others.'

'Wow! How did you...I mean, you don't seem the type, somehow.'

'What, wrong accent, is it?' He feigned offence.

'No,' she said with a laugh. 'Well, maybe yes. They're portrayed as right school, right background, type people, aren't they?'

'Well, I'll have you know I earned my masters at Cambridge,' he said, with a Queen's English accent. 'I graduated Cum Laude in Russian studies from Edinburgh, and was invited to go to Cambridge. Whilst there I was head hunted, so to speak,' he chuckled. 'By the MI. Seems I'd shown exceptional aptitude in a few key areas! It was exciting stuff for a young man from the middle of nowhere in rural Perthshire, so it was.'

'I can imagine. Wow. How come you dropped out then to – to this?'

'Ach, I saw stuff I didn't like. Straight up. Bad shit, you know?' His look said *let's not go there.* 'Enough of that anyway, eh? Now, let's be seeing what's going on where you're concerned, aye?'

'You're a walking, bloody dichotomy, aren't you? A bread making, wine brewing, deer hunting, wild man of the forest who lives in a Hobbit house and was a bloody spy! Unbelievable!'

'Aye, that's me,' he said, with some satisfaction. 'Here now, is that your parents?' he asked, as a picture of Katherine and Geoffrey in a newspaper report appeared on the screen.

'Uh-huh,' she replied, dropping her shoulders. 'That's them.' The story she knew, but this one included a report on the funeral.

'Okay, now this is just the papers. Doesn't mean a thing, okay?' he added, in an attempt at reassurance.

'Okay,' she answered meekly, trying desperately to believe him.

He searched through local hospital records. 'Aye, there we go. Mortuary. Aye. Sorry lass. It's no looking good for them.'

'Thought as much,' she said, coldly, nodding her head. 'Couldn't imagine them accusing me of murder and letting them live. That would be a bit stupid of them, wouldn't it?'

She wandered across to sit on the floor beside Volki, wrapping her arms around his powerful neck, resting her head on his. She felt sick. Her head thumped. Tiredness suddenly smothered her and within minutes she was asleep.

Ranulf began searching, quietly, methodically, making notes as he went, bookmarking relevant pages. The only sounds were the clicking of the keys, the scratch of a pencil and the occasional exclamation muttered under his breath. 'Well, well, well!'

When she awoke it took her a few seconds to remember where she was. She wiped a combination of dog hair and drool from the side of her mouth and looked across to see Ranulf still working away.

'You all right there?' he said, without taking his eyes off the screen. 'You were crying an calling out in your sleep something awful. I didn't rightly know whether to wake you or leave you.'

'Sorry –'

'Don't be daft. I was worried, was all.'

'How long was I asleep for?'

'Couple of hours. Volki's comfy, eh? It's no the first time he's had a body sleeping on him! Done it myself a few times out in the woods, eh Volki boy?'

Volki stood up, stretched and yawned, then padded across to his master, his tail gently wagging. Suze rejoined Ranulf at the table, pulling her chair up close to his.

'Right lass, you ready for this? Wee bit good news!' he said, as he opened the relevant tab.

'Bloody hell, I'm dead!'

'Seems that way, aye!'

She read on past the headlines "Callous murderer dies in botched escape attempt", shaking her head at the barrage of lies. 'Well, that's a pretty thorough character assassination they've done on me, isn't it?'

'Aye, and that's no even the worst o them. What a shower, eh? Still, at least you can relax a bit knowing you're dead, eh?'

'There is that,' she replied with a sardonic laugh.

'Okay, enough of that for now. You must be hungry. Spot of food?'

'Sure. Yes. Thanks,' she replied, although eating was really the last thing she felt like doing right now.

25

'I'm guessing you had a pretty rough time of it in there, aye?' Ranulf asked, as he stoked the fire.

'Yes, it was horrendous,' Suze replied, staring at the logs as they caught and sparkled. She shook her head. 'Absolutely horrendous. I became a number – literally. Number 42 was how they addressed me. They'd wake me up all the time, feed me at odd hours, or sometimes just not bother at all. I saw daylight on a handful of occasions in the whole time I was there. It was what kept me going. The thought of the next time I might get outside. The only things I knew would happen were the drugs and being taken to the so called classroom.'

'The classroom?' he asked, tilting his head to one side as if straining to hear.

'Yes, they'd strap me in this chair, a dentist type thing, and force feed me all kinds of vile propaganda. Videos, really nasty ones. Brainwashing shit.' She shivered at the memories. Volki nuzzled her hand, as if he knew, making her smile.

'Sounds like classic Psychops stuff,' he said, nodding.

'Psychops?'

'Psychological Operations. What we'd do to terrorists, threats, perceived enemies.'

'And you were a party to it?' she asked, unable to

disguise her distaste.

'Not me, personally, no. We, as in the forces.'

'Ah, I see,' she replied, with some relief, but a barrage of questions that weren't for now.

'You've done really well by the looks of you, though.'

'Do you think so?'

'Aye, I do. I've seen people end up in a real mess. How did you keep it together, fight it?'

'Music. I sang in my head all the time. I figured if I kept my mind full of something of my choosing it would keep me sane; keep them out, you know?'

'Smart lassie,' he said, looking up at her with appreciation.

'And I figured music because it was easy. Easy to just keep it going. To build my own mental firewall, so to speak. It took me places too. You know how a song can just take you right back to a certain place and time? Well, yes, it helped me keep it together.'

'Are you up for a wee bit more research?' he asked, reaching for his computer.

'Sure, yes. I'm good.' she replied, nodding. She put her arms around Volki's neck and whispered, 'Isn't that right, Volki boy. All good.' His tail wagged on the rough wooden floor, sending tiny particles of dust up to dance their way through the surreal light emanating from the computer screen.

'Right well, just say if you need a break, aye?'

'Will do.'

'So, what do you want to check on next?' he asked.

'The crash, I guess,' she replied, with a shrug.

'Right, so when was it?'

'The first of September.'

'Where?'

'I don't know exactly. Somewhere near Salisbury, I think. Yes, I remember the doctor saying something about Salisbury.'

'Okay,' he said, opening tabs with fatal accident reports. 'Removal van, aye?'

'Yes.'

'Right. This must be it then.' He swung the screen round for Suze. 'Have a wee read.'

She read the accident report. 'This can't be right,' she mumbled, then read it again. 'Tragic accident...blow out...driver killed...nothing about any passengers. What on earth?' She looked questioningly at him.

'You're sure, lass. The same van?'

'Absolutely! I remember the registration plate, everything.'

'And your pal, Jake?'

'He was a mess. Couldn't move. I was sure he was a goner. So sure that I left him. I fucking left him!'

Their eyes met.

'Survival. Just that,' he said slowly, pointedly, holding her gaze. 'No need to beat yourself up,' he added, before turning back to the screen. 'Right. Let's have a wee peek at the official line, shall we?'

'What do you mean?'

'Homeland Security Forces,' he said, with a conspiratorial grin.

'You can't?' she asked.

'I can!' he replied.

Within a few minutes he was in. He typed in Jake's name – access denied. He tried another route – same result. 'Shit,' he mumbled, 'No as easy as I was hoping. Ach well.' He thought for a while then nodded. 'Worth a try, aye.' He was chatting to someone else online. 'Right, here we go. Naw, that's no working either.

179

Secure as shit, lass, so it is. Shall we try you? Just for a laugh, eh?'

'Why not?'

'Access denied. Well there's a big surprise, eh? I don't know who you've upset, but it's someone pretty powerful and no mistaking. Their feathers will all be in a flutter now,' he said, with a grin. 'Aye!'

'So will they know you've been trying to access?'

'Naw. They'll know someone's trying but no me. No worries on that score.'

'Safe as houses?' she said, with a grin.

'Aye, safe as houses. Right, I'm going to exercise the beasts. You're welcome to come, or you can stay. As you please.'

'Do you mind if I pass?'

'Course not.'

The thought of traipsing through deep snow wasn't appealing and she wanted down time. Her time. A chance to digest this. To think about it. She also wanted to do some digging of her own.

'And the laptop? Can I?'

'Naw, sorry. No that,' he said, as he clicked the computer case closed and locked it. 'We'll look some more when I get back, all right? I'll just be an hour or two.' He pulled on his boots and jacket, adding, 'Make yourself at home, lass.' He whistled for the dogs and off they went into the hills.

She felt awkward, alone in this little house she so desperately wanted to forage through for...well, anything really. But she wouldn't, couldn't. There was something about this man. An honesty, a decency, which she wasn't going to take advantage of. Instead she settled for drifting between reading one of his National Geographics and gazing out at the beautiful

180

solitude of this place. It seemed that the storm had passed, the sky cleared, the view back in place, albeit drifting away again with the retreat of daylight. Her mind churned thoughts of Jake around at unexpected moments. She pushed them back where they came from, not wanting to wonder, to hope. She couldn't afford that right now.

When, at last, the silence was broken by the dogs barging through the door she was relieved and comforted to be surrounded by living things again, deliriously happy ones at that. She welcomed them back with strokes and pats as their tails beat against her legs in enthusiastic greeting.

'Hi guys. Have you had fun?' she asked.

'Aye, they have indeed. Going crazy out there, so they were. Got the scent of something exciting and decided to chase it.'

She laughed at the image. 'What was it?'

'I don't know. Wouldn't be deer this far from the woods. More likely rabbit, or fox, or some such,' he said, as he crossed over to the window and peered out at the darkening sky. 'Snow's on its way again. Feels like another heavy one too.'

'Can I make you a cup of something?' Suze asked.

'Aye, tea would be grand. There's quite a nice wee mixture in that tin next to the stove there,' he said, pointing at the kitchen.

'This one?' she asked, picking up a hexagonal tin with Chinese patterns and writing on it.

'That's the one, aye.'

'Don't tell me, you picked it up whilst on a little foray into deepest China,' she said, only half jokingly.

'Naw, never been,' he replied, smiling at her. 'An the tea's home made.'

'Pretty self sufficient, aren't you?'

'I am that. If I can't grow it or make it I trade for it with the locals. Works pretty well. Hardly ever spend money on stuff, like. Even the power is self-generated. Combination of wind, water, an solar. There's a generator for back-up, but I try an avoid it.'

'Cool!' she said, bringing the teapot and mugs over to the table.

'Now, let's have a wee look an see what's been happening in ether land, eh?' he said, as he opened his laptop back up. 'Hmm... somebody knows how to cover their tracks all right, and would you look at that!'

'What?'

'You've been deleted. Clean as a whistle – gone!'

'What do you mean?'

'From Homeland. You've been erased, deleted. Nothing. It's like you were never on their list. Never under investigation. Never there at all.'

'Is that a good thing?'

'Well, aye, in so far as it sort o puts a seal on you being dead but...it's no usual, like. It would be case closed but file left for the records, you know? It also means it's that bit harder to find out who was after you. Who set you up, which is a shame. Me. I like to know my enemy.'

'Me too.'

'I wonder if you're anywhere?'

'What do you mean?'

'Birth records, school, medical, that kind of stuff. Let's see. Do you mind?'

'No, please. This is fascinating. On you go.'

'Right.' He checked all of the obvious places, then the not so. 'You, lass, were never even born.'

'Bloody hell. I guess someone really doesn't like me.

I'm not too sure how I feel about that.'

'I wouldn't be too upset about it but, aye, looks like you were a serious threat to someone, or something. Any ideas?'

'Not really. I mean we were digging the dirt on plenty of dodgy politicians and the likes but...shit, I could really do with my computer.'

'Where is it, like?'

'Ah, it got taken by New Dawn when they took me in. It's really annoying because we were always careful to have back-ups, you know?'

'Aye. And?'

'Well, usually one person had the computer and the other the external hard drive. That day I had the drive, Jake the computer. But when I ran, I took the computer as well. So, they've got both. We never trusted the Clouds so didn't use them for any kind of back up.'

'Naw, well, you were right about that. So it's all gone then, aye?'

'I'm afraid so.'

'How's your memory?'

'Right now? Pretty shit. There are blanks, you know?'

'That's to be expected, lass. Dinnae worry. We'll work on getting it back in time, eh?'

'Okay.'

'First priority is getting you fit an well, aye?' He smiled warmly and patted her knee.

'And Jake?' she asked. 'What about his file, records, whatever?'

He fingered the keys, glanced at the screen. 'Still there. Oh!' Scratched his head, leaned back in his chair. 'No, he's gone too, well, from Homeland, at least. Reckon somebody's shitting themselves somewhere. Or maybe someone's just feeling all smug and successful, eh? I wonder?'

His fingers chatted more encrypted messages. Replies were speedy. Discussion became more and more excited.

'What's happening?' she asked, the frustration she felt evident in her voice.

He held up his finger to request silence or patience or both. She had to bite back on her impulse to react with annoyance at being shushed, instead raising her eyebrows in subtle silent protestation. He finally stopped and turned to face her.

'Sorry lass, got caught up in a conversation there. Some things have to be chased up right away or they can get lost. So, what I'm wondering is, how did they pick you up after the crash? How did they know you were there at all?'

'I don't know. I'd guessed it was because they knew I was travelling with Jake and they found him.'

'Aye, that would have made sense but...How much time had passed from the crash to them catching you?'

'I can't be sure. I passed out and a lot of it's jumbled, but it can't have been more than two or three hours.'

'That's what I was thinking. So, within a couple of hours the crash gets reported to New Dawn. Jake's ID'd – an that's assuming they did find him there. You're called in as missing and then found by the chopper squad. Really? Doesn't quite add up to me.'

'What are you saying then?'

'I'm thinking something was tracking you? You were so important that someone very powerful put an alert on the satellite system.'

'Which means?'

'Which means that as each satellite picks up a face it

scans it for a most wanted. It's costly and time consuming so only used for big stuff, aye? Known terrorists, enemies o the state type things.'

'Yeah, but, this is just me. Christ, this doesn't make any sense at all.'

'No, it doesn't. Can we go right back? Right back to when you knew something was going on?'

'Sure, yes. That would be the site going down when we were in London.'

'Okay, lass, what I need you to do is tell me everything. And I mean everything. From about a week before then till you got picked up. People, places, conversations, what you had for your breakfast. Can you do that for me?'

'I can try. Sure...' She paused.

The wind had picked up and was slamming against the front of the house. Even the snowflakes were moving at such a pace they clattered against the windows.

'What's up?' Ranulf asked.

'That article in the paper. It had a picture of Jake and me out in a bar a couple of weeks before then. They must have been tailing us or something before that, mustn't they?'

'It would seem so. Right. As far back as...let's say a fortnight before. As much as you can. I'm going to record it all, okay?'

'Shit,' she mumbled.

'Aye, well, you're just going to have to trust me, eh?'

'No, it's not that. I do. It's just, it's going to be really hard, you know? Really hard.'

'Right,' he clicked the record function on. 'Let's do this.'

26

'Okay, it looks like we've got a few wee questions to answer, aye?' Ranulf said.

'I'm listening,' Suze replied.

'First off is this Brian lad. You knew him well, aye?'

'Not me, no. I got to know him through Jake, but they'd been friends since primary school. I can't imagine –'

He interrupted by raising a finger at her. 'First rule of espionage,' he said with a grin. 'Always assume everyone is guilty. This whole innocent until proven stuff is a piece of nonsense.'

'Okay,' she replied, her voice rising with a hint of consternation.

'Surname?'

'I don't know.'

'Right. What do you know?'

'Em, they were at school together, so maybe old school records or something?'

'Now you're thinking. Good lass. School?'

'No idea. Christ, I'm useless, aren't I?'

'Not to worry. We'll search Jake Bateman and – there we go. Brian. That him?'

'Oh, you're almost as good as me,' she replied with a grin. 'Yep. That's him. And that means that Jake's still alive on the internet.'

'It does indeed. Now, let's get Brian flagged.'

'Flagged?'

'Aye. Wee automatic background thingie. Should throw up any anomalies.'

'How can you still do this?'

'Ah, well, I could tell you but then I'd have to kill you!'

'That is so not funny right now,' she said, with a reprimanding tone. 'Really!'

'Aye, well. Right,' he said, embarrassed at his apparent insensitivity. 'Next we have...' he played more of the recording. 'Nah, no them, or them. Okay, the guys that picked you up in the park.'

'But they helped us! Surely not? I mean they could have just handed us in straight off.'

He looked knowingly across at her, his eyebrows raised. 'Guilty until – remember?'

'Sorry. It's a bit hard to get my head round that one. Goes against the grain somewhat!'

'Aye, well. So, what do you know?'

'God; nothing really,' she replied with exasperation. 'But we've got one name from the accident report, yes?'

'We do indeed, if it's genuine, that is. Do you know the address o the house?'

'No, but I'd recognise it, and I think I could work out roughly where we went from the park.'

'Right, let's have a wee look then, shall we?' He opened Open Maps and they walked around the area where she thought it was.

'That's it! Yes, definitely. So now what? Registered owners search?'

'Aye. There you go. Let's see now. There. Dana and Peter Whitestaff.' He took their details and flagged

187

them too. 'And we'll just throw in Roger, what was it?'

'Roger Baczewski.'

'Aye, right, Polish, American laddie.'

'What are you looking for here?'

'Everything and nothing. You never know what might show up. An odd wee spot in someone's history, unusual friends, parents, even blanks. You never can tell.'

'Okay. If you say so.'

'Aye. There's no telling who might have been got at. Folk can do strange things when they're scared, so they can.'

'How long will all this take, do you think? To get the checks done?'

He scrunched his face up. 'Could be a while. Maybe till tomorrow. You could do with a wee break anyway, aye?'

'Yes. Yes I could,' she said, thankfully.

*

After they'd eaten she went for a walk with Ranulf and the dogs. The storm had abated, and despite the dark, the snow made the visibility surprisingly good. The sky was now clear and awash with stars. The moon cast a silver trail across the valley. Little puffs of vapour escaped from the dogs as they panted and yelped in a frenzy of fun. The sound of their feet crunching their way through the frozen crust of snow was almost musical. The bass drum announcing the onset of an overture. She smiled, wondering where such a thought had come from. The contrast between two days ago and now was incredible and she found it hard to believe that she was here, in this white wilderness, in the protection of this incredible man. She wanted so much to believe in him, to feel safe, to relax. But, despite everything, all of his kindness and help, she wasn't quite there, quite yet. Not fully.

They headed up the hill behind the house. The snow was deep and the going slow and hard work, taking its toll on Suze's muscles; on her lack of fitness. She struggled to keep up with Ranulf, but wouldn't show weakness, give up; wouldn't admit defeat. Her relief when they turned back down the hill was enough to make her whisper a thankful, 'Yes!'

'What's that, lass?'

'Nothing.'

When they returned he built the fire up and brought out another bottle of wine.

'I could get used to this,' she said, as she looked into the flames that were now roaring up the chimney. There was a crackle and a fizz as a spurt of green flame leapt out from one of the logs.

'That'll be some poor wee beastie getting toasted, aye.'

'Really? Oh, that's a shame. What a way to go.'

He laughed at her. 'I don't reckon the wee beasties can really compute anything, do you?'

'Probably not, but still...' She took a sip of wine and pulled a face. 'Oo, strong!'

'Is it, aye? Best take it easy then. Cannae be getting drunk, eh?'

'Can I ask something?'

'Sure, fire away, lass.'

'You seem, well, decent. A down to earth kind of a guy. I can't see you being mixed up with whatever it was you were mixed up in. You know? Soldiering, espionage type, stuff.'

'Ach, it was a big compliment, getting recruited like that, and exciting. I felt like I was this James Bond kind of a guy, running off undercover, checking up on people. I really didn't have time to think about what I was doing. I just did it.'

'Hmm. Every schoolboy's dream, yes?'

'Something like that, aye.'

'How long did you do it for?'

'Ten years, three months, or thereabouts.'

'That's pretty precise.'

'Aye, well, a defining moment in my life happened at the ten year three month mark. Makes it easy to remember,' he said, twiddling with a small piece of well worn stone from the collection on the windowsill.

'Oh, I see.'

'Aye.' He polished the stone with a puff of breath and his sleeve, then with great care placed it back in exactly the same spot, moving it a centimetre here and a centimetre there until he nodded that he was satisfied.

'So why the change of heart? Why leave?'

'There's little miss journalist popping up again, eh?'

'Sorry. I can't help it.'

'As I said, bad stuff that I've left behind, an I'd rather it stayed there. It doesn't matter what I did. Who I am now, is good. Fair enough?'

'Fair enough,' she agreed, feeling that perhaps she had overstepped the mark again.

'I think the relevant history right now is yours, no?'

'I guess so.'

He let the fire burn down as she told him about being adopted, her family, being brought up in Cornwall then moving to London. They talked about politics and found they had similar leanings, an abhorrence of the current regime and its overtly racist, neo fascist fervour. They discussed theories of how it had all spread culminating in the belief of the majority of British voters that repatriation was somehow acceptable, desirable.

'There's some new folk taken over your site too. Bit dodgy looking, to my mind. I'll show you tomorrow, if you want?'

'Yes, that would be interesting. Thanks.' She stretched and yawned, suddenly noticing the effects of the wine. 'I need my bed.'

'Aye, getting that way myself. On you go, lass. Goodnight.'

'Night, Ranulf.'

She made her way up the quirky wooden stairs and drew the heavy curtain around her platform. Thoughts spun around in her head as she showered off what was left of the day; her eyes closed, her face pointing up into the blast of hot water. She stretched her arms out and pushed her hands against the recycled glass tiles, enjoying the mix of rough and smooth against her fingertips. 'Wow,' she muttered to herself, trying to get her head around the alive but dead concept. 'Just wow.'

As she lay in bed listening, he worked on well into the night. His fingers clicking on the keyboard, him talking in a muffled whisper. Whether it was to himself, the dogs or someone at the end of a connection, she wasn't sure. She eventually drifted off with thoughts of what if and Jake.

27

Richardson felt that he had just given the speech of his life. His acceptance speech. At last! It was even better than his infamous repatriation speech. He had shut them up, the whining liberal lefties. The proof of the success of the all-powerful ID cards, of New Dawn, of the crackdown on criminals, on terrorists. England was a safer country. A country to be proud of. Illegals, whether foreigners or criminals, had no place in this new society. In his new society. Those that had something to give now had the chance to flourish, and by God they were doing just that. Off-shore bank balances overflowed. The economy was growing at a notable rate. Those that had nothing, that were nothing, had been isolated, as necessary. He had quoted figure upon figure exemplifying the undoubted success of this bold new regime.

'Well, old chap, that was splendid. Put those lentil munching, sandal wearing, melon eaters in their place and no denying!' Charles enthused. He slapped Richardson affectionately on the shoulder as he took his seat opposite.

'Thank you, my man. I'll admit, I worked my bollocks off getting it just so.' He laughed. 'It did go down rather well, didn't it!'

'Indeed, indeed.'

The heavy oak panelling of the walls of the bar of their club was awash with congratulatory conversation. The sumptuous brocade curtains dripped with it. The crystal chandeliers gleamed with it. Other gentlemen sat in their Edwardian seats, sipping the finest cognacs and scotches, puffing on fat Cuban cigars – one had to admit that there was still nothing better, despite all that Cuba was. The socialists at least got something right!

Richardson was relishing in the attention, the congratulations, the absolute power. Could circumstances get any better? He doubted it.

Outside, life carried on in this new normal. People went to work. They used their ID cards to shop, to open their doors, to make use of the medical services, to gain access to universities, to colleges, to schools. The streets were clean – at least in the respectable parts of the country. The scourge of beggars had been removed. This was a good country in which to live.

The process had been relatively simple. Most people were happy enough to need only one card. Let's be honest. Who really enjoyed the inconvenience of a wallet full of unnecessary cards? Oyster cards, library cards, membership cards, discount cards. The list was endless. Most people quite enjoyed having a card swinging around their neck on a company halyard, showing who they were, what they had achieved. This was just a step up. One card, centrally controlled; easier, less-complicated lives.

Those without ID cards only had access to the black market. Ghettos had formed for this sub-culture, sickness was rife, state provision virtually nil. Despite their best intentions, the majority of well-meaning teachers, social workers, medical professionals, had moved on. They had their own lives to lead, their own challenges to face. The risks of getting involved were too great. Of course, some remained, some crept in and out when they could. Those without children of their own who needn't worry about lives being tarnished by parents known to be sympathisers.

It was straightforward enough to smear those who had no voice. Easier now that there was one less loud-mouthed liberal squealing about injustice. *Ah Suzanna. Fare thee well!* There were more of course, but their voices would grow quieter and quieter. Technology was such that they would all be silenced soon enough.

'And what next, eh? When will we see phase 2?' Charles asked, rather too loudly, indiscreetly.

'Hush man,' Richardson whispered, forcing a smile. 'Not here.'

Charles had been a good friend. He was well liked. Had the right contacts. He was dependable. But with one too many brandies he relaxed just that little bit more than he should. Loose tongues were always dangerous, even here amongst political colleagues and party members. One chose one's confidants with the utmost care, and once chosen traps were laid. Security put in place. Richardson had more than enough on Charles to discredit him, if necessary.

Phase 2 was indeed already underway. It had begun with dogs. All good owners wanted their dogs kept safe from thieves, from getting lost. It had been easy to persuade them that an inbuilt tracking-chip would be the perfect guarantee. A simple addition to the registration chips and there we have it. Safety! Next the repatriated, the refugees, had been given the implants. Tracking was working perfectly. There were no known side-effects. The rats could scurry, but they could no longer hide.

194

Of course the English public would be a different kettle of fish. Richardson wanted them on side. It was so much easier to control a population when it was their will. He was already working on that speech. He didn't think it would be so difficult to get the majority of the population on board. The disappearances of children, baby-snatchers, kidnappings, rebellious teenagers. All of the things that so worried people. Imagine always knowing where your loved ones were? Imagine the security, the peace of mind? *The caring parent is the tracking parent.* That wasn't quite right. It needed to be tweaked, but the essence was there. The concept. It was just a simple step-up from ID cards really. Nothing to lose, to forget, to mislay. Life would be easier.

Criminals and protesters, the anti-establishment types wouldn't have a say in the matter. Nor should they! One little chip to set the population at ease. Indeed, it was already underway with the inmates of the re-education camps.

28

The days had slipped into weeks and life here, in the middle of nowhere, had become the norm. Suze was growing in strength physically and mentally, and enjoying it. A feeling of power over her own destiny was returning.

'Okay, lass. I reckon it's about time you got a new identity, aye? We cannae have this ghost walking around now, can we?' Ranulf said, settling down at the table with his laptop. His manner was akin to that of a friendly teacher, almost paternal but not quite.

'I guess not,' Suze replied, pulling her chair close, so that she could see the screen. 'So, how do we go about this. I mean, can you do it well enough to fool the authorities? Is it even possible?' She'd seen it done in the movies, of course, read about it in novels, but this was her, and its consequences were altogether different.

'Aye, it's no that hard. First things first, eh? So, who would you like to be?'

'Wow! Okay, this is weird. I guess someone as close to me as possible would make sense.' She looked at him seeking confirmation.

'Aye.' He nodded in a way which asked that she carry on.

'So, same age, twenty two.'

'Right. Date of birth?'

'Summer. Let's make it July 5th.' Her mother's birthday. A constant connection.

'Okay,' he said as he typed it in. 'Name?'

'I think I'd like to be a Louise,' she smiled. 'I've always liked that name.'

'Right you are. Louise it is. Surname?'

'What sounds good with Louise?' She sat thinking, trying out names in her head, sharing aloud those that she thought were possibilities. This was more difficult than she had thought it was going to be. 'No, no, no. This is me for the rest of my life so...It has to be someone I admire,' she said, half to herself and half to Ranulf, as if he could help.

He shrugged and raised his eyebrows at her.

'Okay, Harringer, Louise Harringer. That's got a decent ring to it.'

'After Joan?' He smiled a knowing smile.

'The very same. I did a project on her at uni. She was a pretty fine journalist, don't you think?' She remembered all of the research she'd done with Jake. How they had talked into the small hours about the things she'd uncovered, the way she stood up for the truth irrespective of how unpopular she might become with the powers that be. They had imagined what they could do once they'd graduated; places they might travel to and uncover dark secrets, corruption, illegal arms deals, human trafficking. All the things that fired them up, and now? Now it was just her, sliding away from her old self.

She wondered how this could ever be beaten. This invisible enemy who had torn everything away from her. How the hell could she fight against it when she didn't even know who or what her adversary was? At least now she was being proactive, taking a stand,

197

keeping her mind occupied on something positive, something over which she had control. She felt Ranulf staring at her and shook herself back to the task in hand.

'Sorry, did you say something?'

He laughed, 'Aye, I did. You all right there?'

'Yes. Just remembering stuff, thinking.'

'Right. Shall we crack on then?' His tone wasn't impatient, but it was enough to encourage focus, progress.

'Sure. Sorry, where were we?'

'I was saying shall we make you an orphan? Keep it simple?'

'Oh, poor me,' she laughed, stopping quickly when she caught the reprimanding look. 'Sure.'

'Place of birth?'

'Hmmm...Cornwall or London?' she said, perusing the pros and cons, tipping her head from side to side, sucking air in through her teeth.

'Why don't you stick with London? More anonymous, aye?' Ranulf suggested.

She was enjoying this now. It was making her feel secure; protected by a new, hitherto unknown persona and one entirely of her making. She was now a work of fiction. It was as if she were being given a second chance at life. A clean sheet with no nasty blemishes, painful secrets or haunting memories. They were no longer hers to deal with and it was good. Very good. The gratitude she felt towards Ranulf was immense. And there was nothing in it for him. No ulterior motive. She looked up at him working away on the computer. No. She smiled. No ulterior motive.

'You've no idea how weird this is,' she said.

'Oh, you'd be surprised,' he replied with a tone expressing otherwise.

198

'Oh wow!' she exclaimed with due excitement. 'You've done it to yourself, haven't you?' She pulled her chair closer to his as if in a conspiratorial conversation. 'Shit! So who were you?' she half whispered. 'Did you kill yourself? Was someone after you? Was that it?'

'Full o questions, eh? You know I can't go there, don't you?' he replied, with a slightly uncomfortable grimace.

'Yes, of course, but still...I have to ask! Wow! I bet it was that thing that happened.' She clicked her fingers. 'You know, the thing that made you leave the service. It was so bad you had to disappear.' Her mind was working overtime now trying to concoct possible scenarios, reasons. She felt a little bit guilty, but her enjoyment far outweighed that. It was like oxygen for her. Life.

'Okay, back to you,' he said slightly curtly, with a tone that implied end of discussion. 'So where in London do you know best?'

'That would be Lewisham.'

'You know schools and all that stuff, aye?'

'Yes, I do. Let's put me at Prendergast Vale.'

'Same class as Jake?'

She smiled, ruefully. 'Yes. That would be cool. Us having been childhood friends. Nice.' She found herself caught in a reverie of the two of them getting into mischief at school, as they undoubtedly would have. Bunking off class, smoking behind the bike sheds. It felt somehow right being able to extend the amount of time they had spent together, to invent stories, re-write their personal history.

'You still with me?' Ranulf asked, with a quizzical expression.

'Sorry, yes,' she sighed. 'Just...yes.'

'Okay then. College? Uni?'

'L.S.E.'

'Studying?'

'Journalism.'

'Okay...now for some wee fun bits, aye?'

She laughed. 'What are you thinking of?'

'Och, things like competitions you've won, holidays you've been on, that sort o thing.'

'Cool! Let's see...'

They spent nearly the whole day creating Louise Harringer until, finally, Ranulf was satisfied with the amount of detail they had invented. She'd chosen to have green eyes and red hair for the pictures he was posting. He told her he'd get green contact lenses sent and they would visit a local hairdresser to make everything correlate. He checked that the necessary links had been created and that everything looked right, authentic. He knew from experience how costly shoddy work, loose ends, could be. The silence was deafening as he went through it all again, slowly, checking, confirming, making sure.

She was desperate to ask about his change of identity, if it was done by him or the secret service; if he'd done something terrible which necessitated him disappearing. It had been made very clear, however, that she wasn't going to be told anything. Difficult though it was, she pushed it aside and tried to leave it there.

'Right. That seems to be that. Are you happy with it?'

'Yes. It's brilliant. Thank you.'

'Ah, you're welcome, lass. Now you just make sure you learn all this stuff inside out and back to front. It'll give you something to do while I'm away, aye?'

She fought back the butterflies fluttering around in her stomach and took a deep breath. 'You're going away?' she asked slowly, trying to sound calm and collected, though she felt sure she'd failed miserably as the words squeaked out as if she were a frightened little girl.

'Aye. Just for a few days. Maybe a week, tops.'

'Okay,' she said, falteringly. 'I guess it had to happen some day.'

'You'll be fine. Look at you. Strong as the proverbial. Besides, you'll have the beasts to protect ye.'

'Oh, you're leaving them with me? Cool,' she said, calming down. 'That's a whole different ball game then!' The relief was palpable. His dogs were attack trained and powerful and she was now one of their pack. To be protected at all costs.

'Aye. Just think o the compliment it is too, eh? There's few folk I'd trust wi them.'

'Well, in that case, I'm flattered,' she added sincerely, slightly bowing her head. 'When are you going?'

'Tomorrow.'

'Shit! That's a bit...short notice.'

'Ach, it doesnae do to put things off, I find. Leave them worrying away in your head and things just compound themselves, don't they?'

'I guess so, yes.'

'You know how things work here. The routines. Just keep it all the same, for you and the dogs, an it'll all be fine, you'll see.'

'Hmmm...' she nodded, looking across at the heap of dogs in their alcove, sleeping, heaped one on top of the other, almost indistinguishable from one another. It took her back to that first time she'd seen them. She congratulated herself. *Yes, you've come a long way, girl. A long way indeed.* 'Are you leaving me tooled up?'

'Aye. Course. They're yours now. That was the whole point. Keep yourself safe.'

'Thank you. For everything, Ranulf,' she said sincerely, taking his hand, looking in his eyes. 'Thank you.'

'Aye,' he replied matter of factly. 'Nae bother.' He rubbed her head affectionately, as if she were his little sister.

The dogs were up now, padding about impatiently, nuzzling Ranulf's arm. 'What is it? Oh Christ. Would you look at that. It's dark out already and they've no had their run. 'Coming?'

'Yes. Of course.'

They kitted themselves up, like always, against the weather and any possible assailants.

'Have you always carried a weapon or is this just for my benefit?' she asked, as they headed out.

'Always. I guess I got in the habit back then, aye? And it's best to err on the side o caution with these things. You never know these days, do you? An there's my history so...aye. Aye ready, as they say,' he added with a grin.

She returned the smile.

They ran through the snow in silence for a while. This was something she loved. A freedom. A silence. A release. It was as if she were connected to something else. Something deep and permanent. Something special. The dogs ran obediently in their wake until Ranulf clicked his fingers and they broke free, running around excitedly, chasing each other, barking. Silence broken.

'You know, if I were a dog...It's not a bad life they have with you is it?'

'I like to think they're well cared for, aye. But you? You'd hate it. Having to do what I told you to do all of the time.'

'Ha! There is that. Speaking of which...'

'Awe, no. What's coming now?'

'What you were saying about changing your identity, you know?'

'Aye,' he said slowly, with precision, with reluctant expectation.

'I get that you can't talk about it but...do I know the real you or the made up you?' she asked apprehensively.

'Does it matter?' he replied.

'I really don't know. Perhaps.'

'Should it? I mean people talk shite all the time, don't they? You just never can tell.'

'Point, but...well, you're kind of crucial to my survival, right now, aren't you?'

'Aye. But you trust me?'

'I do. Yes.'

'There you go, then. Enough said.'

'But your daughters, your wife?'

'As I said, enough said.'

'Sorry. I can't help myself sometimes.'

'Aye.'

Part III

29

It had been six weeks now since he had found her. She had been working out, building up her strength, going for runs with Ranulf and the dogs. He had taught her how to shoot, how to use a knife and how to fight. The power she felt knowing that she could hold her own with most people, with or without weapons, was something new and she liked it. What gave her most enjoyment though was learning how to control the dogs. They responded to her whistles, clicks and calls instantaneously, leaving her with a satisfying feeling of achievement, of success, of control.

That morning Ranulf had removed everything from his hair, washed it and tied it in a pony tail. He was clean shaven and dressed in decent 501's, a smart sweater and Caterpillar boots.

'You scrub up all right, don't you?' she said, unable to hide her surprise.

'Aye, well, needs must, eh? So, are you ready for this?'

She exhaled nervously. 'Yes, I guess I'm as ready as I'll ever be.'

'I'll just be down south, having a wee look around, chatting to some o those people on the list.' He stared into her eyes with a look that sought confirmation. 'You're sure you're okay with this, aye?'

'Sure. We'll be good, won't we guys?' she said brightly to the dogs. 'No worries,' pushing the anxiety she felt away. It was about time anyway. And they had talked about it. How it had to be him, on his own, not associated with her or Jake, and experienced in the art of undercover work.

'And remember, Suze is dead. You're who?'

'I'm Louise.'

'Good. Okay, so if we have to talk on the phone it's Louise and it'll be code, aye? They cannae track it but they can tap it.'

'Yeah, yeah. I've got it. Don't worry.'

'Right then. Keep them in the house until I'm well on the road, all right?' he said, nodding at the dogs. 'And any problems you can get me on the satellite, aye?'

'Okay, will do. Take care, Ranulf,' she said, as she gave him a big hug. 'Please take care.'

She stood on the doorstep and watched as the Jeep disappeared down the snow clad valley; listened until there was nothing any more. Silence. Absolute silence. There was no hum of distant traffic, no intrusion of other people's lives. Nothing. There wasn't even any birdsong. She had never felt so completely alone and the sensation was a peculiar one. There wasn't fear, or loneliness, but a strength, a determination.

The dogs had settled themselves down for a sleep, but she was restless. She flicked on the satellite connection of the rugged phone he'd left for her and fought hard against the urge to call him, just to check everything was working. It was all okay. She chastised herself. Of course it was okay. This was Ranulf. He wouldn't have left her with anything that he wasn't completely sure of. The loaded gun was on the table in front of her, as were the two blades. Picking them up in turn, she studied them, gripped them, aimed them at nothing. She laughed aloud, thinking back on who she was. The CND campaigner. The woman who abhorred violence. The peace lover. And now? Here she was checking that she was ready to kill, if necessary.

She began her now daily routine of weights, push-ups, sit-ups, squats and skipping, followed by yoga and meditation. Her body and mind were more finely tuned than she could ever remember them being. It was good.

The minute she reached for her jacket the dogs were up and trotting around her, nuzzling at her hands as she tried to do up her boots. Ranulf would have told them off; told her off for being too soft. "You need to control them, lass."

'Sit,' she called, in the deep authoritative voice she had been taught to use with them. They obeyed and waited patiently, tails sweeping the floor, as she hooked the gun into her belt and slid one of the knives into her boot. She opened the door and whistled for the dogs to follow.

The snow still clung defiantly to the ground and a fairly strong wind was stirring up trouble. It whipped at her face and made her smile. This wasn't adversity, wasn't problematic. This was now the essence of life. They ran off up the valley. The dogs obediently followed in her tracks for the first two hundred metres or so. Then, as instructed, she signalled their release with a click of her fingers and they charged off, barging into one another, yelping, barking, chasing. Suze worked her arms, pumping, pushing herself, focussing, controlling her breath.

By the time they headed for home the light was fading and the hills were blending with the ominous clouds in the darkening sky. The wind had pummelled its way up to gale force and roared through the valley – no silence now – carrying scents which tantalised the dogs, causing them to stop and sniff the air at regular intervals. Each time they did so she would draw her gun and take aim, remembering Ranulf's training – speed, stance and certainty – pretending to fire. She had run further than she had intended, perhaps further than was wise, so she stepped on it on the way back. Thankfully, the wind was at her back, making the trek through the snow easier and she reached home just as dark was falling. Once inside she slid the bolt of the door, exhaled deeply and sat, resting, looking out of the window, until the wilderness outside was black and her total solitude confirmed.

'Okay guys, dinner time,' she said to four pairs of eyes staring at her from their nook. 'Come on!' They all fed on various concoctions of deer and vegetables, hers cooked, theirs raw. She found herself unable to settle and paced around the little house as if marking out her territory, checking her boundaries. Finally she decided on some of his wine to help relax her. It was a guilty pleasure as she sat sipping in front of a roaring fire until her eyes felt heavy and she made her way up to bed. Day one down.

Her days continued with the pattern she had become accustomed to. The only difference was that she was on her own. That didn't bother her as much as she had thought it would. The frustration of not knowing what was going on did. He had said they'd only speak in emergencies, just in case. Shit! She was used to being the one doing the investigating, the one searching into someone's past for dirty secrets. She hankered after her computer. It was agonising. Years of research, notes, thoughts, all of it on her computer or on the external hard drive. All of it gone and into the worst hands possible.

Ranulf had encouraged her to start writing down as much as she could remember. Every day she had been adding to her collection of memories. As she wrote, more tumbled out of their hiding places. Good or bad, she wrote. Her childhood became more lucid. The status of memories of her parents had sharpened their way out of the receding greyness that had been smothering them. They became vivid once more, as if she were bringing them back to life.

She took the pad of paper she had been using from his stationery area and prepared to work.

'Okay, let's see what we can add,' she said to the dogs. She sat down at the table and began to add to the brainstorm she had begun of what might have been on her computer, scribbling down everything that came into her head. She reread, circling, underlining and scoring out where she thought prudent. The cathartic element wasn't lost on her. As well as helping her gather her thoughts, carry on her investigations, it was very therapeutic, cleansing.

'Ah, shit,' she said, as she used up the last page of the notepad. 'Sorry Ranulf, I need to rummage.' It struck her then just what a compliment it was for him to leave her here, in his home. He was such a private person. A man who had turned his back on everything and retreated to this hideaway with the few things that were important to him. He had entrusted it all to her. The dogs, his home, everything. She couldn't let him down.

On the highest shelf she could see a white box which looked like it might have contained paper. It was out of her reach so she pulled one of the wooden chairs over, stood on it and stretched up. Her fingertips only just reached the corner of the box. She tentatively inched it off the shelf, bit by bit, unsure of what its weight and contents might be. Finally it toppled towards her and she snatched at it, losing her balance and jumping, unsteadily off the chair.

The dogs jumped up, alert, staring at her. 'It's okay guys. It's all okay,' she confirmed. 'Bed!' They obediently slunk off and lay down again, eyes still trained on her.

She took the box to the table and sat down with it. Inside she found a ream of paper and a bundle of pencils – artists pencils. Underneath the paper were pencil sketches; really good ones.

'Huh, I wonder who drew you then?' she said to one of the drawings.

It was a disturbing portrait of a teenage boy sitting on a piece of waste-ground. There was a darkness to his face, to his expression, and it made her uneasy, made her question. Flicking through them, she found more of the same. The same child in different situations. She felt guilty, disrespectful, and hurriedly replaced them, covering them with blank paper, taking a handful for herself and putting the box back where it came from.

'Shouldn't have done that, guys,' she said to the dogs. 'Bad Louise.'

She went over the notes she had made with Ranulf about her new identity. He had been very meticulous, going over every detail of this fictitious life. If you searched her online, she was there, winning prizes at school, graduating university, medical records, the lot. He had even given her a criminal record, well, a speeding ticket, just for authenticity. He had said he'd bring back all the physical elements she needed on his return.

She found herself creating stories about this new person she'd become, Louise Harringer. It was fun, inventing scenarios from her childhood, imagining what her life might have been like.

'So what do you think guys?' she said to the dogs. 'A happy childhood, or abuse filled and nasty? Hmmm. Might as well keep it realistic. A bit of both, eh?'

30

The dogs sat up all of a sudden. Their ears were pricked, muzzles raised, sniffing. Something had them on alert.

'What's up guys?' Suze whispered, straining to hear. Nothing. She checked out of the windows. Still nothing. The dogs were making for the door so she followed, trusting to their instincts, picking up her gun on the way. An unwelcome nervousness had crept in. Her heart was racing as she slid the bolt and slowly opened the door, checking, listening. The dogs barged past her, running off into the white wilderness, barking.

She whistled return. They didn't react. 'Get back here. Now!' she called. 'Volki! Come!…Shit.'

She grabbed her jacket and ran after them along the valley. For the first time since Ranulf had left they were completely ignoring her, charging off out of sight, oblivious to her calls. She ran on in silence, grateful for the reassurance offered by the gun in her belt. About a mile on, the valley twisted its way around the riverbed. They could have gone up or down the valley. Thankfully their paws left an easy track to follow. They were following the curve of the river, and again. As she looked along the valley, coming round a bend in the distance, she could make out a vehicle. She stopped, crouched behind a rock and squinted at it, trying to

214

focus in the harsh glare of the sunlight bouncing off the snow.

'Oh, thank Christ!' she mumbled, as Ranulf's familiar Jeep took shape. The dogs had caught up and were running alongside as if it were one of their pack. They were emitting joyous yelps, their tails wagging furiously. She rested her hands on her knees and exhaled deeply, taking control, slowing her breathing back down.

She looked up again. Ranulf wasn't alone. There was somebody else in the Jeep; somebody in the passenger seat. She fought against the trepidation that was creeping its unwelcome way into her thoughts. There couldn't be anything to fear, surely? This was Ranulf, and the dogs weren't behaving as if they were anxious. Nevertheless she allowed her fingers to feel their way around the gun in her belt. She drew the weapon and took her stance; her arms locked in position; the stranger in her sights.

The Jeep stopped and Ranulf called out of the window to her. 'Glad to see you're remembering what I taught you, lass, but it's meant for the bad guys, aye, no me an your friend here. No need for that!'

She smiled and put the gun away. 'Well, you never know, do you?' she called back. 'You could have warned me!'

'It was meant to be a nice wee surprise, aye? Permission to approach?'

'Granted,' she said with a laugh.

When the Jeep pulled up she caught the smile. It was unmistakable. Finding it hard to believe what she was seeing, she stood welded to the spot, staring. She briefly closed her eyes, but he was still there when they reopened. Jake clambered out and grinned at her,

215

holding his arms wide open. She ran at him, leaping up, wrapping her legs around his waist. He fell backwards and they landed in the deep snow with a thwump. They lay there, clinging on to each other, laughing and crying in a violent wash of emotion. She breathed in that smell; that smell of him.

'Right, you two. I'll see you back at the house, aye?' Ranulf called, as he drove on, the dogs following in his wake.

'You look fucking amazing, Suze!' Jake said, holding her at arms length by the shoulders. Taking her in. 'I can't believe it.'

'I thought...Shit, Jake, I thought you were dead. I'm so sorry. I–' She hung her head and sobbed.

'Shhhh. It's okay. I know. I know.'

*

'I need to pay a wee visit to one of my neighbours up the road. Let him know I'm back and he's off duty,' Ranulf said when they finally got back to the house.

'Off duty? You mean you've had someone watching the place, watching me?' Suze asked, with a combination of incredulity and upset.

'Aye, well, it wasn't that I didn't trust you, lass, just wanted to make sure you were safe, was all.'

'I see. Huh!' she said, with her hands on her hips. 'Can't say as I noticed anyone.'

'Naw, you wouldn't. It was just a discreet wee link, like, at the outside here. Nothing too intrusive. See you in a couple of hours, aye?' he said, as he closed the door behind him.

They were sitting at the table, watching the figure of Ranulf trek through the snow towards the distant hills, the dogs joyfully alongside him. Suze turned her attention back to Jake.

'I don't believe it! He's had a bloody web cam on me somewhere. Well, actually,' she shrugged, 'I do. I really shouldn't be surprised at all.'

'Quite a character, isn't he?' Jake said, with a wry grin. 'And as for this place. Wow! Like wow! Some guy!'

'Yes, and no mistaking! I'd have died if it hadn't been for him, you know? I owe the man my life. Anyway, I guess you've heard that story. What about you? What in hell happened? I mean the van was mangled, you too, and Roger...dead.'

'Apparently they always have someone following the van on runs like that, just to make sure, yeah? Anyway, the couple they had in the car behind managed to drag me out before the police came, and they got me away.'

'Cool.' she rubbed at her forehead and looked at the floor. 'I waited until I heard sirens. I was watching from the bank, and then...I ran, Jake,' her voice was breaking and she lifted her eyes to meet his. Her stomach knotted. 'I ran away like a fucking coward. I've never felt so shit. Oh, God, it was all so horrible. You were a state, Jake. All mashed up.'

'Don't even go there, Suze,' he said quietly, gently. 'You had no choice.'

'Nah, we always have a choice.' She looked away. 'Anyway. Tell me.'

'You know what they're like. They've got such a network. It's amazing. They got me checked into the hospital by a couple of their friendly policemen. Injuries sustained in a farming accident, they said. No questions asked. Nothing. They had a false name and an ID made up for me, the lot.'

'A proper, fully functioning ID?'

'No, but good enough. Like our ones. Flashable but

217

not cashable!' He laughed, cocked his head.

'Brilliant,' she said with a smile. 'So how long were you in hospital for?'

'A few weeks. I've got pins holding me together all over the place. You should see my scars!'

'Go on then, macho man. Show me,' she said with a laugh, disguising the internal wince.

He showed her the scars on his arms, legs and back.

'Shit,' she said, running her finger along the jagged white line up his arm, kissing it like a mother to her child. 'They've done a good job though, haven't they? I mean, you're all good now, aren't you?'

'Yeah,' he said, pulling a mischievous face. 'It'll just be a problem getting through security, and my tattoo's all to shit!' He laughed.

'Idiot!' She slapped his arm, playfully.

'Hey! Walking wounded here. Less of that,' he joked. 'And that tattoo was a work of art. Priceless, man.'

'Yes, but just think of all the cool stories you can make up now. Apparently girls go for that sort of stuff,' she said with a smile, nudging him in the ribs.

He raised his eyebrows at her, reproachfully. 'Oh what, so getting smashed up whilst on the run from New Dawn isn't cool enough then? Just your everyday, run of the mill guy type stories.'

'You know what I mean...So, have you just been staying at Pete and Dana's since then?'

'No, no. They reckoned it was best to stay clear, after what happened to Roger. He was registered at their house and they were expecting quite a few follow up visits from the police and the likes. And, well, I felt guilty as shit, you know?'

'I can imagine.' She shook her head. 'Horrible...just

218

horrible.'

They sat in silence for a few minutes.

'Do they know what happened to the van? Why it crashed?'

'An innocent blow out apparently.'

'Uh-huh. That's what the news reports said too. So, where did you stay?'

'Not far from where we met Magda, as it happens.'

'Really?'

'Yeah. With some friends of Dana's who are part of the same escape route thing.'

'Cool.'

'Yeah. Good people. They did a raid on the farm, you know, where Magda was?'

'Oh excellent. And? What happened?'

'It was like something out of the movies. Really! We snuck up in the early hours and cut our way through the fence with wire cutters.'

'We?' she asked, with some surprise. 'So you went along?'

'I did, yeah. They reckoned my languages might have been useful and, well, they'd have been hard pressed to stop me getting one over on those pieces of shit!'

'Sure. I can imagine.'

'Anyway, there were ten of them, all young women. They took a bit of persuading, you know? I mean, they were all scared, like Magda was, remember?'

'Of course, yes.'

'Magda remembered us, which helped. Meant they could trust us, you know? They'd only come if everyone agreed. No-one left to be punished. Christ. It makes me cringe just to say it.'

He remembered the squalid huts, no windows,

mattresses on the floor, buckets for toilets, nothing to suggest that they were human beings. No possessions, nothing on the stark walls, no pictures, nothing to break up the bleakness. The girls, skinny and pale, bruised and afraid. The security lights, the razor wire fencing, the stench of the place. If you could put a smell on fear then that was it. The memory of it made him shiver.

'Anyway, when they heard about the amount of support they could get they all agreed. So, they came. All of them.'

'Brilliant! I'd have loved to have been a fly on the wall the next day.'

'Yeah! For sure!' He laughed.

'So what happened from there? I mean where did they all go to?'

'I've no idea. They keep it on a need to know level. Safer.'

'Of course. That makes sense. I remember Dana and her need to know thing.'

They hadn't taken their eyes off each other, as if both were afraid to look away. Afraid that this wasn't real.

'What about you? How the hell did you end up here?'

'Didn't Ranulf tell you then?'

'Uh-uh. Other than that he found you in a forest and that you were safe, nothing.'

'Yes. That sounds like him, come to think of it. So you don't know about the re-education centre, or any of that?'

'No! Shit! So they caught you then?'

'Yes, yes they did, bastards.' She motioned a spit at the floor.

'You look so good. I just didn't think you'd been through anything. Sorry. Shit. What was it like?'

'Can we talk about this some other time? Do you mind? It's just so good to see you.'

He smiled at her and squeezed her shoulders. 'Course, and likewise. Shit, you've no idea.'

'Well, I think I probably have,' she said, raising her eyebrows at him and smiling.

'Yeah,' he replied, taking her hand, 'Yeah, course you have. Awesome place this, isn't it?' he said, finally looking away, glancing around. 'Did he make it all himself, Ranulf?'

'As far as I can make out, yes. He doesn't talk about his past too much. It's strange, sort of like I really know him, but I don't know him at all. Does that make sense?'

'Yeah, sure.'

'He was a spy, you know?'

'You're kidding me?' Jake glanced around the little house again, as if looking for clues, signs.

'Uh-huh. He's got a dark past. Bad stuff, apparently, but he's one of the best people I've ever met, so...yeah.' She shrugged her shoulders.

'You and he haven't, aren't...are you?'

She threw him a disdainful look, muttered, 'Fuck's sake,' under her breath, then got up to put a couple of logs on the fire. An uncomfortable silence was threatening.

'Friends?' he asked, embarrassed, as she sat down again.

'Of course,' she replied. 'Just...well, you know. I'd expect more from you. A, he's old enough to be my father. And B, I don't jump into bed with my hero like some stupid princess!'

'Sorry. I know. I mean, I just wasn't thinking. I didn't mean anything. Ah shit. I'm sorry, okay?'

She smiled. 'Accepted.'

There was a knock on the door. 'Just me,' Ranulf called.

'Why on earth are you knocking on your own front door?' Suze asked.

'Acht, just a wee bit tact. Didn't want to interrupt, like.'

'No, no, we're just friends. Close friends,' Suze said with a laugh.

'Is that right? Well! Don't know about you two but I think a wee celebration's in order, eh?' He rubbed his hands together. 'Now, what'll it be, the elderberry or the bramble? What do you reckon?'

'I don't think I've tried the bramble,' she giggled, 'Good is it?'

'It's no too bad, though I do say so myself,' he replied, puffing his chest in a show of mock pride. 'Main thing is it does the trick, aye?' he added with a wink. He returned with three glasses and a couple of bottles and plonked them on the table.

'Fancy glasses,' Jake said, smiling.

'Aye, the lassie thought it funny too.' He shook his head. 'Anyway,' he said, holding his glass up. 'To happy reunions.'

They clinked glasses.

'Thanks, Ranulf. For everything,' Suze said.

'You're very welcome. The pair of you.'

'Yeah, cheers, man. I can't believe how well she looks.'

'Acht, that was all her, eh lass?' he said, in the manner of a proud father, lifting his glass at her. 'Quite the fighter, aren't you?'

'More so now, yes. All tooled up and ready for action.' She laughed along with Ranulf.

Jake sat looking perplexed. 'Yeah, the whole gun thing was kind of a shock. I mean you! With a gun? What's with that?'

'You're not going to believe this but, turns out I'm a pretty mean shot.'

'Yeah? Well, you certainly looked the part!'

'Yes, and I can throw a knife, and, I'm not too bad at Krav Maga.'

'Which is?' Jake asked, cocking his head at her.

'Military self defence. An Israeli specialism,' Ranulf answered. 'You'll no be wanting to get on the wrong side of her now.'

'Oh, I would never do that anyway,' Jake said, with a hint of laughter. Hands up. 'No worries on that score!'

'Hey you, I thought you were my friend?'

'Always, Suze. Always.'

31

Annabel took her seat, in row H. Discreet enough, she thought, as she settled down to watch the concert. It was a stunning venue with starlight in the domed ceiling, three tiers of seating, a circular stage. A place that could lift one out of one's reality. Allow dreams. This was Annabel's dream. To be here, watching this. Just this. The music was loud and not what she would normally choose to listen to, but this was different, wasn't it. It was difficult to keep her emotions in check as surges of pride and loss fought their own private battle inside her. The passion, so evident in her daughter with every note she played, was striking. A woman completely lost in her music. It was sublime. Beautiful. She hardly noticed the other band members. The audience cheered and roared asking them back on stage for three encores.

'Thank you,' Sophie mouthed, as she walked backwards, off the stage, her violin held aloft in one hand, her bow in the other, swathes of silk and chiffon trailing around her.

The lights came full on; the crowds filing out in an excited buzz. Annabel sat there with her eyes closed, her head bowed, unaware of the hubbub around her.

'Excuse me ma'am. We're closing up now,' came the voice of a young male usher.

'Oh, I am so sorry. I became so lost in it all.' She smiled up at him, embarrassed.

'Yeah, good concert, wasn't it?'

'Yes, yes it was. I wonder, might I be allowed backstage?' she asked timidly, as if she had no right.

'It's not our policy ma'am. The artists do need their privacy after a show. I'm sure you understand.' He smiled somewhat patronisingly at her.

'Perhaps if you could pass on a message? Tell Sophie, the violinist, that her mother is here?' she said, this time with more conviction.

'Oh, I see.' His attitude changed, his smile becoming genuine. 'Is she expecting you then?'

'No, no she isn't. It's a surprise, you see.'

He studied her face. 'Now that you mention it I can see the resemblance. Sorry! Look, I'm totally breaking the rules here, but if you want to follow me to the stage door, we'll check okay?'

'Very well. Thank you, young man,' she said appreciatively, hoping that she held a calm exterior which belied the panic she truly felt.

He returned within a couple of minutes and led her backstage to Sophie's changing room. Annabel stood, with her hand ready to knock, momentarily frozen. He knocked for her and smiled.

'Thank you,' Annabel said, with an appreciative smile.

He nodded, 'You're welcome!' and walked off as the door opened.

'Mum,' Sophie said quietly, staring. 'I...wow...'

'Sophie. So –' Tears began to fall through the well made up face.

'Come in,' Sophie said, looking up and down the hall. 'What on earth, Mum? What's wrong? What's happened?'

Annabel held up her hand to ask for a minute to compose herself. 'I've...left him dear. I've left...the bastard,' Annabel managed to squeeze out through sniffs and faltering inhalations.

'Well, I'm glad,' Sophie said, then hesitated and held her mother's gaze. 'Is it for real this time? I mean, permanent?'

She nodded. 'Yes. I...yes.'

'What happened? I mean, after so long? No. Wait. Let's get out of here. You'll come to mine, yes?' She squeezed her mother's hand and looked into her eyes with expectation.

'I would love to, dear. Of course.'

The chauffeur dropped them at a chic warehouse conversion in New Concordia Wharf. They took the stairs to the top floor.

'This is beautiful, dear,' Annabel said, as she took in her daughter's home for the first time. 'All these windows. The light is just splendid.'

'Isn't it? I was lucky to get it. They're in such demand, these old conversions.'

'Yes, I can imagine. So it's just you then?' she asked, looking around for signs of a partner. There were a couple of framed posters on the wall and a montage of newspaper clippings and photos from many different countries. In an alcove two photographs sat amongst some crystals. One was of Sophie as a toddler with Annabel, the other as a young adult, with Annie, at the retreat.

'Me and my cats, yes. Speak of the devils.'

Two elegant cats padded their way across the wooden floorboards, tails held high, mews expectant. They wrapped themselves around Sophie's ankles, rubbing and nuzzling.

'Hi guys,' Sophie said. 'Just let me get these two fed and I'll be with you, okay Mum?'

'Of course, dear. May I,' she asked, gesturing to the settee.

'God, Mum, you don't need to ask. Treat the place as yours. Please!'

Annabel sank into the ethnic cushions and closely watched every movement her daughter made as she feed her cats. The elegant fingers twisting the can opener. The flick of a strand of misplaced hair. The gentle stroking of each cat as they greedily devoured their food. The wrinkle of her nose as she smiled at them. The dimples. The scar above the right eye. She never knew the truth behind that, but she could guess. The familiar pangs of guilt revisited her as she thought of all the years she had missed.

'Wine?' Sophie asked, holding up a bottle of Bordeaux.

'That would be lovely. Thank you,' she replied.

Sophie brought the bottle and two glasses over and placed them on the old wooden sea chest which she used as a coffee table, then came and sat beside her mother, curling her long legs under herself.

'That's nice dear,' Annabel said, running her fingers along the chest.

'Isn't it? I picked it up in a second hand shop in Camden. I love rummaging around those places. So much fun.'

'Yes, we used to do that a lot, didn't we? When you were small.' She smiled at the memory.

'We did, didn't we. I remember.'

'I've been wanting to see you play for years. I've got all of your CDs, of course but...I was just too scared of

227

what he might do if he found out.' Her voice began to break and she dropped her head.

'No need Mum. It's all okay. Look at me. I am who I am and I like her.'

'But I'm so sorry...about all of it...you know?' she said, looking up at her daughter and forcing a smile through her tears.

'Yes, I know you are,' she said, taking her mother's hands in hers. 'So, is this definitely it then? A fait accompli?'

'Yes, I promise. It's been a few weeks now. I just left without telling him.' She smiled at the thought. 'Took what I believed to be mine and left. It felt so good; so very good. I'm sure he thinks I'll come crawling back again, but I won't. Not this time. This is different.' Her voice had taken on a firm tone of resoluteness. 'He has no means of contacting me and I, well, I shall not be contacting him.'

'That's great, Mum, I'm so glad! But why now?'

'He went a step too far...hmmm.' A shadow darkened her face.

Sophie sighed. 'Well, in my view that happened a long time ago. Anyway, I'm very happy for you. And the others, the children, do they know?'

'Yes. Yes they do. I told them after I'd left.'

'Aren't you worried? That they might tell him where you are?'

'Oh no dear, no. They don't know where I live. Funny. They've never asked.' Her smile was melancholic.

'Do you see them at all?'

'Hardly. I've met them for coffee, briefly, but that's it. They seem to see things from their father's point of view.'

'Yes, I remember.' she said distractedly. 'He could do no wrong, could he?' Sophie didn't like the feeling that was revisiting her after so many years. 'Anyway.' Brightening up. 'Where are you staying now?'

'I'm in a small hotel in the West End. A touristy place, nice and inconspicuous.'

'Right. We'll get your things tomorrow and move you in here.'

'No, I couldn't dear. I would be such an imposition.'

'Nonsense. It's not as if I haven't got the space and we've got a lot of catching up to do. Besides which, I can keep an eye on you here,' she said, squeezing Annabel's hands. 'No arguments. Do you hear me? And, you can cat-sit when I go off on tour. You'd be doing me a favour, Mum, come on, at least until you've got yourself back on your feet.'

'Then thank you.' She smiled, a wave of relief washing through her. 'I would love to.'

'Talking of which, how are you financially?'

'Oh, I'm quite comfortable, dear. I've been putting money aside for a long time, paying myself a salary, one might say. It amounts to a decent little nest-egg.' She smiled in a self congratulatory sort of way.

'Well done you. It's not as if you haven't earned it over the years.'

'That's exactly what I was thinking, besides which, can it be classed as stealing? I mean –'

'It definitely can't, no! Neither legally, nor morally. But you must say if you need something. My CDs have brought me in a small fortune.'

They worked their way through two bottles of wine as Sophie told stories of her travels, lovers past, friends, but mostly about her music. Annabel listened, mesmerised by this beautiful, successful woman, her

229

daughter. They talked about when Sophie had left. The people at the retreat who had kept her through her pregnancy and arranged for the adoption. The music school which had offered her a scholarship and accepted her as a boarder.

'Did you ever hear about, um, the baby? Did you keep contact?' Annabel asked awkwardly, looking away.

Sophie sat in silence for a couple of minutes.

'I'm sorry, I shouldn't have asked. Foolish of me.'

'No, no, it's fine. It's been so long, that's all. I don't think about it too much. It doesn't do to dwell.'

'No, of course, you're absolutely right. It doesn't.'

'I talked it all through with Annie, at the retreat. She was amazing. Such a good person. Anyway, I decided it was best to let it go completely. I left a letter with the lawyer. Just in case, you know? In case she ever wanted to know who her mother was. I'm glad I've heard nothing. It makes me think she must be happy with her lot. Don't you agree?'

'Yes, I imagine so. Are you still in touch with her? Annie, I mean?'

'No, didn't you hear? She died in the summer. There was a dreadful accident and her car burst into flames. She stood no chance.'

'Oh, I am so sorry. How awful. She was like a mother to you, when I...well, I wasn't.'

'Come on, Mum. We've been through this. You had no choice.'

'Perhaps, but even so...'

32

'Here's your new ID and paperwork, as promised,' Ranulf said to Suze, handing her a manilla envelope.

'Wow! A new life, just like that. Amazing. Thank you,' she said sincerely, holding his gaze. 'Thank you, Ranulf. I don't know what to say.'

'Well, have a wee look then, why don't you?' Ranulf replied, expectantly.

She turned the envelope around in her hands, began to open the seal and stopped. 'Shit,' she mumbled. 'This is all a bit weird, you know? It's like a final seal on everything. The deletion of my family, of me. It's...well...it's weird.'

'Maybe try and think of it as a new beginning, lass, not an ending. Come on. It'll not bite you.'

'Ah, shit. Okay. I guess you're right.' She tipped her new self onto the table and spread the documents out, picking them up one at a time. Inspecting them. Digesting them. 'They're perfect.'

'Aye. Nothing but the best for the two of you.'

'Oh,' she said, surprised. 'You've done one for Jake too? She turned to Jake. 'You never said.'

'Yeah. We, well, Ranulf thought it best. Just to be on the safe side.'

'Cool. Yes. Of course. Show me then?'

They sat and chatted about their new personae,

familiarizing each other with the details, sharing made up stories and histories. Jake felt the knot in his stomach twist and turn with his emotions as she told him about the school she'd chosen, being in the same class as him, childhood friends. He tried to hide it but was sure his ears were turning red. He twiddled with his leather bracelet, hoping they couldn't see.

'We'd have been so bad, wouldn't we? Can you imagine the trouble we'd have encouraged each other into?' he said.

'Exactly what I said! Didn't I Ranulf?'

'You did that, lass.'

'Did you find anything out down there?' she asked. 'Are we any further on with our wee investigation?' she added, mimicking his Scottish accent.

'I couldn't find anything unusual about any of the folks on our list.'

'Really?' Suze replied, despondently. She was desperate for answers, reasons; something that might help her get her head around this. Something that would give her an outlet for her anger. A definitive thing to fight against. She needed an enemy that she could see. A target. 'So what now then?'

'Well, they all seem squeaky clean. All except one,' Ranulf added, looking intently at her.

She felt uncomfortable, as if something awful was about to be exposed. 'Okay, so don't keep me in suspense. Who?'

'Well, it's a wee bit...sensitive, like,' he replied, with uncharacteristic hesitance. 'It's your mum, lass.'

'What?' she said, her expression showing the disbelief she felt. 'My mum? But she's...'

'Naw. No her. Your birth mother. Do you know who she is?'

'No. No, I don't. As far as I'm concerned Katherine and Geoffrey are...were my real parents. I never wanted nor needed to find out.'

'I think you should, considering.'

'Considering what? Just because they're dead doesn't stop them being mine,' she cleared her throat. 'Does it?'

'Course not, Suze,' Jake interjected, 'but maybe you should listen.'

'So you know?' She was angry now. 'Shit!'

'No, no. Ranulf wouldn't tell me a thing, but you trust this guy, yeah? So –'

'Sorry, Ranulf,' she said, backtracking. 'No offence, it's just...well. No offence.'

'None taken, lass. Shall we?'

'Okay, I suppose so,' she said, with a telling exhalation of pent up anxiety. 'So, enlighten me.' Her voice was harsh. Bitter.

Ranulf spun the laptop round to reveal a picture of Sophie Cunningham, violin in hand.

'Bloody hell! For real?'

'Aye, no doubt.'

'You can see it. You've got her eyes and her cheekbones. Look,' Jake added, squeezing her hand in reassurance. 'And her talent too, by the way.'

'Oh, you play, do you?' Ranulf asked.

'Yes, yes, I do,' she said impatiently. 'Okay, so my mother's this super cool violinist. What's that got to do with any of this? I still don't get it.'

'It's who she really is that's interesting and, hmm.' He raised his eyebrows, met her eyes, lowered his voice. 'You're not going to like it, lass.'

'Shit, how bad can it be?'

'Pretty bad, considering your political beliefs. See,

her name was changed when she was thirteen. She used to be Sophie Richardson.'

'And? I'm still not getting this.' Frustration was beginning to get the better of her.

'Daughter of the right honourable Sir Nigel...' Ranulf said slowly, carefully, hesitantly.

'No fucking way!' she shouted, thumping the table with her fist, jumping out of her chair. 'There is no fucking way I'm related to that piece of shit!' Her face became flushed. Her eyes angry.

'Fuck me,' Jake mumbled and looked at the floor.

'And you're absolutely sure? No doubt at all?' she asked, pacing up and down now.

'Sorry, lass; absolutely.'

'How the hell did this come to light then?' she asked sharply.

'Your parents', Katherine and Geoffrey's, lawyers were given a letter from her, your mum, Sophie.'

'And they let you see it?'

'No, no. I broke in.' He grinned sheepishly at her. 'Hope you don't mind, eh? Thought it best to know everything, considering.'

'Sure, yes. And you have it? Here?'

'I do. Do you want to see it?'

'No. Not right now, no.' She shook her head. 'This is just too much.' She kicked at her foot. 'Shit.'

'You all right?' Jake asked, wrapping his arm across her shoulders.

She shook it off, stepped away, not wanting to be weak, to be needy, to be any of the things she felt right now.

'Yes. I guess I'll just sit firmly on the nurture side of the whole nature, nurture argument from now on.'

'That's my girl,' Ranulf said, patting her warmly on

the back.

Jake twitched.

'So what now, Ranulf? You're the expert here, aren't you? What the hell's going on, and what do we do about it?' Suze asked.

'The first part, I don't know, but I do think you should go and talk to Sophie Cunningham. When you're ready, like.'

'I need a day or two to get my head around all of this, okay?'

'Of course, lass. Take as long as you need.'

'And you'll come with us?'

'That's a wee bit tricky, you see. The dogs an all, aye?'

'Yes, but you saved my life and –' She looked expectantly at him. 'Your philosophy, not mine.'

He laughed at her. 'Aye, right you are. We'll see then, but I think you can handle this by yourselves, the two of you.'

'Dunno about that,' Jake said. 'Our track record's not so good to date.'

'It's not, is it?' Suze added with a wry smile. 'Pretty disastrous, actually.'

'Well, you're two different people now, aren't you? Anyway. Like I said. We'll see.'

33

'Can I take the dogs out, Ranulf? I need to clear my head.'

'Course you can, lass. Off you go.'

'Company?' Jake asked.

'Yes, of course. Are you up to running?'

'I am.'

They headed off on her usual run along the valley. She loved how this made her feel, running with the pack in the wilderness. It was so cleansing, elemental, and somehow right. Jake ran in her wake, struggling to keep up. He'd been working on his fitness since getting out of hospital, running, working out, but this was a whole different ball game. The snow. The hills. It was tough.

Suze took a detour and veered away from the valley, running on to the top of the hill where that waterfall ran down, almost vertically. The flow was stronger, faster than she remembered, the ice had crept back as the earth began to thaw. The sound of crashing water was all consuming. As she stood looking at its descent she was taken back to the first time she had been here with Ranulf, when she had just escaped. So much had changed. She had changed, and not just in name. That girl felt like a distant friend. 'Beautiful isn't it?'

'Yeah,' Jake replied, breathlessly. 'Fuck me, you're

fit!' He stood behind her and wrapped his arms around her waist, thankful she didn't twist herself free.

'I am. I like it. It makes me feel...powerful.'

'I can see that. Suits you.'

'Do you see the forest over there?' she said, pointing to a hazy tree line in the distance. 'That's where he found me. Apparently I had hypothermia and was almost dead. I couldn't believe it when I came to in this tepee type affair, deer hide everywhere, a pack of monster dogs smothering me, and a wild man of the forest tending the fire outside. He had tiny wee skulls and feathers threaded into his hair and home made clothes of skin and shit. Totally weird. I thought I was hallucinating at first. Really.'

'I can imagine. So what was he doing out there?'

'Hunting. He hunts deer all around here. Spends days away being part of the wildlife, as he calls it. I was so lucky his dogs picked up my scent or I'd have been a goner, for sure, or back in the centre if they'd found me in time.' She paused running things around in her head. 'But, then again...come to think of it, no. I'd be dead. Hmm.'

She took a minute, gazing towards where she had escaped from. Remembering Donna and how easily they had taken her life. How easily it could have been hers. Who held so much hate?

'Apparently he set it up to look as if the dogs had eaten me, my body being dragged off into the forest amidst a trail of blood.' She laughed at the thought. 'Clever huh?'

'For sure. So he knew you were on the run then?'

'Yes. I was dressed in prisoner's uniform. Well, re-education camp uniform. They were shooting at us, you know? Like we were...animals or something. They got

Donna.'

'Donna?'

'My cell mate. She got me out, knew the codes, and they shot her in the back. Just like that. Bang. Disgusting!'

'Slow down. I'm not following you here. What codes? How did you get out?'

'A warden dropped her key in our cell. An electronic thing. I noticed and slid it under the bed then checked what it was the next day. Donna knew I had something and asked to see it. She was totally loopy, acted like a cat, I mean totally. Anyway, because she was loopy they never bothered that much about her and she had learnt all the codes for the doors. That's how we got out. And it was New Year so there was just a skeleton staff who were having a drink to themselves. It was surprisingly easy. Until she got shot, that is.'

'Did you not wonder? I mean the chances of the key falling, and your cell mate knowing the codes?'

'Yes, yes I did, but I really didn't care. It was vile in there and if I thought there was even the tiniest chance of getting out I'd take it. What did I have to lose, you know? Everyone I cared about gone. You, as far as I knew, my parents. I really didn't care any more.'

'Yeah, that would be you. I can see that.'

A shadow drifted across the sky and she stared up at it.

'Oh wow, look,' she said, excitedly, pointing to the sky where a huge bird was looping and plunging through the air. 'It's a golden eagle.'

'Really?'

'Yes. It's displaying for its mate. There are a couple of nesting pairs hereabouts. So cool. I've seen him a few times.'

They stood quietly, watching as it danced around, a black silhouette against the crystal blue sky, until it eventually flew off beyond the horizon.

'What do you reckon to this whole Richardson thing?' she asked. 'Are we on to something or not? And, perhaps more importantly, do I really want to go there, you know?'

'I was wondering that too. You could just turn your back on it all and start afresh, couldn't you?'

She turned to look at him. 'I could. We could.'

'But you know you're not going to be able to let it go. It's just not you, is it?'

'No. No, it's not. Did you know that I'm officially dead, by the way? How's that for cool?' she laughed. 'Beat that! You're holding on to a ghost.'

'Well, if this is how a ghost feels it's all right with me.'

'Idiot!' she said, turning and mock punching him. 'Race you back.'

'No fucking way!' he replied to her back, as she ran off down the hill, the dogs bounding behind her yelping their delight. 'Wait up. Ah shit.'

She was waiting for him, hands on hips, at the foot of the hill, barely out of breath. When he got close enough he began pelting her with snowballs. She ran at him and knocked him over. The dogs danced around them barking.

'They're not gonna bite me are they?' he asked, half seriously.

'No. Not unless I tell them to,' she replied, with a villainous grin.

'You've got this thing about knocking me over, haven't you?'

'Perhaps,' she laughed. 'It's fun.'

239

'Suze?'

'Yes?'

'Ah...nothing.'

'What? Come on.'

'I'm just so god dammed happy that you're okay. It wasn't good, you know...being away from you. Not knowing, you know?'

'Yeah. Yeah, I do, Jake.'

Part IV

34

'Right you are. You two take care now and let me know, aye? Keep me posted like, and don't forget who you are. Louise, Zack, take care now.'

'Will do Ranulf. Thank you. For everything. You're the best,' Louise answered, feeling a surge of melancholy sneak its way up her spine as she pulled back from the window. She waved at the retreating Jeep as it headed away towards the little house which, despite the brevity of her stay, had come to feel like home to her.

'This is weird,' Louise said, looking at the people milling around the station. 'It feels completely alien to me now, being amongst people like this.'

Zack felt her tense up as a couple of patrolling policemen glanced their way. He pulled her close, as if they were lovers about to be separated by their journey, and whispered, 'Hey, it's okay. You're Louise and no-one's looking for you. And we're still in Scotland. Relax.'

'Easier said than done,' she replied, pulling back, forcing a smile.

They picked up a couple of coffees and headed for the train. No-one looked twice at their fake IDs as they swiped them for payment at the kiosk, for tickets on the train, or for formal identification as they crossed the border back into England. You could almost feel the change in atmosphere. The tension. People spoke less, more quietly. The train was patrolled by a New Dawn guard after every station. IDs were scrutinised, biometrics checked, faces scanned, over and over again.

Louise practised the techniques she had learned over the last few weeks – had it really only been that long? It felt like years, a lifetime – breathing deeply, calming herself. It was difficult and she found herself regularly having to focus on slowing her heart rate down. She stared out of the window at the blur of life which trailed behind her. Zack tried to help by chatting about things of no consequence, things to make her smile, but it was hard going and he eventually gave up. They both knew they were heading into unfamiliar territory, despite having lived in London for so long, it was all very different now. There was no comfort, no sense of returning home.

Four hours later they were in Euston station. Louise worked on her frame of mind, instilling a cold, steely determination. Despite everything, or perhaps because of it, she was stronger than she had ever been. She could face this. People would be ignored. Nothing would distract her. They made their way to the underground, pulsating with its anonymous swarm. Amongst the familiar advertisements for movies, theatres, and books, were propaganda posters. Posters listing who to contact if you were suspicious of someone's ethnicity. Posters expounding the virtues of New Dawn. Posters of smiling happy families secure of their place in this new England.

Zack put his arm around her shoulders and gave her a squeeze. 'You okay?' he whispered.

'Yes. Fine,' she answered. 'I'm fine.'

'Ready for this?'

'I'm as ready as I'll ever be, I suppose. I feel like a stranger, you know?'

'Sure, yeah. Different people in more ways than one, aren't we?'

'You can say that again.'

'Sure, yeah. Different people–'

'Dickhead!' She laughed and pushed him, thankful, yet again, for his ability to lighten the situation, make her laugh irrespective of what was happening around them.

They got off at London Bridge and headed towards the Jubilee Line. It was only a couple of minutes before they reached Canary Wharf. They had to show their IDs and have their travel passes checked as they left the station. Each time they had to show them their anxiety lessened. They knew by now that they were good. The biometrics matched up. Everything worked. And most importantly, they were on nobody's radar.

As they walked through the maze of waterways, steel and glass, that was the financial district, it all seemed unaffected by the disturbances, sparkling and glinting in the winter sun, shouting decadence and wealth. There was a light police and guard presence which they ignored. The security here was more surreptitious, cameras everywhere, drones hovering around, ensuring safety, surveillance. Criminals, illegals, the underclass, would never consider coming to this part of the city.

Louise and Zack walked confidently, arm in arm, with the air of a couple who had every right to be there. Their talk was of the weather, imaginary friends, new cars and shopping trips. Louise smiled at one of the policemen who was watching their progress with a little more attention than she would have liked. It seemed too purposeful, intimidating.

'Chilly one this evening, isn't it officer?' she called to him, rubbing her hands together.

'It is indeed, ma'am,' he replied. 'Where is it you're headed?'

'The Gun. Just around the corner.'

'Right you are. You take care now and get home by curfew. Can't be too careful these days, can you, eh?'

'Indeed, indeed.'

She turned her gaze back to Zack, smiled and whispered, 'Shall I shoot the tosser?'

He found it hard to stifle his laugh, turning a chortle into a cough.

They turned the corner to Coldharbour and walked into the pub. It smelled of furniture polish and old food. A row of empty bar stools, red, padded, brass studded, and highly polished, stood against the traditional wooden bar. The drinks display behind housed a row of pewter mugs and an impressive array of bottles. Zack ordered two beers and brought them to the table. His reflection shone off the highly polished floor, his footsteps self-consciously echoing the pub's lack of patrons. There was only one other couple, two men in suits, who sat, apparently deep in conversation, at the far end of the bar.

'That's it, across the street. There,' Louise said, looking out of the window, nodding her head towards the warehouse conversions. She took a couple of sips of her beer then stood up. 'Okay, better get this over with.'

'Already? Not going to finish your beer first? A bit of Dutch courage?' Zack asked, surprised at her haste.

'No,' she replied confidently. There was no more waiting. This would be done now. 'I won't be long,

246

okay?'

'Sure you don't want company?'

'I'm sure. It makes it easier to escape this way, doesn't it?'

'I guess.' He shrugged, trying to mask his disappointment, his concern. This would have been so much easier had he been going with her. She was walking into the unknown. Yes, Ranulf had made the initial contact, checked things out, but nonetheless this could be dangerous. Those who had the most to lose were often the least reliable. This woman, her mother, had everything. Wealth, success, fame. They just had to hope that she also had integrity.

Louise turned back and smiled at Zack as she left through the swing doors, which squeaked their farewell.

He blew her a kiss and watched as she walked resolutely to the entrance of the block where her mother lived. Watched her check in her pocket for the gun; her new permanent companion. Wished he didn't feel so useless.

35

Louise pressed the buzzer, ran her ID through the scanner and waited. The door clicked open and she stepped into the glass and chrome of the entrance. Almost immediately the door closed itself behind her. She didn't look back. There would be no panic. No state of alarm. The security guard nodded at her and gestured towards the lift. She shook her head.

'Thanks, but I'll take the stairs.'

'Right you are, miss, if you're sure. Ms. Cunningham's expecting you. Top floor on the left.'

'Thank you.'

She took her time as she climbed the stairs up to the top floor. Of course there were cameras. She would ignore them. They would show her as calm and confident. When she reached the top floor her mother was waiting at the door.

'Hello.' Sophie smiled, raised her eyebrows. 'We do look alike, don't we? Come in, come in. Can I get you something. Wine? Beer? Coffee?' A waft of expensive perfume trailed in her wake.

'No. No thanks. I'm not stopping,' Louise replied curtly.

'Oh–oh, all right then,' Sophie said with forced gaiety, tainted with disappointment, surprise.

'Yes. Someone's waiting for me.'

'Oh, I see. You don't mind if I do, then?' she asked, gesturing towards the opened bottle of Bordeaux that sat on the marble worktop.

'No, of course not.'

As Sophie poured herself a glass of wine she glanced down at the street below. The street lights had flickered on adding to the feeling of an evening chill. Mist was creeping up from the water, snake like. She shivered. A young man stood outside The Gun, smoking an e-cigarette, talking to a security guard. He was shrugging his shoulders. She turned from the street and walked back to the lounge area, curling her legs under her as she sat beside this stranger who was her daughter.

'You know, I guessed you were happy.' She paused. Took a deep breath. 'Because you hadn't tried to find out about me, your mother. Were you? Happy?' Sophie asked awkwardly.

'Yes. Yes I was. Look. I'm sorry, I'm not here for any big emotional thing, you know? My adoptive parents were amazing and honestly, you hardly crossed my mind. There was no need. Can we just cut to the reason I'm here.'

'Of course,' she replied, taken aback by the brusqueness. 'I'm glad, truly. All I ever wanted was for you to be happy. I was just so young, and–' she stopped for a minute and thought, staring at her daughter. 'So why is it you are here? What can I do for you?'

'It's a long story but basically,' Louise cleared her throat. 'They were killed. My parents. Murdered,' she said matter of factly, surprised by the distance she felt from the words.

'Oh my God!' She drew her hands up to her face. Withdrew them again. 'I am so very sorry. How terrible for you.'

'It was my fault,' she shrugged, dismissively. 'These people, this person is trying to kill me. Somebody wants me dead and people keep dying around me so, yes. I need to know who that might be. I thought perhaps you could help. Perhaps you knew something.'

'I really can't imagine. I mean. Oh my God.' She shook her head.

'Oh my God, what?'

'Just your situation. Look, if there's anything I can do. Anything at all.'

'Did you know who they were? My parents, Katherine and Geoffrey. Did you know them?'

'No. No I didn't.' She looked at the ground. A grey cat jumped up onto her lap and she stroked it, smiling at it. 'Ksh, ksh,' she said, as it nuzzled her chin. She looked back up at her daughter. 'I trusted the person who found them for me implicitly though. I knew you'd be well cared for. Loved. I was only thirteen, you see. It was such a vile situation. Your father was insisting, you see, that I had an abortion.'

Louise cocked her head, as if she'd misheard something.

Sophie continued, 'I wouldn't, so I had to leave, had to hide. My mother took me to a retreat and they took me in. It became my home.'

'Hmm. So my father? Who was he?'

'Richardson. Nigel Richardson,' she said, barely above a whisper.

'No, not your father. I know about that. I mean my father,' Louise replied with unintended impatience.

'Richardson...isn't my father. My mother met him when I was six.'

Louise felt an immense sense of relief and smiled broadly. 'So he's not any blood relation of mine then?'

Sophie hung her head and began to cry. 'Oh, God. This is so hard. I never wanted. Oh God.'

Louise stretched across to reach her mother's hand. It felt damp and clammy. 'What the hell? What's wrong?'

'That bastard.' She shook her head. 'Excuse me.' She walked, almost ran, to the bathroom, sniffing.

As Louise glanced around the impressive flat she noticed the screens on a panel beside the entrance. Cameras were recording the stairwell, lifts, and street outside. She could see the pub's sign. It reassured her, knowing that Zack was sitting in there waiting for her.

Sophie returned, a tissue in her hand, her previously perfect face now looking blotchy. She sat down on the settee and tossed her head back, ran her fingers through her hair and exhaled.

'I'm sorry. It's been so long. I thought–' Sophie sighed. 'I thought it had all,' she waved her hand. 'Gone.'

'It's okay. Don't worry on my account. But I don't understand any of this.'

Sophie's voice broke and she coughed. She looked down at her hands which were twisting the tissue around and around. 'You see, he abused me. From when I was nine he started staying in my bedroom longer than he should have. He said it was our little secret –'

'Oh my God!' Louise's hands clenched the settee. 'Richardson?'

'Yes,' Sophie confirmed meekly. 'And yet, to everyone else he was this loving stepfather who took the time to tuck me up in bed. It's a peculiar thing isn't it? How people see what they want to see?'

'And this–this went on until you left?'

'Yes. It did.' She stopped and looked at her daughter,

251

looked in her eyes. 'You see –'

'No. Wait! You're not telling me I'm his daughter?'

'Yes. Yes, you are. I am so sorry.' She shook her head, squeezed the tissue. 'I –' She lifted her head so that her eyes met her daughter's. 'I never wanted you to know.'

Louise stared, keeping everything hidden, everything down. 'And does he know? Does he know about me? That I'm alive?' The stoicism she felt was a welcome surprise.

'Well, at the time he was told I'd had an abortion. He'd told Mum that I was this awful little slut and that he never wanted me to darken his doorstep again. Can you imagine? What kind of a man?–' She took a deep breath to help regain her composure. 'Thankfully there were some friends of Mum's. They ran this retreat place and, well, they looked after me.'

Could he have found out? I mean I found you,' she asked urgently. 'And you're so famous! He could have recognised you.'

'It would never occur to him that I might amount to anything, besides which the man is so self absorbed I doubt if he'd notice. My name's been changed, I look very different.'

'But it's possible?'

'Yes, it's possible, but extremely unlikely. There were only two people who knew about it; my mother and Annie. Annie's dead now. She died in a car crash.'

'Annie?'

'My second mother, so to speak, from the retreat.'

'Okay. So when? When did she die?'

'It was last summer.'

Louise was churning over events, times, in her head. Last summer, when it all began in earnest. When the person she used to be died. 'Uh-huh. That fits.'

'Fits? I'm sorry? I'm not following.'

'That's when the shit hit the fan for me.'

'In what way?'

'It's too much to go into right now but, basically, I've been on the run since then, barring a brief stay at his majesty's pleasure.'

'You were in prison?' She couldn't disguise the shock.

'No, no. Nothing so ordinary for a Richardson, eh! It was a Re-education camp.'

'Oh my.' She briefly closed her eyes. 'I'm so sorry. How did you end up in one of those places? I've heard they're horrendous.'

'Yes, they are. At the time I thought it was because of the site we had, my colleagues and I. We had a news website – Utell – and New Dawn didn't like it. They'd closed us down a few times. We thought this was just more of the same.'

She shouldn't have said that. The plan had been to remain anonymous and here she was offering her background, her story, unnecessary and dangerous connections. She wished she could just step back, swallow her words, begin again. Shit!

'Oh my God. That was you! Of course, of course. You were all over the news.' Her eyes were wide with disbelief.

'It was all lies. All of it,' Louise said firmly, keeping her mother's gaze. 'Lies.' She began to feel uncomfortable, panicky. She rubbed the back of her neck.

'You're dead. That's what they said. That you were dead.'

'Officially I am, yes. Look, I've taken a huge risk

253

coming here, you know? But I have to finish this–this bullshit. I'm trusting you here. I need you to keep this between us. No-one else.'

'My dear child, of course I will. Of course,' she said, as reassuringly as she could. 'You do look very different. I wouldn't have known. I mean, I didn't make the connection until I was told.'

'Good.'

'Your secret is absolutely safe. I swear. And, you know there was a fair amount of scepticism at the time, amongst right thinking people, about what the press had written. The people who had contributed to your site published a lot of articles and posts decrying the press' stories.'

'Yes, it was good to hear.'

'Of course they were countered, dismissed, but the seed was there. I'm very proud of who you've become. Of the work you've done.'

'Thank you,' she said earnestly. 'I saw you, your band, you know, at the "Rock Against" gig. I had no idea...'

'We were more than happy to play, I mean, it was an honour to be asked, actually. I felt like I was secretly getting my own back at Richardson as well, which was an added bonus.' She smiled a rueful smile.

'Funny, isn't it? Life?'

'Indeed, indeed.'

'And your mother? Is she still there? With him?'

'No. Thank God. She's finally left him. She said he'd gone too far. She's not talking about it, but considering everything that I already know about, this must be something truly heinous. She's staying with me now. She went out. Didn't want to get in the way of...us.'

'Oh, I see. Look, do you know anything about him?

254

About what he's up to these days?'

'No. Nothing beyond the public face. Why on earth would you want to know anyway?'

'I have my reasons.'

36

'Louise!' Zack beamed, as he met her with a hug outside the front of the bar. 'You wanna come back in for a drink?'

'No. Let's just head off,' she said, looking around nervously. 'Plus,' she checked her phone. 'Time's getting on.'

'Was it okay, then? How did it all go?'

'It was fine. Sorry. It all took longer than I expected. Thanks for waiting. I owe you one,' she replied in a tone strangely devoid of feeling, linking her arm with his and heading back up the road. 'You're not going to believe what happened.'

'So, do tell.'

Sophie was watching them from her window, waving at their backs, her hand on her mouth.

'It's–I don't know where to start–shit! It's not for sharing with the world either.' She looked back at the empty window as the lights were switched off and the glass turned icy black.

'It can wait. You sure you're okay?'

'Yes, I'm fine. Shocked but...fine.'

'Ranulf's flat, then?'

'Yes. If there's one person I trust right now it's him.'

'Oh, so I've been demoted then?'

'Idiot!' She giggled and pushed him away.

He laughed and put his arm around her shoulders, pulling her close. 'Okay. Fine by me. I know when I'm beaten.'

'Him, I trust with my life. You, you get my soul, okay?'

'Okay. I can deal with that.' He squeezed her and kissed her head.

Curfew was imminent and the streets were almost deserted, bar the increasing number of police and security patrols. Security cameras spun, silently tracking their progress. A drone hovered above them before flying off again. Louise and Zack hurried on, heads down, to Ranulf's flat which was only a ten minute walk away. Ranulf had been quite insistent about timing. They had to arrive between nine and ten and make sure they spoke to Jim. Louise swiped her ID at the entrance and the steel door clicked open. They were welcomed in the foyer by the security guard who checked their IDs against his list, double checked the photographs against their faces, slipped their cards into his computer, nodded his approval and smiled.

'Are you Jim?' Louise asked, somewhat concerned over what was happening between card and computer. It wasn't just a simple swipe. Something more was going on. She didn't want to ask. Didn't want to appear nervous, suspicious, but she most definitely was.

'I am that, Ms Harringer. Now, if you can just sign here.'

She had to check herself; remember the practised signature of Louise Harringer.

The computer beeped and their ID cards were spat out. Jim handed them back, smiling, nodding. 'Penthouse flat. Very nice. Great view up there. Staying long?'

257

'Oh, we're not sure. We're just visiting. You know how it is.' She smiled in return, gratefully taking hold of her card again.

'Right you are. Now, if you need anything just you let me know. Always happy to help.'

'Thanks but we're fine. If we could just have the key?' she said, perhaps a little too impatiently.

'No need. It's already on your ID,' he replied with a nod, showing them to the elevators. 'I'll need to show you how it all works though. Mr. McKenzie has his ways.'

Has his ways? What is this? She was wondering about what they had come down to. This all seemed very strange. Very un-Ranulf. She was trying hard to focus on the now. Not to dwell on what she had just found out about her parentage. But how can you let something like that slide? Pretend? Ignore? Move on?

Inside the elevator there was no button for the thirty-second floor, where the penthouse flat was, and nothing else to indicate how to get there.

'Now. There are only three cards for this contraption here. Mr. McKenzie's, the one I have, and this one,' Jim said, holding a card up and handing it to Louise. 'What you do is you slip it in beside the panel, here. Do you see?' He slipped his card in and waited until it was automatically ejected. 'Then, hey presto, and you're away.'

Louise raised her eyebrows at Zack. 'Wow,' she mouthed.

'Now, just make sure you don't take it all the way out until the doors open. If you do the lift won't work. Simple as that. It's a one stop lift so no-one else can get in once it's going. You got all that?'

'Yeah. That's great. Thanks,' Zack replied.

The lift silently glided its way up to the thirty-second floor and the doors slid open on their arrival. They stepped out into a small corridor with two doors leading off it.

'That one's a service room, cleaning stuff and the likes,' Jim said, pointing to the smaller one. 'And this one's Mr. McKenzie.' He showed them how to use the security system and how everything in the flat worked. 'If you have any problems you can just call me. The number's on the card, okay?' he said, as he bade them goodnight.

'Right. Thanks again. Night,' Zack said, thankful to be finally closing the door behind him with a feeling of almost safety. Not quite, but close enough. He could relax for a while. This had been quite a day and yet there was more to come. Whatever revelations were waiting he would be ready. There for her.

The flat was in complete antithesis to the man they had come to know. Glass and chrome, minimalist and flash.

'Wow!' Zack exclaimed. 'Talk about extremes.'

'I know eh? That man is just so full of surprises. And the secret floor,' she said with a laugh. 'We could be in a spy movie. It's cool.'

'Do you reckon it's actually his?'

'So he said. Maybe from his spying days,' she said in a silly voice. 'I wonder if he's got it wired? He could be watching us, you know?' she added with a grin.

'That is altogether too freaky! Are you being serious?'

'Not really, but hey. You never know, do you? He was filming me at the Hobbit house, wasn't he! And that place I was in just now, my mother's. Nah,' she shook her head, 'Sophie's,' she corrected. 'It had cameras all over the place. And she's just a musician.'

'Fuck's sake,' he said, scanning the ceiling and walls.

I know, eh? But then again, I guess she has her reasons to be paranoid.'

'More so than Ranulf?'

'Hmmm...' She picked up a couple of takeaway menus from the glass coffee table. 'Hey, as we're back in the land of the living, fancy ordering a take-away? I'm starving.'

'Okay. Sounds good.' He checked the front cover of the menu. 'And they've got curfew clearance. Cool. Your usual?'

'Please.'

As he was calling she had a nose around. 'Sorry Ranulf,' she whispered into the air as she checked through drawers and cupboards. 'But you knew I would.' To her disappointment there was nothing other than kitchen equipment, bedding and towels. No surprises, no personal touches, nothing. The feeling was more like that of a hotel room than someone's flat. There were changes of clothing for both of them, including underwear. 'Just weird!'

'What's weird?'

'Look!' she said, holding up the clothes. 'Right sizes, right style, right everything.'

'Okay. Yeah. That's weird.'

260

37

'Oh my God. It's been so long!' Louise said, as she peeled back the corners of the takeaway containers. 'It smells gorgeous. Mm-hmm.'

Zack smiled at the enjoyment she was getting out of her meal. She was like a child at Christmas. He couldn't help but wonder at what life must have been like for her since September; how much she had suffered on top of everything that they had been through together. And now there was whatever she had just learnt. Of course he was itching to find out, to understand. He didn't want to push it. She would tell him soon enough. He cleaned up after they'd eaten and gave her a bottle of Cobra beer.

'Funny, isn't it? How you get used to being without. I'd forgotten about all of this. Beer, curries, stuff! Stuff which I thought I couldn't do without and...well, yes. Strange.'

'I'm afraid I was spoilt. Pampered, you could say! Great food, comfort. They were really good people.' He grinned sheepishly at her.

'I didn't miss it though, at Ranulf's. It was cool and natural, I guess, living like that.'

'So, when all of this is over? You'll be dropping out? Living in a Hobbit house in the middle of nowhere?'

'Maybe.' She laughed quietly. 'Who knows? I could

think of worse things to do with my life.'

'For sure, but I couldn't see you giving up your job. Reporting, investigating, fighting for the rights of the downtrodden and all that. It's so much a part of you.'

'No, probably not, but there's no need to be here, is there? In the city?'

'I guess not.' He shrugged, smiled across at her. 'I can see the attraction. It was very cool up there.'

'Yes, it was, wasn't it?'

He was growing so impatient. It was too much not to ask. 'So what now? You haven't told me what happened yet. What we're up against.'

'Sorry, no I haven't, have I? It's kind of...difficult.' She pulled a face of distaste. Her eyes clouded with a darkness that made Zack uncomfortable.

'Okay, and?' His look was a cross between concern and question. 'I can't help if I don't know what you're– what we're dealing with.'

'Let's see, who is the most cretinous person, politician, we've been investigating over the past year, or so?'

'Easy. Richardson, and he's your grandfather, which is pretty fucked up.'

'It's a lot worse than that. Turns out he's not my grandfather at all. He's my father. How about that, eh?' She laughed a strange, cold laugh.

'What?' He choked on his beer and wiped the drips from his chin with the back of his hand.

'Yes. Sophie isn't his by birth. He's her stepfather. He abused her. Raped her. He's my fucking father!' She jumped up from the settee and did a ballet type twirl and a curtsy. 'Enter Suze slash Louise. The product of quasi incest and rape. Pretty special, huh?'

'Oh, shit, man. Can this get any worse? You must

be–ah fuck, Louise.' The anguish he felt for her bounced off the walls.

'It's all right. I'm beyond upset. I'm thinking retribution. Nice word that, don't you think? Has a certain ring to it. Retribution. Another beer?' she asked, making her way to the fridge.

'Sure.'

'To retribution,' she said, raising her bottle.

'Not sure about this but...yeah...' he added, clinking bottles. 'To retribution. Cheers.'

'Cheers.'

'What sort of retribution did you have in mind?'

'I really don't know. I know what I'd like to do but–I have to think about this. No messing up allowed, Zack my friend.' She raised her bottle. 'This has to be good.'

'It's a damned shame we lost all that stuff on the computer, isn't it?'

'Tell me about it! I spent hours and hours trying to claw it all back from my memory at Ranulf's. Everything I could think of. At least now I can focus on that slimy excuse for a human being. Well, that's what makes most sense, if anything does. It has to be him.'

'Change the I to we please. You know you're not getting rid of me again.'

'Of course. That's a given. Well, I was assuming that was a given.'

'Once more unto the breach, dear friend, once more,' he began in Shakespearean timbre. 'Or close the wall up with our English dead.'

Louise laughed as he continued.

'In peace there's nothing so becomes a man as modest stillness and humility: But when the blast of war blows in our ears.' He stood up and punched the air. 'Then imitate the action of the tiger; Stiffen the sinews,

263

summon up the blood.' He sat down beside her, smiled at her and clinked beer bottles. 'Tigers!'

'Tigers!' she laughed.

'So what do we need to know about Richardson then?' Zack asked.

'I want everything. Everything it's possible to find. From the colour of his socks to his latest concubine.'

'Yeah, yeah. I remember. You were working on that, weren't you? The whole sex scandal thing.'

'I was indeed. I didn't think much of it at the time. I mean, it's not exactly shocking these days, is it?'

'No. For sure. Sadly mundane. Do you remember anything unusual though? More pervy than the run of the mill shit?'

'I wish I could. That's one thing I haven't got back yet. My recall, you know? They gave me such a mental bashing in there. There are bits...missing...messed up.' She sounded hollow, confused.

'Well, we're all tech'd up now, thanks to Ranulf, so we can start again. Start with what we can remember and take it from there,' he put in, reassuringly. 'It won't take long once we get started.'

'Yes. Thank you,' she said sincerely.

'For what?'

'Just being you, being here, being my friend.'

'So, when are you going to thank me properly?' he asked, wiggling his eyebrows up and down. Grinning.

'And what do you mean by that?' she giggled.

'Oh, you know. Take me to bed. Ravish me. Stuff like that. I wouldn't mind, really!' He cocked his head.

She laughed. 'Yeah. That's what's best. You always know how to make me laugh.'

'No! I'm being serious.'

'Yeah, yeah. Idiot!'

264

38

Louise slept fitfully. Nightmares of what had happened between Sophie and Richardson refused to stay away, except the face wasn't Sophie's, it was hers. Richardson walked into her room and slowly began taking his clothes off, a foul grin on his face. She tried to scream, but no sound came out. She tried to get out of bed, but she couldn't move. It was as if she were stuck to the mattress. It became wet cement, tightening its grip, hardening around her. He was laughing as he entered her. Laughing and grunting. Her mother, Katherine, came in and smiled then turned around and left, closing the door behind her. The girl cried, silently. No sound, only pain and terror. She could taste his sweat, taste his breath.

The relief of waking up was immeasurable. She decided against trying to sleep again – fearful of more visions taking over her mind – despite the inappropriately early hour. The first hours of the morning were often the most productive workwise. She would research, dig, do all of the things that kept her ticking. Fight against it all.

'Wow, you're up and working already?' Zack said drowsily, as he walked across to the bathroom in his boxers, his eyes still adjusting to the harshness of the artificial light.

Louise was sitting on the settee with one of the laptops Ranulf had left for them open beside her. There were pages of notes scribbled in a pad on her knee. She looked up and smiled. 'Yes. All this stuff was whizzing around my head and I wanted to get it on paper. You know?'

'Sure. Embarrassingly enough, I slept like a log. Must be the city air,' he said with a sleepy grin. 'I'm just going to wake myself up with a shower then I'll be with you, okay?' His voice trailed off into the porcelain and glass. She could hear him groan as the blast of the shower brought him back to life. Other than that he seemed strangely quiet. No singing today.

She walked over to the kitchen area and stood looking out at the lights of London as they flickered on with the waking of the working populace. The view was quite stunning from where they were, with all of the city stretching out before them. Nothing overlooked the ceiling to floor windows which made up the entire exterior wall. Beyond them a balcony stretched its way around the building. Glass floor, glass walls. She slid the windows open and stepped out onto the balcony, gingerly at first, slightly disconcerted by the glass, the height, the distance to the hard ground. Gripping the metal rim of the glass surrounds she leaned over and stared at it all.

She could see why Ranulf had chosen this place, so high, so removed, so anonymous, yet beautiful in its own way. It was like his own private crow's nest in the middle of London. Pictures of people going about their ordinary business, far below, trickled through her mind. People waking up, going to work, doing what they do; keeping it all going. Others hiding in the shadows of their illicit lives. Funny, she thought, how she had slipped from one to the other. Journalist to criminal. Daughter to murderer. Living to dead. And now who

266

was she? Something in between. Something new. Something else. Whatever, she was going to fight.

The espresso machine hissed at her, its smell beckoning, breaking her out of her reverie. 'Hmm,' she mumbled, as she filled her tiny cup with strong black elixir, remembering how Ranulf had said he was a mug man. 'Cheers Ranulf,' she said, smiling to where she imagined a camera might be, and returning to her place on the settee.

Zack soon joined her and they began to sift through their memories of previous research, poring over her notes, checking dates, times, people and places.

'I don't feel like we're getting anywhere,' Louise said with frustration, several hours later, throwing her head back and closing her eyes. 'There's nothing– nothing out of the ordinary.'

'Yeah, but remember how deep we had to dig before? We'd been after him for months, and that was then, you know? Before all of this shit. Don't expect too much too soon.'

'I suppose so. I think we need something else though. I'm thinking something dodgy. A wee hack perhaps?' she said with fake coquettishness.

Zack laughed. 'Yeah. We can do that. Ranulf was adamant the tech here was totally secure so, why not? Where would madam like to start?' he added, with a servile bow.

'That's my boy! I'm thinking phone, browsing history, easy stuff like that,' she said with a grin. 'Nothing too challenging.'

'Okay. I could get so far but Brian was always the expert, you know?'

'Yes, he was, wasn't he? I haven't even asked–' She hung her head. 'Shit. What have I become?' She looked up at him, fighting the disappointment she felt in herself, fighting against this person she barely recognised. 'Your oldest friend and I haven't even asked. I am so sorry. How is he? Do you know? And your Dad? What happened to them?' she asked. 'Christ, talk about self-absorbed,' she added, with mental castigation. 'It all seems so very, very, long ago.'

'I know. It's okay.' He took her hand reassuringly. 'They're both fine. They were pestered for a while, but a couple of days after the crash it all stopped and they were left alone.'

'Have you seen either of them. I mean, I guess it's safe. Ranulf said Brian checked out, and your Dad, well, that was a no-brainer.'

'No. Not yet. I spoke to my Dad, on the sat-phone. I'd planned heading back to town, but then Ranulf turned up and...well...'

'Hmm. And Brian? What happened that night? Do you know?'

'Yeah. I finally got through to him. He'd left his external hard drive at the pub and ran back for it. Didn't want to hold us up so didn't say anything. Then he had to hide from the patrols so couldn't make it to the lock up.'

'Yes. That sounds like him. So, were they in the bar then? New Dawn? How did he manage to get past them? I mean, it sounded like they were right on top of us.'

'They were. He only got as far as the car park then realised he'd have to forget it. The place was swarming with them. He just hoped they wouldn't find the drive or be able to get through the encryption, if they did.'

'Horrible who you doubt, isn't it? When the shit hits the proverbial. You know, we even checked you out,' she added with embarrassment.

He shrugged, dismissing any guilt she felt. 'So, do we get Brian involved?'

'Don't take this the wrong way but I'd rather not. The less people that know...you know?'

'Sure. No probs. So just us then?'

'Just us.'

Several hours later they were still plugging away. Searching. Keeping themselves going with too many cups of coffee.

'Hey, it's already getting dark again.' She turned to look out of the window. 'Jeez. Take a look at that.' she added, shivering at the scene which stared at her through the glass. Torrential rain had begun flowing down the window in cascades, making it seem as if they were underwater. A wind was howling around the high rise; the song of a siren. The building seemed to move, to sway slightly with the wind. She hugged herself against the foreboding she was feeling.

'Take-away again then?' Zack asked.

'Absolutely!'

'Beer and pizza?'

'Ha, ha. Love how the beer gets top priority!'

'Well, you know me.'

'Yes,' she said with a smile, 'I do. Beer and pizza would be grand.'

There was a knock at the door half an hour later. Louise jumped then laughed at herself as she remembered the pizza they'd ordered. Zack opened the door for Jim.

'Brutal out there tonight. Wise to stay in, the two of you,' Jim said, with a fake shiver.

'Yeah, that's what we were thinking.'

'Here's your take-away. Gave the driver a nice, big

tip. Horrible job on a night like this.'

'Right. Cheers. How much do we owe you then?'

'Nothing. It's on Mr. McKenzie's account. His instructions.'

'Really? That's...very decent.'

'Decent man, Mr. McKenzie. Not too many about like him these days. You two enjoy your evening.'

'Cheers. You too.'

Zack locked the door behind him and slid the chain.

'We need to be careful, you know?' Louise said, looking at the order.

'What do you mean?'

'The name on the pizza slip – Jake – and you're meant to be Zack. It's Louise and Zack for everything. We can't afford to be sloppy.'

'Shit, you're right. Yeah. Louise and Zack,' he reminded himself.

They sat silently at the chrome and glass table eating their food, both seemingly mesmerised by the weather, both lost in their own mental wanderings. After they'd eaten, Louise tidied. She was unusually fastidious in keeping the place spotless, almost obsessive. When she was satisfied she sat beside Zack on the settee and smiled at him.

'So,' she said conspiratorially. 'Unless we come up with something tonight, I think tomorrow we should up the ante.'

'Okay,' he replied slowly, the word drawn out like a piece of elastic. 'Anything specific in mind?' he added, with an obvious note of apprehension.

'I think we have to get out there and see what he's up to ourselves.'

'What, tail him you mean?' His apprehension shouted through staring eyes; his voice raising an octave.

'Something along those lines, yes.'

'Jesus, Louise, that's so dangerous it's suicidal.'

'I know. But this is killing me. I want an end to it. You know? I want that retribution and the release it's going to give me. I need it.'

39

Whatever he felt, or said, he knew that this was going to happen. Richardson was going to be hers, one way or another.

'I get that. I really do but–' He took her hand and squeezed it, held her eyes. 'We need to be very, very sure.'

'Are you with me or not?' she asked, with a mix of frustration and determination. 'I'm going after that piece of shit and nothing is going to get in my way. You know that, don't you?'

He smiled ruefully at her. 'Yeah, I do. So, what are you thinking?'

'A couple of bikes? Nice and speedy; skid lids to hide behind? We've got permits and cash so...?'

'I guess. Shit. Are you sure about this?'

'I'm never sure about anything these days. But hey, it'll be fun. Come on,' she said, nudging him in the ribs.

'Fun?'

*

The next morning they checked where the nearest bike shops were and headed off to make their purchases. They decided on a small place that belonged to a biker, not some corporation, some big manufacturer, just someone who loved bikes and spent their days tinkering with them, doing repairs, doing up old wrecks.

They walked slowly up to the entrance of the alleyway. Both nervous, both wary.

'You sure this is the place?' Zack asked.

Louise checked what she'd written down. 'Yep. This is it.' She shrugged.

A quick glance behind them. A nod of confirmation before heading in to the alley that was only just wide enough for a motorbike to travel along, senses on high alert, eyes scanning, ears tuned in, voices silent. This was a no way out place. Once in they could be trapped. The perfect place for a set-up. They breathed in their anxiety – this would be okay. Redbrick walls, heavily graffitied, echoed their footsteps. Ground level windows were protected by iron bars, but smashed nonetheless. The light at the far end was beckoning; the temptation to run to reach it strong. Zack reached for her hand. Held it tight. *Keep cool, keep cool, keep cool.*

As they reached the lane's end a smell of neglect mingled with petrol. Peculiarly enticing. The alley opened up into a small, seemingly abandoned, courtyard. One of the two doors opened to reveal an overall clad young woman wiping grease encrusted hands on an oily rag. She grinned at them and held her hand out in greeting.

'We're looking for a couple of bikes,' Louise said, shaking the woman's hand in return.

'Ain't no other reason to be heading on in here,' she replied with a laugh. 'In you come then.'

She had a couple of old trail bikes that she'd been working on that were ready to go; fast and manoeuvrable on any terrain.

'Great getaway bikes,' she said, with a grin.

Zack and Louise both laughed too readily, too

heartily, but it didn't matter. Her tattoos were all the confirmation they needed that she was okay.

'Do you have any riding gear, jackets and the like?'

'Sure.'

She let them rummage through a box of leathers and waterproofs, well worn but still serviceable. That was fine. It didn't take them long to find what they needed.

'What about skid-lids?' Zack asked, glancing up at a shelf of them.

'Full face?'

'Uh-huh.'

'With intercom?'

'Now that would be very cool! What do they run on?'

'Red Spot. Totally secure. It's what I use.'

In other times they would have struck up a conversation. Allowed information to drip that confirmed they were allies, but those days were past. Trust no-one!

The woman stretched up and brought down a couple of lids for them to try.

'Perfect!'

There was something reassuring about being in second-hand clothes. It was as if it gave them a genuineness; the legitimacy of bona fide bikers. They both raised their eyebrows at the apparent blood stain on Zack's jacket.

'Is that what I think it is?' Louise asked.

The mechanic shrugged. 'Shit happens! The jacket's too good to ditch, don'tcha reckon? Years of riding left in that one!'

'I suppose so,' she answered, not entirely convinced, and glad she wasn't the one wearing it.

'Pleasure doing business with you guys. Enjoy

274

yourselves,' she said, handing them their keys.

Louise had thought about offering a cash transaction, but decided against it. It would probably have been preferred, but she didn't know for sure. They couldn't afford any slip-ups. Louise swiped her card in payment. She didn't know how Ranulf had done it, created accounts with a seemingly endless supply of money in them, but he had.

'Aye well, that's a need to know, and you just need to spend,' he had said, with a customary grin, when she had tried to push him on it. She knew better than to question him further. This was all about trust, and she had that.

'And you take care now,' the mechanic called after them, waving her hand, as she turned back into her workshop.

'Okay?' Zack asked.

'Okay,' Louise confirmed.

They pulled their visors down and started their bikes up, both of them enjoying that feeling, that excitement. The urge to rev up, to speed away, had to be suppressed. Instead they slipped slowly, cautiously, along the cobbles and out onto the main drag.

They rode off making for the countryside. It seemed to take forever. A slow, tedious, nerve-ridden ride through city streets, past cameras, under drones, alongside menacing New Dawn patrols cruising the streets looking for troublemakers, lawbreakers, people like Zack and Louise.

At last they reached the forest, with its well-used trails, where they could practise; get to know their bikes; prepare for all eventualities. For a while it was just pure fun. Like the old days. The two of them, innocent, out dirt tracking, racing each other, getting covered in mud, getting lost. For a while they left it all behind them, secure in the knowledge that if they did get stopped they would check out. No-one was after them. They had become normal. Not part of the sub-culture, the rebellion, but normal functioning good citizens. And for a while they would relish it, enjoy themselves. But that was how it started. That was how people changed. That need for normality. I'm all right. My life is good.

'You know, this just feels wrong,' Zack said, as he skidded to a halt beside Louise. 'Fun, for sure, but wrong.'

'I know,' Louise confirmed. 'It doesn't sit well, does it?'

'Nope. Shall we go?'

'Yep.'

When they returned to the reality of Ranulf's flat they spent the evening going over possible routes, rendezvous and hiding places. Places where they could escape to if spotted; if they felt threatened. Where they could meet up again if separated. Places where they would find Richardson at some point. Get it all in motion. Everything had to be covered, committed to memory. They would be invincible.

Louise showed Zack the trackers that Ranulf had given her.

'They're cool,' Zack said, as he turned one of the tiny magnetic discs over in his fingers. 'How do they work?'

'We just plant them, activate them, then track them. They hook up to the phone and computer.'

'So what are you thinking?'

'One for each of us.' She looked up at him. 'Just in case, and one for Richardson's car.'

276

'And how exactly do we get his car? I mean, he has security, a driver...'

'I don't know. We'll follow him and see what happens.'

'Follow him from where?'

'Tomorrow's Friday, so his club. At lunch time. Check the place out and...see...'

'This is crazy; you know that, don't you?' he said, with his eyebrows raised.

'I know,' she replied, with a smile. 'I know.'

40

Louise and Zack sat in the window recess of a small, independent, West End coffee shop, whose tantalising aroma perfectly matched the intended ambience of the place. The comforting security of times past, of relaxation, of just being normal. It was a place of idle chatter, of laughter amongst friends, of gentle privilege.

Their table gave them a good view of the private club Richardson frequented. It was one of the things he openly boasted about and therefore an easy place to find him. Lunch on a Friday was seldom missed. Friday, they'd discovered, was also the day he drove himself, so the threat of security was lessened. Louise nervously played with the edge of her coffee cup, making the stylised leaf the barista had so lovingly created tremble and break apart. They made innocent conversation, trying to seem casual; a couple of friends out for a coffee and a chat. Louise found it difficult to draw her eyes away from the door of the club. Trepidation was fighting, successfully, against logic. She felt somehow conspicuous and vulnerable.

'Come on. Where are you?' she mumbled.

'I don't know about this, Louise. I've got a bad feeling,' Zack said quietly.

'I know, I know. Me too. It's probably just because we're getting so close. Let's just sit tight a bit longer and see, okay?' she replied, not taking her eyes off where their intended target should appear. 'All we need to do is clock the car and where it's heading, then we can try and tail him.' She sounded irritated and anxious all in one volatile bundle. She sipped at her coffee; the buzz from the hit of caffeine a superfluous, unnecessary addition to the tightly wound up coil that was her.

The heavy wooden door of the club was held open by a doorman dressed like something out of a century long since past. He bowed and a man exited.

Louise held her breath and stared.

'That's him,' she whispered. 'This time it's him, for sure.'

His gait was unmistakable. The well groomed arrogance exuding from every hand-sewn stitch of his tailor-made suit. She had always despised the man due to his politics and lifestyle, but now? Now it had taken on a whole new level. He looked different, dirtier.

He was heading towards the coffee shop.

'No, no, no. Where's his car? What the hell is he doing?' Louise whispered, her voice rising with each word. 'He can't have–'

He was looking straight at them, smiling, as if he had a purpose for them. She felt sick; the dream, the visions, the deed.

'What do we do now, Zack? What the hell do we do?' she hissed, as a trickle of sweat dripped down her spine.

'Nothing. We sit here and chat, okay?' Zack replied calmly. 'It's all okay. Look at me and smile. That's my girl.' He took her hand and kissed it. 'He doesn't even know you exist.'

'Maybe. Maybe not. Oh Christ!'

A light rain had begun to fall. Richardson flicked

open his black umbrella and tilted it, gesturing for someone to join him in its shelter. A young woman, dripping designer from head to toe, stepped in front of the window and returned his smile, accepting his offer. He was so close Louise could have touched him were it not for the glass separating his world from hers. Richardson turned and he and the woman walked off together along the pavement.

'Let's go,' Louise said. 'See where they're headed.'

'On foot? That's not the plan, Louise. That's too fucking dangerous!'

She was already leaving, heading out the door. Zack caught up with her and put his arm around her shoulders, keeping his eyes on the umbrella. His ears picked up the click of stilettos, the confident stride of brogues, the rain pattering on the umbrella. There was no way Richardson could have known who she was. In his world she was dead. If things got dangerous, risky, Zack's instincts would kick in – he would know what to do – at least that was what he told himself.

Richardson and the woman turned up a side-street and into a private basement car park, whose metal security gates strummed open with the click of a four digit code.

'The bikes,' Louise called, as she turned and ran, pulling Zack by the arm. 'We need the bikes. Shit!'

They raced back towards where they had parked their bikes, ignoring the glances of passers by. It was dangerous to run in an area like this, drawing attention to themselves, alerting cameras, security. There was a good chance something or someone would have picked them out of the crowd, scanned their faces, checked their IDs. But it would be all right, they convinced themselves. It had to be all right.

The bikes were only a block away. Reaching them they jumped on, started up and rode back just in time to see Richardson pull out onto the main road in his Jaguar sports. They followed at a safe distance, taking turns at being the lead, twisting in and out of the traffic, trying to remain inconspicuous, checking back, checking above, all as subtly as was possible. Both were full of adrenalin, hearts pumping, breath short, minds racing. Conversation between them was almost constant. Keeping each other safe, alert. Instructions on when to take over the lead, when to fall back.

They hung back as the Jag turned into Pavilion Road in Knightsbridge, waiting at the corner, watching, as it slowed and drew up outside a very swank little mews house. Bright white walls, glossy black door and frames, barred windows, cobbles. Richardson opened the door for his lady-friend and they hurried inside, his hand squeezing her buttock. The door closed with a solid clunk. The turn of a hefty key. Windows illuminated before curtains were drawn.

Louise saw her chance and took it.

'I'm going in. You wait here. Keep an eye out.'

She pulled off before Zack had a chance to try and convince her otherwise.

'We should wait a bit. Make sure they're staying. Don't rush it, Louise. Don't rush it.'

But perhaps she was right. Time spent in a place like this was dangerous. They stood out. They should get in and out as quickly as possible. He watched as she pulled the bike up behind the red sports car. This was it. This was the point of no return. The hunt would be on and there was no backing out of it now. He knew that.

'All clear, Louise. Just hurry up for Christ's sake.'

'Shh. It's all good.'

281

The calmness she felt as she casually tilted the bike on its stand and dismounted was pleasantly surprising. She bent down at her front wheel as if to check it. As she stood up she delicately slipped the disc on to the inside of Richardson's wheel arch. She couldn't look around to see if anyone was watching, anyone had noticed. Unnecessary attention would be drawn. She had to look natural, unworried, as if she had every right to be here, doing this.

'Done!'

She mounted her bike, started it up, and drove off, glancing back over her shoulder one last time. All clear. Or so it seemed. Zack caught up and they headed back to Canary Wharf. They rode home in silence.

'Do you have any idea how totally insane that was?' Zack asked, as he closed the apartment door behind them, finally feeling able to speak.

'Fun though!' she laughed, ditching her helmet, peeling off her leathers. 'Admit it. That was one hell of a buzz.'

'Admitted,' he replied, cocking his head.

'What a stereotypical tosser. A red sports car and a bimbo shacked up in a posh little mews flat. I mean. Jesus!'

'I know, eh? You couldn't make it up. Well, you could but it would be boring.'

She laughed. 'So, let's activate this thing and see what he's up to.'

She flicked open the laptop and activated the tracker, calling it "Tosser".

'Subtle,' Zack laughed.

'Well–'

It was still at the mews. She set it to alert so that it would beep when it began to move. Theirs were also

282

activated just to make sure they were ready to go at a moment's notice. She turned to Zack and he smiled as he watched her type their tracker names in. John and Yoko.

'You okay?' he asked.

'I'm just fine. Do we need to plant one on his official ministry car as well? What do you think?' she asked.

'I reckon not. I can't imagine him doing anything dodgy in that, can you? Tosser he may be, but stupid? Doubt it. Besides which it's going to be regularly checked, scanned. It's not like we're his only enemies, now is it?'

'You're probably right. So now we just wait and see.'

She didn't know what she was hoping for. Journalistically it would be to uncover something so heinous that it would bring him down. Irrevocably and permanently reduce him to nothing. A man destroyed, humiliated, cast aside like the hundreds of thousands he had condemned to a life worth less than nothing. Privately, personally, she wanted him to lead her to a place where he was vulnerable, unprotected. A place where she could inflict pain on him and, yes, kill him. She wanted to see him dead.

41

They tracked the movements of the Jag; of Richardson in private mode. His forays became predictable, from house to club or house to hooker, nothing which piqued their interest. Their days were spent in the solitude of the apartment. A peculiar separateness from everything else had settled on them. When sunlight hit the windows they darkened, slowly, subtly, the process reversing itself with the passing of clouds, of nightfall. There were blinds that closed with the press of a button. Despite being higher than all of the surrounding buildings, having no onlookers, they would close them. It felt somehow safer, more private. Time dragged as their impatience grew. Something had to happen.

'That's a new one,' Zack said, a couple of weeks later. 'Look.'

They followed the tracker as it moved west. A few miles later and he stopped.

'Hmm. Let's have a wee explore on Search, shall we? See where he's visiting.'

Their search led them to an area just outside of London. They tried to zoom in, but it was blank.

'Odd. The place is out of coverage,' Zack said, scratching his head, thinking, exploring other searches, but still drawing up blanks. 'There must be a deep black-out over it. Even the best of the alternatives can't get through.'

'What do you reckon? Governmental or something private?'

'Because of the car I would guess private, but it's definitely weird. Definitely some heavy shit if he can get a blanket this deep over it. Maybe some covert government meeting place? Something ultra sensitive for a select few?'

They decided against going there now. It would be wiser to wait; to see how long he stayed; to find out something about the place before putting themselves at risk again. Difficult though it was, they slept in shifts so that nothing could escape them. Whatever was going on in this place it felt important, different, valuable, and they didn't want to lose track of where he went.

Richardson stayed until the following day before heading back to his family home.

That morning they sat mulling it over. Both of them had cabin fever and were itching to get out again. To be doing something other than watching the flicker of a tracker.

'Can we go and check this place out?' Louise said. 'I don't know why but I've got a feeling...something's not right here.'

'Journalist's instinct?' Zack asked.

'Journalist's instinct,' she confirmed, with a smile.

'Right now?'

'Yes. I reckon this needs to be checked out in a hurry.'

'Agreed.'

Both of them felt the excitement build as they got ready: leathers, gloves, crash helmets, weapons. It was peculiar how quickly it had become normal. Tooling up was just part of getting ready, like throwing on a coat or pulling on boots. Louise kept the gun. She'd been taught how to use it and was a decent shot, so it made sense. Both of them had knives.

A smile and a wave for the security guard as they left.

'You two take care now.'

They walked out into the blinding sunlight of a spring day, flicking their visors down before riding off. It felt good being proactive again. Doing something.

42

The ride took longer than they had anticipated – lights were against them, traffic too – but finally the sat-tracker told them they had arrived.

'I'm so not sure about this,' Zack said apprehensively, as they parked the bikes in the cover of an unkempt beech hedge that stretched to a good two metres above them. It would offer decent cover.

'I am,' Louise replied, clipping her crash helmet to her bike and pulling her balaclava down. 'Are you coming?'

'Of course I am but...just be careful, okay?' he said to her back.

They checked that the bikes couldn't be seen from the road, then looked up and down it, listening for an engine, watching for headlights. It was deathly quiet. They ran across the road to the walled exterior of the lodge. Louise aimed the grappling hook gun at the bough of a tree which hung over the ivy-clad wall. She pulled on it, making sure it was secure, then hoisted herself up the wall. She hadn't noticed the broken glass that had been cemented onto the top of the wall until she stretched up those last few centimetres. *Shit!* The force she used had been enough for the glass to pierce through her leather gloves. She winced at the pain, thankful that it hadn't been worse. Not daring to use words she tried to signal to Zack what was up there. Warn him. He nodded, mouthing, 'You okay?' She nodded in reply. Checking behind the wall first, she then signed the all clear to Zack, who climbed up after her. They crouched awkwardly on the top of the wall and listened again. Silence.

They recoiled the grapple and used the tree and ivy to make their way onto the ground inside the property, landing on mud and leaves which smelled like they belonged to autumn, not spring. It was musty and evocative. Childhood adventures. Muddy knees. Scratches and scars. Bonfire nights and sparklers. Baked potatoes and hot chocolate. Louise threw her backpack back on and they stood in the shadows, watching, listening, taking their time.

They heard the snapping of some twigs and looked at each other, anxiously. Louise could feel the adrenalin pump its way around her body. She focused on it, savouring it, feeding off it. Slowly, discreetly, she felt in her boot and drew her knife, waiting, holding her breath. A deer scampered out of the undergrowth, stopped and stared at them for a peculiarly long time, its eyes wide and vacant, then skipped off across the lawns and into the blackness of the night. Louise smiled to herself and moved on.

They kept meticulously to the plan. Zack had insisted. No hot-headedness, no rash moves. There was no room for mistakes and no need to hurry. They skirted the entire perimeter, checking for exits, dangers, and security, in total silence. When they had reached their starting point again they doubled back to where there appeared to be most cover; to where the woods crept closest to the house. They waited. The lights were now turned off, bar the one which came on above the front door, guiding the way along the gravel entrance. A woman came out, locked up and climbed into a Mercedes, driving off towards the road. Electronic gates clicked open. They listened as the sound of the engine trailed off into the distance leaving silence in its wake, and the gates clicked themselves closed again, before making their move.

It was about fifty metres to the house across open lawns. They ran, keeping as low to the ground as they could, trying to blend in, praying that no lights would jump to life and pick them out. Security seemed surprisingly lax, considering the blackout they had witnessed on their computers. Their progress was similarly easy. There was no sign of working cameras, alarms, dogs, nothing. When they had reached the house itself they crept around to the window furthest from the road. Louise teased her knife between the fastener and frame. It clicked aside and the window slid open. They looked at each other as if to say, "Is that it?" Half expecting an alarm to go off, they waited for a couple of minutes. Nothing. They climbed in.

They kept balaclavas and gloves on as they walked from room to room, checking for the duplicitous flickerings of cameras and security beams. When they scanned the area around the front door, there was indeed a panel of CCTV screens, but deactivated, as was the alarm system. They shrugged their confusion at each other. *Strange.* Through the light of their torches they could see gaudy golds and voluptuous velvets, though nothing personal; nothing to hint at owners or inhabitants. Erotic artwork adorned the walls; Klimt's 'Frau bei der Selbstbefriedigung,' Bosch's 'Garden of Earthly Delights,' Hokusai's 'Dream of the Fisherman's Wife.' It looked like an upmarket whore house.

Louise halted momentarily after she had opened the door to a bedroom. Her mind was assessing a multitude of possible scenarios. None of them good. There were cameras in here. But not discreet ones. They were overt. Intimidatory. She checked quickly. They weren't connected. Her flash light scanned the bed. She froze. Zack tapped her on the shoulder and gestured towards the window. Headlights crept towards the house; tyres crunched along the gravel. Her chest thumped. She felt faint. She wanted to throw up. He gestured to the way they had just come. She nodded and they left, sure that they had covered their tracks. Left no clues. After they had climbed back out of the window Louise slid her knife through and closed the latch as the front door opened.

They ran across the lawn not looking back, just running; all too familiar. As they sped away on their bikes Louise's head was full of questions. Questions about the cameras, the handcuffs, the masks, the whips, but mostly about the child's bloodstained body which lay lifeless at the foot of the bed.

43

The ride home had dragged on and been done in silence, neither Zack nor Louise able to express what they were feeling, nor wanting to. Thoughts cluttered, words stuck, visions broke in to steal any semblance of comprehension. Flashbacks of what they had just seen pushed their way in front of everything else. It was relentless. Finally, back in their territory, they secured their bikes and hurried up to Ranulf's flat as if being back in there could wash away what they had witnessed. Make them feel safe. Clean again.

Zack finally broke the silence. 'What the fuck was that all about?' he asked, slumped on the settee. 'This is...I don't know! What the fuck?' He ruffled his hair with his fingers, his expression beyond incredulity, beyond revulsion. His face was pale. He felt sick.

'It looks like his penchants for raping little girls has stepped up to murder too,' Louise replied coldly. Her eyes inscrutable. She knew from previous investigations that there was nothing they could do. The van that pulled up as they were leaving would have been cleaners. The body would be gone. The place spotless. Richardson off the hook. 'It's like some sick movie, you know? If this wasn't happening to me I wouldn't believe it. Any of it!'

'Unreal. Totally unreal. What do we do? Jesus!'

'I'm going to get shit faced is what. Are you up for that?'

'Sure,' he replied gently, with the closest thing he could muster to a smile.

'I need to just get drunk. Get very, very drunk.' She poured a shot of vodka and downed it in a oner, slamming the glass down on the kitchen counter, followed immediately by another. 'I feel dirty. Just...dirty,' she mumbled. 'I need a wash.'

She stood in the shower, her hands pressed against the heavy glass tiles, her head bowed, water streaming through her thoughts. *Who the hell am I...?* Images spun around her head; the lodge, the cameras, Richardson with the child, the body, the blood, Richardson. They fought for supremacy. She felt faint. Drowning in it all. Struggling...

'You all right in there?' Zack called from the hall. 'You've been ages.'

'Shit.' She shook her head. Her skin was wrinkled, the air thick with steam. 'I got–lost–sorry,' she called back. She wished she had a key; a restart button. Something to change all of this. Any of this.

'No problem. Take as long as you want. I was just concerned, that was all.'

She wrapped herself in a thick, towelling robe and joined Zack in the sitting room. He smiled at her, his eyes concerned. Poured her a vodka. They got drunk. But there was no fun in this. No laughter or idle chatter or amused reminiscing. No release. Nothing but the dulling of senses. And even that didn't happen until they were barely able to speak coherently. They fell asleep where they were; Louise on the settee, Zack on the floor at her feet.

The following day the hangover from hell negated

any serious work being done. They watched old movies on cable television. Hid away from it all for a day. Pretended life was normal. For a day.

*

Their minds had to be kept busy, focused on something else. They began burying themselves in research, checking histories, news reports, anything at all related to Richardson, his family, his background, his rise to power. They had done all of this before. Neither of them expected anything new to come to light. They began to narrow it down to while they had been out of action. Last autumn to now. What had he been up to?

There had been another of his infamous speeches. More bile. More lies. More applause from his supporters. Louise baulked at every photograph, every picture of him smiling for the cameras as he preached the virtues of his all encompassing ID card system. How much easier life had become. The efficient functioning of the state and the economy. It flowed seamlessly. But was it really that simple? Louise and Zack doubted it. There had to be more, but they couldn't find it. Neither could they work it out. They both knew that they weren't operating at their best; weren't being as critical, or as thorough as they should be. Both knew that what they were really doing was waiting, killing time until Richardson went back to that little lodge house in the country.

Days turned to weeks with nothing of any consequence revealing itself. Their frustration was mounting and they had begun niggling at each other; the obsession of needing something to happen, something to offer a solution, had taken over. They fought to keep rationality to the fore, to not lose focus.

293

44

Louise stretched as she stepped away from the computer; her back was stiff, her shoulders clicked.

'Coffee?' she suggested.

Zack pulled his face taught, made his eyes stare, chattered his teeth. 'Sure. Need more caffeine!'

She laughed. 'Nutter.' She cleaned out the coffee machine; refilled it for the umpteenth time that day, and stared out at the vista before her. Lights flickered on in apartments, creating a surreal chequerboard in the darkening sky. An orange aura snaked above the city as street lights hummed on. Slivers of light escaped from the edges of drawn curtains. As she had done every day since her arrival here she wondered at what everyone out there was doing. How normal were their lives? Was it all just okay? Going along with this was okay? Could she imagine life ever feeling normal again? No she couldn't.

'Oh yeah,' Zack said excitedly.

She flicked her attention back to him, to here.

'Louise. Look, look, look. He's going back.'

The tracker was heading out of town in the direction of that little country lane. They both stared as it drew closer. It turned sharp right. He would be there in a matter of minutes.

'Are we ready for this?' Zack asked.

'Are you kidding me? I have never been more ready for anything in my life.'

Louise left the pre-written note for Ranulf so that there would be a record of what they had uncovered if they didn't make it back. They donned their biking gear and the backpacks that had been sitting ready in the hall. She set the alarm and nodded as she pulled the door closed behind her.

'Everything all right?' Jim, the security guard, called after them as they hurried through the entrance hall.

'Yeah, yeah,' Zack called back over his shoulder. 'Just gotta meet someone.'

'Right you are, son. Take it easy now,' Jim said, with a wave. As soon as they had left the building he picked up his phone and pressed auto dial.

The traffic was horrible, as always, but they were able to weave their way through the congestion, driving carefully, following the rules, not drawing attention to themselves. Despite its frustrations, for them, and others like them, rush hour was the best time to travel as there were fewer checks. You had more chance of avoiding detection. People wanted to get home. Traffic had to be kept moving. The regime wanted to have control, but they needed the compliance of the people. Keep frustrations to a minimum. Allow traffic to flow rather than tempers to fray.

They kept an eye on each other, chatting through the headsets in their helmets, passing comment on any warning signs, dangers, secure in the knowledge that their conversation couldn't be intercepted.

'Something's going on up there,' Zack said. 'Best pull up.'

'Yes. I see it. Okay.'

There was a commotion up ahead of them and the

road was blocked by military looking vehicles; open-topped Jeeps with armed men in uniform. Zack pulled up, Louise behind him. A crowd had gathered. Some held placards, others sang and shouted. New Dawn, in riot gear, were pushing them back to the cheers and sneers of the Union Jack waving mob behind them. Shaved heads, tight jeans, khaki bomber jackets, Doc Martens, yeah, she knew that uniform well.

In the harshness of the spotlights they could see a little suburban house behind the barricades being emptied of its occupants; two adults clinging to their children, being dragged into the back of an unmarked van. The children cried. The adults stared with eyes wild. They had been hiding there for the past five months. It hadn't been easy, especially for the children, but they had clung on to the hope that something might change. If they could just stay hidden for long enough there was always the possibility, a chance. Anything was better than the repatriation camps; the return to the war-torn rubble of what had once been a place called home. The ghosts of dead friends and relatives. Behind the family came two more figures with bags pulled over their heads. They stood tall. Trying their best to be defiant. They had been the keepers of the safe house.

The majority of raids were carried out at night, or very early in the morning, quietly, unseen by most. Not publicised. It was easier to get things done that way. Dispose of the problem with the minimum of fuss. Occasionally however, New Dawn would make a show of it, particularly if a ring had been uncovered, as had happened in this case. Too many organised sympathisers were a danger and they had to be taught a lesson, humiliated. Ordinary people wanted the reassurance that everything was under control; that the threat of illegals was almost over. Dealt with. Friendly press would be forewarned, a few local Nazis invited. A last minute leak would be dropped for the liberals. It was vital that government showed its strength, its power to keep the streets clean; its people safe. Participating in the hiding of migrants, illegals, would result in being caught and sentenced to a lengthy stay in a re-education camp. Your property would be removed from you. None of your old life left for you to return to. The Nazis and the liberals weren't kept apart. A contained amount of public disorder was good. Look at the trouble they cause. Look at how well we deal with it.

Louise fought against the urge to go down there. To do something. *Fuck*! She looked to Zack who grimaced, reading her thoughts, sharing her frustration. They turned their bikes around and rode off, feeling shit.

45

The detour they had been forced to take was an inconvenience, losing them time, altering their plan slightly, but they were confident enough that Richardson wouldn't be going anywhere in a hurry. If their thinking was right he would stay until the early hours at least, probably until the morning. The city lights now a subdued dusting behind them, they hid their bikes in the cover of the same hedge as last time and climbed the wall at the same place.

Once over, they knew they had to be even more careful than they had been on their last visit. This time lights were on, two cars were parked out front, and one of them was Richardson's Jaguar. They were sure security, of some sort, would be in operation tonight. They doubted bodyguards as this wasn't official business; far from it. It was something to be kept secret, hidden from all but those taking part. But you never knew. Best to plan for the worst.

Louise enjoyed the feel of the shoulder holster which held her gun, the confidence it gave her, the power, the confirmation of why she was here. The change in her circumstances. Prey to predator. Now she held the upper hand.

They repeated their circumnavigation of the grounds, clinging to the shadows of the trees and the cover of the wall, checking, taking no chances. Louise started as a couple of deer took flight when the security lights glared at them for encroaching into forbidden territory. They scampered off to join the rest of their herd at the wood's edge. She exhaled deeply and shook her head, stifling a nervous laugh.

She felt Zack's hand firmly on her shoulder. 'Okay?' he whispered.

She nodded. 'Yes, fine. I should have remembered from last time. Let's wait here a bit. See what's going on,' she answered in tones so hushed they were barely audible.

'Sure. At least we know that the deer turn the lights on and by default, so would we.'

'Yes.'

They sat in the cold, the dark, and the damp, their backs against the crumbling stone of the wall, their breath seeming loud and intrusive. The heavy musty scent of the ivy that smothered the wall, clutched at the trees, was almost unpleasant. They watched and waited, searching through the darkness at each rustle of leaves, snap of twig, until an innocuous reason was confirmed. For once Louise was inwardly cursing the wildlife.

Finally something was happening at the house. Zack nudged Louise in the ribs. She nodded. The front door opened and two small figures ran out, caught in the spotlight of the security lights. They were children, a boy and a girl, dressed only in their underwear. The lights in the house flicked off. It was suddenly pitch dark until their eyes became accustomed and shadows appeared. A man's voice could be heard counting down from ten.

'Ready or not!' it bellowed.

'Here we come!' Richardson added with a laugh, as

299

they ran after the children.

'Tally-ho!' the first voice called.

The children bolted for the cover of the woods. They had no idea of what they were running to, what lay beyond the shadows, but they knew full well what they were running from. The girl stumbled and fell, letting out a cry. The boy dragged her to her feet and pulled her silently onwards. When they reached the woods they slipped from tree to tree, trying to be invisible. The boy thought about staying still, just hiding. Or should they run further? To where? To what? The girl began to cry. The boy wrapped his arms around her. Urged her on. They had to keep running.

Richardson and his partner split up, sweeping the woods from both sides, calling to each other, to the children. Their footsteps were heavy, rough, no attempt at stealth. They were drawing closer to the children; closer to Louise and Zack.

The boy whimpered as something sliced through his foot.

The girl spoke with her eyes. Staring. *Shh*. She tugged at the boy's arm and pulled him on, leading him deeper into the cover of the trees. They were running blind, with no idea of where they were, who was chasing them, why this was all happening. It seemed that all they had spent their lives doing was running. They could remember nothing but that. Running. Being afraid and running. When they had been with their parents they had been running from war. The swoop of aeroplanes. A tide of bombs. Snipers taking aim from abandoned buildings. Death, and danger all around them. Years of it. One makeshift stopping point to another. One camp to another. Home wasn't even a memory. It didn't exist. A concept that was alien to them. And now there was this. Was there anything other than this?

They heard something. A movement too close. It was right there. They froze. The boy squeezing the girl's hand; part in an attempt at reassurance, part in fear. They barely dared to breathe. Hands clamped their mouths and held them tight.

Louise tugged off her balaclava with her free hand, crouching down to their level, and tried her damnedest to force a friendly smile. An attempt at some form of comfort. 'It's okay. It's okay,' she whispered. 'We're here to help you. Shh.'

The children stared through drugged eyes. Fear and confusion.

Louise and Zack took off their jackets and draped them over the children's bruised bodies. No words. They formed a chain – Louise at the front, then the children, then Zack – and slowly, quietly, crept along the wall. The two huntsmen drew closer together.

'Can't see a bloody trace of them Nige. You?' a voice called through the silence.

'Cunning little buggers. Makes the hunt all the more fun though, what? The tougher the chase the sweeter the reward.'

'Indeed!'

The voices sounded far enough away. They had time to get the children out of there. Louise fired the rope at the wall, clambered up, and with Zack's help hoisted the children onto the wall. Zack held on to them; pointed out the glass. They stood on trembling legs, their small bare feet precariously balanced on either side of the glass. Louise leapt down to the other side. She stood arms outstretched, as first the girl, then the boy jumped into them. Zack stayed on the wall, keeping watch.

An unnerving sound. The hum of traffic. Louise listened intently. It sounded like a solitary vehicle. Headlights split up the night. She pulled the children tight against the wall. Possible scenarios flew through her head. This could be another of Richardson's number, security of some sort, a patrol. It could also be an innocent driver. Someone to help. To take the children to safety. No. She couldn't take that chance.

The car drove on by. She ran across the road holding on to each of their hands. Small vulnerable hands that didn't cling back, as if they had no strength left in them. Nothing more to give. She sat them down beside the bikes, covering them with the jackets. The scurry of a night creature in flight scratched its way through the hedge. Something small and fast. A stoat perhaps. Then the swoop of an owl. Powerful wings beating through the air, almost touching them. A squeal. Prey caught.

'You must stay here, okay? Just stay here and help will come.' She had no idea if they had understood or not and gestured with her hands as best she could to reinforce the words. Pulled her finger to her lips. 'Ssh.' They had just stared as she tugged at the hedge, trying to draw it further around them. She bolted back across the road, ran at the wall, reached for Zack's outstretched hand, caught it. He pulled her up and they let themselves slip back down into the grounds.

Once more they kept to the wall. They knew they had the advantage as they tracked the cumbersome footsteps and heavy breathing. The one they were on the trail of wasn't Richardson. He was squatter, fatter, clumsy. They crept in his footsteps, doing their utmost not to make any sound. The snap of a twig. The man stopped. Listened.

'Okay my sweets, come to daddy,' he whispered, cocking his rifle. He turned around, caught a shadow flit behind a tree. Heard a breath. 'Over here Nige!' he called in triumph, sure that he had found them. He lunged at the tree. There was nothing. 'Confound it!' Another shadow, this time on the other side. Had they split up? Plucky little things! He leapt towards the shadow. 'Got you!'

Only he hadn't.

Louise let fly at the man's arm and kicked the rifle out of his hands. She spun and aimed another kick at his face, sending him slumping to the ground. Blood dripped out of his broken nose.

'You bitch!' he hissed.

She stood above him, smiling, her gun pointing at his forehead and stamped on his groin. *Thank you Ranulf.* – Always play dirty, he'd said. Mean and dirty, cos sure as hell they will. – The man curled into a whimpering, foetal ball. 'Shut it!' she hissed. Zack had already taken the duct tape out of his bag. They wrapped the tape around the man's mouth more securely than necessary so that it cut into his ruddy cheeks. They bound his legs together and secured him to a tree.

'Fuck you,' Louise whispered venomously, as she spat in his face before heading off to find Richardson.

She crept from tree to tree, keeping her footsteps light, as near to silent as possible. She could feel Zack right behind her. No need to check. It was taking longer than she would have liked – she was so close, so god-dammed close – but she couldn't slip up. Wouldn't allow herself to slip up. Retribution would be hers.

'Jeremy?' Richardson called. 'Where are you, old boy?'

Silence.

'Stop playing silly buggers will you? Show yourself man!'

Silence.

'Bugger.'

46

She was so close now that she could smell him. The whisky on his breath, his expensive cologne. Barely breathing, barely moving, she crept closer until she was absolutely sure. Timing it perfectly, she lunged at him and swept the legs from under him.

He tried to aim his gun at her as he lay on his back, the disbelief screeching from his face. Who the hell would dare to do such a thing? He could see little more than a shadow, but it was most definitely an adult one.

She kneed him in the throat and he curled into a ball moaning. The satisfaction, the pleasure it gave her to see him writhing in pain. Zack stomped on Richardson's arm. A crack, perhaps the break of a bone. It didn't matter. He picked up the gun. They handcuffed his arms behind his back and hauled him, face first, across the lawns. Louise smiled at the groans he let slip as his protesting body bounced off the steps and into the lodge. They threw him onto the floor in the corner of the kitchen. Marble and steel, everything sparkling, everything fitted, everything top of the range, bespoke, now splattered with blood and dirt.

They distastefully searched him, as if he carried some contagious disease, removing his mobile, house and car keys. This car didn't operate through his ID, neither the lodge. Some things were best kept secure, even from security.

'Unlock the phone!' Zack demanded thrusting the sliver of precious metals in Richardson's face.

'Over my dead –'

'Easily arranged,' Louise said, aiming her gun at his head.

'Unlock it!'

This time he obeyed. These people, whoever they were, had no time for games. They meant business and he valued his life more than what was on his phone. He would get through this, get out of this, and finish them soon enough.

Zack scanned through the recent calls and texts. No contact names, only numbers and emojis. He raised his eyebrows at Louise. 'Interesting,' he said quietly, pocketing the phone.

'Do you have any idea who the bloody hell you're dealing with here? Any idea of the kind of trouble you're in?' he coughed at them through a painful windpipe.

Louise smiled. 'Oh yes, Daddy dear.' She kicked his head and it slumped forward, chin to chest. 'The question is do you?' She peeled off her balaclava.

He lifted his head slowly, squinted, tried to focus, stared at her. A contemptuous smile began to spread across his face as he recognised the bone structure, the perfect curve of her lip, the shape of her eyes. 'You're dead,' he said, forcing a laugh. 'You were supposed to be already, but you most certainly are now!'

'Wrong on both counts. You see, I'm very much in charge here and you? You're going down. Predator to prey just like that. How does it feel, huh?' She stroked the gun across his sweaty forehead. 'Knowing. Your. Time. Is. Up.' Each word precise, slow, threatening.

'Look. Let's get things into perspective here, shall we?' Richardson blustered, momentarily losing his cool, dragging it back. 'No need to blow all of this out of proportion. As you well know I am a very wealthy and powerful man. You could start a new life. Wealthy expatriates somewhere exotic. Wouldn't that be nice? Hmm? A delicious little island far away from all of this.'

'Let's get a few things straight, shall we? You've lost...this,' she twirled the gun around. 'Whatever this is. You've lost. And I'm going to so enjoy pulling the trigger.'

He sneered. 'Really? You'd turn your back on a second chance like that? Don't be a fool.'

She kicked him in the ribs. 'Yes, really!'

His head slumped again.

'I wouldn't mess with her if I were you,' Zack interjected. 'You don't want to make her angry.'

Richardson lifted his head back up, took a deep breath. Composed himself again. 'You do realise security are on their way. Automatic, you see, when the code isn't pressed,' he said smugly. 'Last chance. Name your price and this will all be forgotten. You have my word.'

'No price,' she sneered. 'And even if there was, your word's not worth shit.'

'Two million,' he offered.

'As I said.'

'Ten million. Come on now. Don't be a fool all of your life. Ten million. Imagine it.'

'You know not everyone stoops to your level,' Zack said. 'The lady said no deal.'

'Oh, how touching. He really does stick up for you, doesn't he? Is that the attraction then? A little lap dog?'

He turned to face Zack. 'What is it you're calling yourself these days?'

'None of your god-damned business,' Zack replied.

'I would imagine another two minutes, or so, and you, my little half cast immigrant friend, and my beloved daughter, will be taken care of. Properly this time. I may even do it myself,' he said, with a self congratulatory smile. 'Good fuck is she? Her mother certainly was. A little wild cat, that girl. Sad to see her go really. Convenient, in your own house, you know? But she was getting too old for my tastes.' He winked salaciously at Zack.

Zack cracked the side of Richardson's head with the butt of his gun. He was out cold. 'I so fucking enjoyed that!' he said, with no enjoyment at all.

'That shit about alarms. You're sure you disconnected it all?'

'Absolutely.'

'Let's try and bring the bastard round then.'

47

Richardson came to gasping for breath, spluttering through bowlfuls of water which Zack was dousing him with. He lifted his head up with great effort, as if it had somehow become too heavy for his neck. Louise took hold of his hair and pulled his head up, forcing his eyes to meet hers.

'How did you know? How did you find out who I was?' she demanded.

His eyes seemed to struggle to focus, then closed again.

'Ah, shit! Give him another will you?'

Zack willingly obliged. It didn't work. He was out cold again.

They waited, impatiently, both just staring at him, willing him to come around. The red light of the clock on the oven pulsed off the worktops, flicking away the minutes. Five. Ten. Fifteen.

Finally his eyes opened. His head shifted. He stared at her.

She kicked at his leg, asked again. 'How did you know?'

'It was your grandmother,' he spluttered, spitting out a mouthful of blood. 'Stupid woman,' he added boorishly, pulling his faculties back, bringing his strength to the fore. Rising above it all. 'Beautiful, but stupid. Kept clippings, notes and dates in her sewing basket. How pitiful.' He laughed as if remembering the punch line to a joke. 'Came across them one day. Thought I should pursue it. Paid a visit to her friends at that God awful retreat. They always blab, those types, hippies, earthy mother nature types. She blabbed. Told me all about the little deception; your existence.' He smiled at her.

'And so you killed her?'

'Now, now.' His words dripped with condescension. 'She had an accident. A traffic accident, wasn't it?'

'What about my mother? Your wife's daughter? Do you know where she is now?'

'I do indeed. Heroin addict. Quite common amongst these musician types. Overdosed a few weeks ago I believe. In a morgue somewhere, perhaps even buried. I wouldn't know.'

'You bastard!' The shock hit her in the stomach. No, the woman hadn't meant anything to her, but she was her mother. There was that connection. It hurt. Another layer of pain inflicted by this man. But she wasn't going to let him see it. She wouldn't allow him that satisfaction. Anger was an easy emotion to saturate herself with. Its supremacy clung fast. She stared at him, unflinching. Cold.

'Oh, come now. None of this would have had to happen if she'd simply aborted the thing.' He smirked. 'Aborted you!'

'Shut the fuck up,' Zack interrupted, kicking him in the stomach. 'She's worth a million of you, you disgusting excuse for a human being. I can't believe you had any part in her creation.'

'That was just it, wasn't it? My flesh and blood, my DNA. I wasn't about to allow a little sexual escapade to

310

ruin everything for me, now was I?'

She kept her cool. It would have been easy to kill him there and then. Satisfying. But she wanted to know more. She wanted to be sure of what had been ticking away in her mind; the sequence of events.

'You knew before, didn't you? You knew about me before we ran to Cornwall? You put them on to us, on to me.'

He smiled. 'Clever girl. That was such an exceptional piece of luck, don't you think? You being a little trouble maker. Everything falling into place. Click, click, click.' His fingers danced to each word. 'Our splendid security forces mopping up for me.'

'Only they didn't.' She pointed the gun, aiming it at his head. 'Did they?'

He smiled, looking through her; looking behind her.

'I wouldn't do that if I were you, lass,' came a voice she knew from behind her.

She turned and stared, unable to believe what she saw. There stood Ranulf. The man who had saved her life. The man to whom she had bared everything. The man she had grown to trust implicitly. He was dressed in the uniform of New Dawn.

'I did tell you. The alarm. I wasn't bluffing, you know?' Richardson said with customary conceit.

'But we disabled it,' Zack said.

'You did that, lad, aye. Quite impressed with it all. Quite a team!'

'I don't get this at all and I don't give a shit,' Louise spat. 'He.' the safety clicked off as she turned and took aim. 'He dies.'

'Naw, dinnae, lass. And you, lad. You put the gun down now.' His voice was controlled, authoritative.

Zack looked at Louise and shook his head. 'No. I'm

311

with her. Whatever she says goes.'

'The two of you listen, and listen good. The uniform's fake. Best way to get around these days, no questions asked, aye? I'm on your side, guys. You know that. Inside of you, you know that. But you need to think. Keep him alive. Expose him for the murdering paedophile that he is, along with his pals, and the pieces start to crumble. He's worth far more to you, to us, alive than dead. And neither of you are killers now, are you? Come on, behave yourselves. That wee note you left for me at the flat – dynamite. When we link it all up he's a goner. You know what they do to paedophiles in prison. What do you reckon they're going to do to the likes of him, eh? If he lives, he's going to be wishing he was dead, like.'

'He's got a point,' Zack said quietly.

'I think not,' Richardson interjected. 'You have nothing on me other than hearsay. A note?' he scoffed. 'That won't get you far. Your word? Any of you? A couple of illegals. A disgraced drop-out from the forces. Not a chance in hell.'

'Aye, well, I beg to differ on that one,' Ranulf replied, though in truth he was concerned. Of course he was. These people spend their lives squirming their way out of trouble. The Teflon brigade. Too much power. Too many friends in high places. Too many people not wanting to look; not caring. He kept his doubts to himself.

'How did you know where to find us?' Louise asked.

'A friend called me. Said he thought something was up. I followed the trackers and hey presto! Now, are you going to put the guns down, or what?'

'So, you've been here, in London, the whole time?' Louise asked.

'Naw, up and down. You didn't think I'd want to miss out on all the fun now, did you?'

She lowered her gun and put the safety back on. 'So why lead me here? Tell me about my mum, about Sophie?'

'You had a right to know and I wasn't one hundred percent sure about him,' he nodded towards Richardson, being behind everything. Thought he might enjoy telling you about it. And surprise, surprise, he did. I think you needed to do this anyway. To see the bastard suffer, aye? See him done for. Come on now. Weapons.'

He gestured for them to hand them over.

Zack did. She didn't.

'This is mine, remember?' she said, eyebrows raised, eyes fixed on his. 'Keeping it.' She tucked it back into its holster.

Ranulf laughed. 'Aye, no surprises there. Right you are. Now, let's get the polis, that's my polis, not his, and put an end to this.'

'The kids! Shit. They're still out there,' Zack said.

'What kids? Where?'

'The two this fucker was chasing are hiding out by our bikes.'

'Right. You two go. Get the children into my Jeep and off you go. Let me deal with this. My territory, aye? Go!'

'There's another one of his–his type, tied to a tree somewhere out there,' Louise told him.

'Right you are. Away home.'

48

Ranulf watched Louise and Zack from the open door as they hurried out of the grounds, and disappeared around the corner. He turned back to face Richardson, rubbed his chin, narrowed his eyes, chewed on his lip.

Richardson laughed. 'What the bloody hell's happened to you. Got a thing for her or something?' he said contemptuously.

'It's got fuck all to do with you, pal,' he sneered, as he knocked him unconscious again. 'Fuck all and everything.' He pressed call on his mobile. 'Aye, it's me. Those coordinates I sent you. Get a team over. Aye, keep it low key. Quiet. Just a hundred percenters. This one's big.'

As he waited he stared at the man who had caused so much damage. He remembered the orders. He remembered the threats. Mostly he remembered the death of the kid he'd promised something to. A promise he'd failed to keep.

*

It had been a messed up operation out in the Middle East. Sometimes that happens. Things just don't go to plan. He'd been getting help from a young local. His informant (too young really but you took what you could get, and kids, well, they could move around more freely without raising suspicion) had been exposed.

314

Right from the outset he'd been promised a way out. If it all went wrong there was an escape route planned, UK visas and citizenship for him and his family. It was the best way to ensure compliance, also the only way Ranulf would operate. They had done their best; done what was asked of them. The mission was over and he was about to return. When his final orders came through they read, "Subjects to be terminated." He'd read and re-read. This had to be wrong. He tried contacting Richardson. Again and again he had called. This was wrong. This wasn't the way things were meant to work out. He had given his word. Finally when he was put through all Richardson said was, 'No discussion here. Termination, or you know the consequences. Do it.'

Ranulf had refused to carry out his orders. He was a lot of things but not a murderer. A life would be taken if his was at risk, if he got caught up in a gunfight, an attack. But not like this. When he went to the boy's house that night he was going to try and smuggle them out somehow. Sneak them onto a plane. Bluff it. It wouldn't be the first time. Deals could be reneged upon; rules could be broken in both directions.

As he walked along the dusty road towards the house he could sense that something was wrong. There was no noise, no chatter, none of the usual sounds drifted out on the heavy night air, only the plaintive barking of the dog who was pacing up and down as if somehow demented. He cowered when Ranulf approached.

'It's okay, boy,' Ranulf whispered softly, though clearly it wasn't. He held out his hand so that the dog could sniff that he meant no harm. He was not an enemy.

The dog began panting heavily, his eyes bulging, staring in terror. Ranulf stroked the dog's head. 'Ssh

315

boy. Ssh.' He crept forward inching closer to the house, his gun drawn. The door was hanging ajar. When he tapped it further open he knew the escape wasn't going to happen. The air was heavy with the buzz of flies. He could smell blood. He could sense death. It hung there like a dirty monstrosity. He struck a match, fearing what would greet his eyes as the flickering light broke through the blackness. He lifted the match high, it's light stretching along the walls, across the floor. It had been dinner time. The low table was set with bowls of untouched food, glasses of water, a bowl of fruit. He cursed as the flame burned his fingers. He dropped the match, struck another. His eyes settled on body after body. Despite his repugnance he had to check every one of them. There were thirteen in all. Three generations of the family wiped out. But the boy wasn't there.

He went back outside and waited, the dog's head settled across his lap; both of their senses finely tuned to every noise, every flicker of movement. By morning he realised that the kid wasn't coming home. He moved on to the wasteland where they would meet in times of danger. Once a vibrant suburb, it was now a desolate ruin. Sure enough, the boy was there, sitting against a wall in the remnants of someone else's home. Pictures still clung to the bullet ridden walls. A curtain flapped against broken glass. Rubble and forlorn furniture, ruined lives and mortar shells. Rats scuttled amongst the debris. A pair of vultures tore at the flesh of something unidentifiable. Crows fought for the scraps. The boy stared, waved weakly, then got to his feet, wiping the tears from his face.

'I'm so sorry, lad.' What else could he say? Words. Only words.

'You promised. You said –'

The boy slumped to the ground. A bullet in his head. Ranulf ran, ducking behind collapsing walls, twisting through abandoned alleyways, jumping over debris. He had no way of knowing who was behind this. All he could do now was get out. He did.

49

Ranulf found the security hub, overrode the system and opened the gates. The lodge was soon being gone over by special forces. People he knew. People he trusted. He watched as they searched for evidence: fingerprints, DNA, photographs of all of the rooms, the cameras, the shackles. When they were done they took Richardson to their HQ. Ranulf followed in his Jeep.

'Good to see you back, McKenzie,' the officer said to Ranulf, with a salute.

Ranulf smiled at him. 'Not back, just making a wee delivery,' he said, with a wink.

'You sure?'

'Oh aye. I'll just see this lot being checked in and be on my way.'

'That's a shame. We've missed you, mate, you know?'

'Aye well... Just make sure none of this goes astray, including them.' He gestured towards Richardson and his accomplice who were being led down to the basement.

'Right you are. So this is as big as you thought, is it?'

'Bigger. He and a few others are going down.'

'That is who I think it is?'

'Aye.'

The officer exhaled with a heavy whistle.

'Don't let him out of your sight. No calls. No nothing. Got that?'

'I'll do my best, but –'

'No. Just do it. You'll hear from me, or one of the team, soon enough.'

'Right you are. Old style?'

'Old style!' he winked.

Ranulf looked back as he headed out through the door. Back on his old life. A life very different. A life he didn't miss. He climbed into his Jeep and stroked Volki's head. 'Good lad,' he said. 'You been watching the bairns for me?' He smiled at the two children huddled in the back seat. 'Now you sit nice. Just a wee bit longer.' They were back at his flat in no time.

'I need clothes for these two, Jim,' Ranulf said to the security guard in his apartment block.

The children, barefoot, were still draped in leathers far too big for them.

'Oh, deary me. Poor little mites. I'll get right on it. Call the missus.'

'Excellent. Thanks. And not a word eh? Witnesses.' He tapped his nose.

'Well, I'll be blown. You know you can trust me, Mr. McKenzie sir.'

'Aye, I do that.'

*

'Have they said anything yet?' Louise asked.

'Not a word. Could be trauma. Could be they don't speak a word of English,' Ranulf replied.

Louise knelt down in front of them and smiled. 'Do you understand me? Can you speak English?'

The girl turned her head into the boys shoulder, hiding her face. The boy looked blankly at her.

319

'Vy ponimayete?' Zack tried in Russian.

'Is okay,' the boy replied in a broken whisper. 'I know little English.'

'Good. You know you are safe now, with good people?' Zack continued.

'Yes.'

'Okay. Are you two family?'

'Yes. She my sister, Ilinca.'

'And you? What's your name?'

'Bogdan. I Bogdan.'

'Okay, Bogdan. Good. Look, would you like to get cleaned up? Have a bath? A shower?'

'Yes. Together. We stay together.'

'Okay. No problem. Come on then,' Zack said, as he led them into the bathroom.

An hour later the children were washed, dressed in new clothes and asleep.

'What do we do with them now?' Zack asked.

'We need to talk to them. Keep them safe. See what unfolds,' Ranulf replied. 'I'm hoping this'll all go through quickly, aye? We need to see.'

'What do you reckon? All Richardson's powerful friends? Are they going to drop him like a brick when it all comes out?'

'I wish!' he shrugged, grimaced. 'There's no way to predict these days, is there now? Folk like that, New Dawn. Aye, well, you just don't know. But meantime all of us. That's me, that's you two, that's the bairns. We all need to stay low for a while. Stay safe.'

'Here?'

'Aye. Safe as anywhere here. No-one's getting in without me knowing and we need to keep close by. Statements to make, evidence to give and the likes, aye?'

'Right,' Louise said. 'I don't know how I feel about that. Talking to the police, you know?' She looked at Zack whose expression shared her concern.

'Yeah, know what you mean,' he replied to her questioning look. 'Our experiences with the law haven't been too good to date, in fact, ever.'

'Aye, right enough. But there's polis and there's *polis*, if you get my drift. You trust me, don't you?' Ranulf put in reassuringly.

'Of course, yeah.'

'Right then. It'll all be good. You'll see.'

50

Two days later the children were called in to make their statements. The investigation wasn't being carried out by the Metropolitan Police or New Dawn but by an elite unit set up by people Ranulf could trust in the secret service. Ranulf drove them to the covert control centre. Press and official police hadn't been informed. This was going nowhere until they were absolutely sure that there was no way out for Richardson or anyone else involved.

'Right, Bogdan lad, there's nothing for you to worry about, aye? Just tell them what happened. Tell them everything you know. They're the good guys,' Ranulf said through a forced smile and with as much reassurance as he could muster.

They were met at the entrance by four plain-clothed officers. All armed. All on high alert. Two of them hurried Ranulf, Louise, Zack and the children in through a heavy, metal, unmarked door which stood in the red brick wall of an industrial unit. The other two checked the street before following them in and bolting the door.

'Scary as shit,' Zack whispered to Louise.

'No kidding! Do you even know where we are?'

'No clue.'

Ranulf was ahead of them, in conversation with one of the officers. The other took up the rear. Louise and

322

Zack each held the hands of the children, who were strangely passive, quiet, just accepting. They were led along a bleak corridor, concrete floor, concrete walls, no windows, angry strip lighting. The sound of footsteps and heavy breath echoed along the corridor. Another door, another corridor, steps down to a basement. A small room with a handful of desks, computers clicking, a hive of activity. Cold, sterile, efficient.

They were greeted by a female officer. She smiled. 'Right, you two. If you'll just come with me?' she said, reaching for the children's hands. 'This shouldn't take too long. If you just take a seat here?' she said to Louise, Zack and Ranulf, gesturing to a row of plastic chairs against the wall.

'They're not going to do this on their own. We're coming too,' Louise said firmly.

'Sorry, miss. Regulations. You're not their parents so _'

'Screw regulations. We're the closest they have to parents right now and we're going with them. End of!'

The officer looked to Ranulf who shrugged and smiled. 'She's got a point there, aye? Doubt you'll get a word out of them on their own anyway. Best if we all just stick together.'

'Okay. On your head,' the officer said.

Ranulf laughed. 'Aye, right you are then!'

They were taken into another small room. It smelled dusty and unused. There was a table and four chairs, two on each side. The children were seated opposite two plain-clothed officers. One male, one female.

'Okay. Now, if you can just tell us what happened. From the beginning. As much as you can,' the female asked.

'From this night only or from when they take us?'

Bogdan answered, his little sister clinging to his arm. He had been the only one to speak since that day. Ilinca remained silent, withdrawn, frightened.

'From when they took you, sweetheart. If you can. Where was that? Where they took you from?'

He hesitated, biting his lip, hanging his head. 'It was camp. Immigrant camp. I not know where. My mama and papa was gone. I not know where.'

'You're doing great. It's okay,' Louise comforted him, standing behind him, her hands on his shoulders.

'It was many days and we not see them. Many children with us. All same. All with no mama, no papa.' He took a deep breath and straightened his shoulders. 'We are put in car with lady. She take us to house. They wash us, in garage with pipe and bad smell things. It burns.'

'They? Who were they?'

'This lady and one other. I not know. They give us injection. Medicine, they say.'

'This house. Was it the house where we – her eyes glanced up to meet Louise's – where they found you?'

'No. Different house.'

'Was it nearby? Near to the other house?'

'No. It very far. They not let us see. They keep us in boot of car. It is black. All I hear is engine noise. This noise of wheels, banging like this.' He thumped his little fists on the table in a fast rhythmic beat. 'Smell of benzine and bad smell. Smell of medicine. They tie us like this.' He held his hands out in front of him, his wrists together. He stared at the officer as if asking for an explanation. 'Our legs too, same. They put tape over mouths, like this.' He gestured tape being roughly secured over his mouth. He was angry.

Despite the fact that Louise had heard this all before,

it didn't make it any easier, any less uncomfortable. It had come out in tiny pieces over the past two days, odd moments when Bogdan felt courageous enough, strong enough, to talk to them. To let them in. Of course, she had heard about atrocities like this. She was a journalist, it was her job. But to be a part of it. To be here with the children that she'd been taking care of...this was different.

'Okay. That's fine. Are you all right, Bogdan? Can I ask you a few more questions?'

'Yes.'

'This lady. Did you see her?'

'Yes. I see.'

'Can I show you some pictures?'

'Yes.'

'Just point to anyone you recognise,' she said, as she placed a succession of pictures on the table in front of them.

Ilinca wouldn't look. Wouldn't participate in any of it.

Bogdan shook his head. 'No. No.' He sighed. 'No.' Then he stabbed his finger at the latest one. 'This one. Yes this one.'

'Well done. Okay. Just a few more.'

He had pointed to two pictures of Clarissa Knightley, provider of select prostitutes to the rich and famous. They had already been pretty confident that it was her. Her fingerprints had been found at the lodge. Her number was on Richardson's phone. This gave them the confirmation they needed.

'I know this isn't easy Bogdan, but we need to know what happened at the house. Can you tell us what they did to you? The men at the house.'

He did his best to tell what had happened to him and

his sister. The beatings, the repeated rapes, the hunt. It was difficult, partly because his memory had been affected by the drugs he had been given, partly because recalling it was painful, humiliating, disgusting.

A few hours later they went after Knightley. There was no-one at her residence. Signs of a rushed departure. Her clients were powerful. Politicians and peers. She felt they had more class, more discretion. She also knew that if she talked that would be the end of her. There was no option left for her but to accept the escape route she had been offered. A stranger in an anonymous car. No words. No explanations.

Twenty four hours later there had still been no sightings of Knightley. They decided it was now best for all of this to go public. U-tell had the story up first. The abuse and murder of a child. The pictures Louise had taken that first night. The probability that this wasn't an isolated incident. Despite the protestations of the best solicitors money could buy, Richardson remained in custody, as did his co-accused. There may not have been any evidence to link them to the murder, but Bogdan and Ilinca had identified them. Surely that was enough.

*

Louise, Zack and Ranulf were watching events unfold from the seclusion of the penthouse.

'Is this really it? Is it all over?' Louise asked.

'Getting there, aye. I don't reckon there's any way back for Richardson now. The rest of that shower? Who knows. But you?'

She cocked her head. 'Me what?'

'You need to think about what you want to do. Do you want to tell the whole story. Get it out there then, well, you're safe, aye? It's done and Richardson has absolutely no power over you. Up to you, though.' He shrugged, raised his eyebrows, part in question, part in suggestion.

'That would mean I'd have to come clean about what he is to me. That's hard. That's really, really hard.'

'Aye, and you're a tough wee lassie!'

'Hmm. And there's the police to deal with, his lawyers, interrogations. I don't think they'd just let me be. Do you? I mean, seriously?'

'Probably not. Up to you, lass. Up to you.'

She sat in silence for a while, weighing it all up. It felt like she'd had enough.

'What name are you going to go by now? Do you want to go back to Suze or stay with Louise?'

'Louise, I guess. It feels safer somehow. A new me.'

'Right then. You could tell your story as Suzanna. No pictures. No-one except for us three know about Louise and Zack. Safe as–' he smiled.

'You could also do it anonymously, couldn't you? I mean it makes no difference to anyone who you are. Just what he did and who your father is,' Zack said, hopefully. He caught her gaze. Took her hand. 'You're done in, aren't you.'

She fought back a tear. Stood up and walked across to the window. The view that had helped her focus, gather her thoughts, make the right decisions. She turned back to them.

'You know what? I am. Done! I need to get my head together again somehow. Cleanse myself of this. Become me again.'

'Fair enough,' Ranulf said. 'And you know what these bloody journalists are like, eh?' Ranulf added with a grin. 'They'll not give you peace.'

'Cheeky bastard!' Louise said, laughing back at him.

327

'I'm heading back up north tomorrow, aye.' Ranulf declared. 'How about you two? You can stay here as long as you want. I'll not be seeing this place again for a while.'

'They couldn't tempt you back then?' Louise asked.

'Naw. Enough of that. Done my time.'

'Dogs and stuff?' Louise said with a grin.

'Aye. Dogs and stuff.' He grinned back.

'Can I ask you–?'

'Aw, here we go. Aye? What?'

'What happened? Back then, when you jacked it all in. What happened?'

'Acht. There was a family. A wee boy. They were helping me. I'd been told they were protected, but... Aye, turns out they weren't.'

'And Richardson? There's some history there, isn't there?'

'Aye. Hate the man, probably as much as you. Enough said, eh?'

'But did you work for him? He was secret services for a while, wasn't he?'

'I did and he was. For a long while. That's how he was able to wangle all that nonsense with you and Zack there. Friends in the right places. Knowledge of the system. Aye.'

'But you personally?'

'Christ she's like a bloody dog with a bone, eh?' he said to Zack, with a wink. 'Not letting it go are you, eh? Sometimes you should just accept it.'

'Accept what?'

'Defeat, lass. Defeat is what.'

'Oh come on. This is going to eat away at me. You know that. It's why I'm good at my job.'

'Speaking of which. What ARE you going to do?

328

The pair of you?'

'I could write a book!' she laughed.

'You could.'

'But I think I'll stick with journalism. There's still plenty work to do. Plenty slime bags to expose.'

'One thing though,' Ranulf said.

'Yes? What?'

'I need to stay hidden. My part in everything, where I live, here and up north. No-one gets to know, aye? I need a promise on that one.'

'Absolutely, Ranulf.' She looked at him quizzically. 'Is it Ranulf? Ranulf McKenzie? Or McKenzie? Or something else entirely?'

'That you'll never know,' he said with a finality. 'And after tomorrow, when I leave, no contact.'

'But—'

'No contact.'

Part V

"Now the earth goes on,
slackening its interrogation,
the skin of its silence stretched out."
Neruda

51

When Louise woke up the following morning Ranulf had already left. He'd left her a note:-

You take care of yourselves. It was a pleasure to meet the pair of you. I'll be looking forward to reading more of your exposés! Two things I want you to do. First is drop in at the address I've put in the satnav for you. Second is get your act together. You're like two peas in a pod and that's how you should be living. You don't get many chances—take them.

All the best,

R x

Under the note was a car key. She smiled and put the note in her pocket then went to wake up Zack.

'Come on you,' she scolded him. 'Things to do, places to go. Get up!'

She was about to call the number Ranulf had left for the safest place to leave her story. They were waiting for her. It would all be very discreet. A brief interview, a

DNA sample and she would be free to go. She decided against it. It was over.

That afternoon they took the car Ranulf had left for them and drove west, following the satnav's directions. There were still check points, still the presence of New Dawn, but to them it felt somehow lighter, easier. The oppressive air seemed to be lifting, as if they could sense an end to it all. They drove on in a strange silence. There was so much to say but now wasn't the time.

*

She recognised it straight away. The tidy little cottage in the middle of nowhere. Zack took her hand as they walked towards the gate. He opened it for her at the same time as the front door opened. A black and white ball of hysteria charged at her, almost knocking her over.

'Yoko! Oh my God, I've missed you so much.'

'Hello, my dear,' the doctor said, with a warm smile. 'She's missed you too.'

They stayed for a cup of tea and a chat. Lizzie was full of questions and comments. Louise guiltily allowed Zack to do most of the talking. Her focus was on her dog.

'So where to now?' Zack asked, as they drove off, waving goodbye. 'Your place? My place? Some other place?'

'What would you say to an our place?' Louise suggested, nuzzling Yoko's neck.

'I'd say that would be fucking spectacular!'

52

Richardson had been locked up for three weeks. Three interminable weeks of hell! The cell door finally opened and he was released. He was met on the steps by his personal secretary who had a satisfied smile on his face.

'Sir!' he said, as he held the limousine door open for him.

'What in damnation took you so long?' he bellowed down his phone. 'Christ! Those places. Those people. You have no idea!'

'It was just a tad problematic. Knightley was easy enough to dispose of, but those children had been well hidden.'

He sighed as he sat back in the comfort of the leather seats. The smell of cleanliness and wealth. He was home!

The End

If you enjoyed this story you can help other people find it by writing a review on the site where you bought it from. It doesn't have to be much. Just a few words can really help spread the word and make a big difference to its visibility. Thank you!

Acknowledgements

Special thanks to Nicola Curnow, Pauline Doig, Dave Wilson, Hannah Shipman, and Jude Mondragon for all of their help, encouragement and support.

About The Author

Fiona was the winner of the Federation of Writers (Scotland) short story competition, 2023. She was born in the Outer Hebrides of Scotland. She graduated with an honours degree in primary education in 1996, after which she spent fifteen years teaching in international schools, predominantly in Eastern Europe. She now lives in East Lothian, Scotland, where her days are spent walking her dog and writing.

Also From This Author

The Unravelling Of Maria
Lovers separated by the Iron Curtain.
Two women whose paths should never have crossed.
A remarkable journey that changes all of their lives.

Maria's history is a lie. Washed up on the shores of Sweden in 1944, with no memory, she was forced to create her own. Nearly half a century later she still has no idea of her true identity.
Jaak fights for Estonia's independence, refusing to accept the death of his fiancée Maarja, whose ship was sunk as she fled across the Baltic Sea to escape the Soviet invasion.
Angie knows exactly who she is. A drug addict. A waste of space. Life is just about getting by.
   A chance meeting in Edinburgh's Cancer Centre is the catalyst for something very different.

Dan Knew
A puppy born to the dangers of street life
A woman in trouble
An unbreakable bond

A Ukrainian street dog is rescued from certain death by an expat family. As he travels with them through Lithuania, Estonia, Portugal, and the UK he learns how to be a people dog, but a darkness grows and he finds himself narrating more than just his story. More than a dog story. Ultimately it's a story of escape and survival but maybe not his.

The world through Wee Dan's eyes in a voice that will stay with you long after you turn that last page.

Don't Get Involved
Ukraine 2001
Three street-kids
A Mafia hitman
A deadly chase

Dima, Alyona and Sasha, three street-kids with nothing but each other, stumble on a holdall full of cocaine. This could be it. A way out. Leonid, a Mafia hitman who will stop at nothing to achieve his goals, is sent to retrieve the cocaine and dispose of the children. Failure isn't an option.

Nadia, a naive expat is looking for a new beginning. She wasn't expecting this!

As their paths get tangled up in the biting cold of a ferocious winter in Kyiv all of them will need to find more strength and courage than they ever imagined they had if they are to survive. What do you call on when you have nothing left to give?

Before the Swallows Come Back
Writing as Fiona Curnow

Perfect for fans of *Where the Crawdads Sing,* by Delia Owens, *The Great Alone,* by Kristin Hannah, and *Sal,* by Mik Kitson, with its celebration of the natural world, its misunderstood central characters living on the outside of society's norms, their survival in the wilderness, and the ultimate fight for justice.

Before the Swallows Come Back is a story of love, found family, and redemption that will break your heart and have it soaring time and time again as you sit on the edge of your seat desperately hoping.

Tommy struggles with people, with communicating, preferring solitude, drifting off with nature. He is protected by his Tinker family who keep to the old ways. A life of quiet seclusion under canvas is all he knows.

Charlotte cares for her sickly father. She meets Tommy by the riverside and an unexpected friendship develops. Over the years it becomes something more, something crucial to both of them. But when tragedy strikes each family they are torn apart.

Charlotte is sent far away.

Tommy might have done something very bad.

Printed in Great Britain
by Amazon